BEACON STREET GIRLS

This book belongs to:

VERITAS AMICITIA GAUDIUM
truth friendship fun!

™

Who's Who

Katani Summers
a.k.a. Kgirl ... Katani has a strong fashion sense and business savvy. She is stylish, loyal & cool.

Avery Madden
Avery is passionate about all sports and animal rights. She is energetic, optimistic & outspoken.

Charlotte Ramsey
A self-acknowledged "klutz" and an aspiring writer, Charlotte is all too familiar with being the new kid in town. She is intelligent, worldly & curious.

Isabel Martinez
Her ambition is to be an artist. She was the last to join the Beacon Street Girls. She is artistic, sensitive & kind.

Maeve Kaplan-Taylor
Maeve wants to be a movie star. Bubbly and upbeat, she wears her heart on her sleeve. She is entertaining, friendly & fun.

Ms. Razzberry Pink
The stylishly pink proprietor of the "Think Pink" boutique is chic, gracious & charming.

Marty
The adopted best dog friend of the Beacon Street Girls is feisty, cuddly & suave.

Happy Lucky Thingy and alter ego **Mad Nasty Thingy**
Marty's favorite chew toy, it is known to reveal its alter ego when shaken too roughly. He is most often happy.

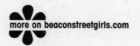

more on beaconstreetgirls.com

BEACON STREET GIRLS

Be sure to read all of our books:

BSG Special Adventure Books:

Coming soon:

ALADDIN MIX

Simon & Schuster Children's Publishing Division

1230 Avenue of the Americas, New York, NY 10020

Copyright © 2004 by B*tween Productions, Inc.,

Home of the Beacon Street Girls

Beacon Street Girls, Kgirl, B*tween Productions, B*Street, and the characters Maeve,

Avery, Charlotte, Isabel, Katani, Marty, Nick, Anna, Joline, and Happy Lucky Thingy

are registered trademarks and/or copyrights of B*tween Productions, Inc.

All rights reserved, including the right of reproduction in whole or in part in any form.

ALADDIN PAPERBACKS, ALADDIN MIX, and related logo are

registered trademarks of Simon & Schuster, Inc.

Designed by Dina Barsky

The text of this book was set in Palatino Linotype.

Manufactured in the United States of America

First Aladdin Paperbacks edition June 2008

6 8 10 9 7

Library of Congress Control Number 2008920652

ISBN-13: 978-1-4169-6427-8

ISBN-10: 1-4169-6427-4

BEACON STREET GIRLS

Out of Bounds

BY
ANNIE BRYANT

ALADDIN MIX

NEW YORK LONDON TORONTO SYDNEY

Out of Bounds

Part One
Over the Top

1

The Soccer Mom

I t can't be *this* cold," Maeve wailed.

"It's like we're in Alaska or something," Katani added, stomping her feet on the bleacher steps.

"My hands feel like polar bear snacks!" piped in Charlotte as she tucked her hands into the sleeves of her favorite hoodie sweatshirt.

"I'm thinking Mexico ... on the beach ... tropical sun beating down ... a cold drink," added Isabel dreamily. "Ooh! You have to try this. Think about sweating and being really, really hot. It helps. Try it."

Unseasonably cold, that's what Kristy B., the most popular weather woman in Boston, said. *Record breaking*. But it wasn't supposed to last. By Wednesday, it would be back in the sixties. That's just what fall was like in New England. What was it that Isabel's Aunt Lourdes said when they moved east to live with her? *If you don't like the weather in New England, just wait a minute.*

But all in all the Beacon Street Girls loved the fall.

"The air is just so crisp and clear," Avery always said.

"It makes you just want to jump around and do backflips." Avery *would* say that because she was the only one of the Beacon Street Girls who could actually do a backflip and land on her feet!

Isabel decided that fall was her favorite season, too. The leaf colors were totally awesome—bright red to intense orange to vibrant yellow and even deep purple. You really had to be totally oblivious not to notice them. And the fall light—it cast the most amazing shadows. They called it northern light, the kind of light that all real painters love. Isabel thought everyone should live in New England at least once. At least all artists, or aspiring artists like her, as Isabel wasn't ready to give herself the honor of being called a real artist yet.

Isabel, Katani, Maeve, and Charlotte were cheering at Avery's soccer game. Well, it wasn't her game exactly. Avery wasn't *on* the team this time; she was an official referee in the fourth-grade girls' tournament. And this game was a big one: the Twisters vs. the Tornadoes.

"Go Twisters, Go Twisters!" whooped Maeve as she stood, raised her arms, and rocked back and forth. It wasn't as if she had any loyalty to either team, but they were sitting in the Twisters' bleachers, so she figured she owed them her best cheerleading efforts.

"Sit down, Maeve," scolded Katani. "You're making Avery laugh, and she has to concentrate. She's getting paid real money for this." Katani was totally a businessgirl type. President of a major corporation was definitely in her future, or at least owner of her own fashion boutique. The Kgirl had some serious style.

They all looked down on the field and saw Avery grinning up at Maeve and shaking her head back and forth.

"Okay," sighed Maeve with a fake sorry look. "I guess my cheerleading abilities are not wanted here."

Charlotte grabbed one of Maeve's arms and Katani grabbed the other. They yanked her down, shouting in unison, "Sit down, Maeve!"

Behind them, a group of little boys repeated, "Sit down, Maeve," and burst into uncontrollable laughter. Isabel, Charlotte, and Katani completely cracked up. "You are so busted," they sputtered in between their giggles.

"The life of a performer is very trying," complained Maeve in her best dramatic voice, and she went back to looking intently at the field. Her friends knew she wasn't mad, though. Maeve hardly ever got mad at anyone. It just wasn't her style. Sometimes her feelings got hurt, but her upbeat spirit always managed to shine through.

Avery once said that Maeve was like one of those wobbly dolls that whenever it gets knocked down, it bounces right back up again. So true, because with a mischievous little grin on her face, Maeve jumped up for one more quick whoop and roll before anyone could stop her. Then she turned and high-fived one of the little boys behind her.

"You are so hyper," Katani said.

"It's all this cold weather," Maeve said, once she settled herself back on the bench. "If I sit still, I am going to freeze to death."

There was a shout from the field. One of the Tornadoes had just missed scoring a goal.

"Twisters and Tornadoes are the same thing, you know," Isabel offered. She had recently moved here from Michigan, where they actually had some seriously big storms. Twisters were one of the only things about the Midwest that Isabel didn't miss. Watching a house fly off its foundation and spin around in the air was a pretty scary sight. Isabel shuddered as she thought about some of the news pictures she had seen.

"I don't think I ever want to see a twister. I mean, it's kind of fun in the movies, but in real life ... no, thank you," said Maeve, handing their adopted little mutt, Marty, to Isabel.

The Beacon Street Girls were taking turns passing Marty back and forth among them like a football. Not only did he seem to enjoy the attention, but cuddling with Marty was helping them all stay warmer. He was like a little heating pad. Everyone was glad that Avery had insisted they bring Marty to the game. If the truth be told, no one was too thrilled to be watching fourth graders play soccer.

"I mean, if somebody's sister was playing, this might be sort of interesting," said Charlotte.

Simultaneously, the girls looked at one another, and as if they had some kind of immediate psychic connection, all said at the same time, "Nah!" Of course, that set off another round of giggles. No, they were there because their buddy Avery was reffing. "You gotta be loyal to your friends," said Katani, when Maeve first complained that it would be too cold. "We would go and see you dance, Maeve, so we have to support Avery, too."

"Well, at least it got me out of cleaning my room," Maeve grinned. "My mother said loyalty to friends was more important than cleaning the Maeve Toxic Waste Dump." She did a perfect imitation of her mother's New York accent.

"Look at how completely cutified he is," Isabel said, hugging Marty for warmth.

"He is just a major charmball, and sooo adorable," Maeve agreed.

"I love those words—cutified and charmball. I think we

should make them official BSG words. I think I'm going to start a BSG dictionary," mused Charlotte, who loved everything to do with being a writer.

Maeve, Katani, and Isabel all looked at Charlotte with amusement.

"I think you should call it 'Word Nerd,'" offered Maeve.

"That works for me," laughed Charlotte.

"I think Marty just smiled at you," Katani said.

"No way," Isabel laughed.

"He did, I swear," Katani said. "See? He just did it again."

The corners of Marty's mouth were turned up in what looked like a grin.

They all laughed, glad the little guy was there. Avery had said Marty needed to get out more. She didn't want him becoming a couch potato. And Marty seemed to think it was fine weather, great weather in fact, but then again, he had a fur coat. Lucky little dude!

It was funny the way the girls always thought they knew what Marty was thinking. Avery, who had been reading up on the subject, said all pet owners give their pets human qualities. But she said that Marty was different from any normal pet. As people in the stands jumped up to see what was going on, Marty jumped up too. Marty was the kind of dog that thought he was a person. You could just tell from the way he looked when someone tried to tell him what to do. It was as if he was saying, "Dude, I'm in charge here." He was definitely a small dog, big personality kind of mutt. Great Danes, stay away!

"I think Mr. Marté is a big soccer fan. Look how closely he's watching all the plays," Charlotte said, laughing. Having lived in Paris for a year, Charlotte liked to frenchify Marty's name. She thought it gave him "panache." That was another of Charlotte's favorite words. She said *panache* was so much cooler to say than *style*!

Marty heard his name and took a running leap into Charlotte's lap.

Isabel saw the surprised look on Charlotte's face and started to giggle. "I guess he's decided it's your turn to hold him," she said.

Marty started snuffling around in Charlotte's pockets, looking for treats.

"All gone," Charlotte said to Marty, but that didn't stop him. Instead, his little legs started digging at Charlotte's pants at warp speed. This set off another round of hysterical giggles. He looked so funny scratching around for nonexistent treats.

Finally, Charlotte emptied her pockets to demonstrate to Marty that she had nothing there. The only thing she pulled out were some golden coins she had been carrying around to practice a magic trick. Charlotte had been studying "great illusionists" for her next English report that was coming up in Ms. R's class. She'd already read one book on the greatest magicians of all time and another that was a biography of Harry Houdini. At the moment, she was reading a *how-to* book on sleight of hand.

Once Charlotte became interested in a particular subject, she read everything she could find on it. Right now, her big thing was magic. It was just so challenging to learn how to make things disappear.

As she flipped the coins through her fingers, Charlotte wondered what it would be like to be invisible. She had seen an old movie called *The Invisible Man* at the Movie House. It was creepy and fascinating at the same time. Being able to walk into a room and hear and see everybody, but they couldn't see you—how completely weird would that be?

Maybe time travel would be better, she thought. You could go visit with Queen Victoria or something. Suddenly, Charlotte was in the English court, eating scones and having tea with the little queen who liked to dress completely in black.

"She looks so tall out there," Isabel said. "It's funny how she towers over everyone."

Oops, back to Earth, Charlotte admonished herself.

"That's because the other girls on the field are fourth graders," Katani said, and they all laughed.

Avery was athletic and strong. The one thing she wasn't was tall.

The wind shifted, and Maeve shivered under their blanket.

Katani, who'd brought a bright pink thermos of sweet tea, handed a cup to Maeve. "Go ahead and finish it," she suggested. "It'll warm you up."

Katani was the only one semi-prepared for the weather. She wore a poncho the girls had named the Kgirl Special. Katani had designed it herself by cutting up a bright yellow fleece blanket, adding a few tassels, and attaching vintage buttons all down the middle. It was the same color as some of the leaves that were falling behind her. With her poncho and her thermos, Katani looked as if she could be on the cover of *Style Girl* magazine. Still, Katani was not all that warm either. Her lips were starting to turn blue.

"You know, Katani, you look kind of cool with blue lips. Maybe you should get some blue lip gloss or something," Maeve offered.

"Maeve, blue lip gloss is for super rock star types. I am going for the New York '*Excuse me, but I own a major fashion empire*' kind of look. You go for the blue. It would suit you to a T, especially if you decide to sing in Riley's band. Think of it, blue lip gloss, red hair, red silk shirt. Don't give me that look. Redheads look fabulous in the right color red ... and blue jeans with rhinestones down the side ..."

"I think we got the picture," said Isabel, nodding her head. Once Katani got on a roll with fashion, there was no stopping her!

Hmm, Riley's band, Maeve thought to herself.

Riley Lee, the class musician, had been asking her for weeks if she wanted to sing with the band. But singing with Riley's band would be a lot of work because Riley was seriously serious about music. He lived and breathed it. Every week, he was talking about some fabulous new band. Maeve just didn't know if she was ready for that yet. She liked hip hop dancing and drama, too. But there were only so many hours in a day. And now there were two places to live ... but she didn't want to think about that now. Her parents' recent separation was too new for her to be comfortable thinking about it even for a second.

By this time, the only one who looked really warm was Avery, who was running the length of the soccer field, blowing her whistle every few seconds. In fact, it looked like someone had painted two really big red circles on either side of her face. Refereeing fourth-grade girls wasn't easy. They were sooo sensitive. But Avery was determined to do a super job. She loved soccer with a passion and had dreams of being a soccer coach someday, that is if she didn't become a senator or a snowboarder in Colorado. "That's the thing about being our age," grumbled Avery the other day. "There's so many amazingly cool things to do. How am I ever going to decide?"

"Avery," Maeve had answered her, "You're not supposed to decide now. You're supposed to try a bunch of stuff first, see what you like, see what you are good at, and then when you grow up, decide on whatever you like best. Besides, if you decide now, you'll get too serious and nothing will be any fun anymore. I mean, geesh, Avery, we're only in seventh grade!"

All the BSG looked impressed. For someone who wasn't the best of students, it was moments like these that made them realize that Maeve had a lot of common sense.

"But," Avery had to add, "what if you like something that you are really bad at?"

"Well," offered Katani in a serious tone, "I suppose you could work really hard at it, and you would definitely get better at it. But I don't know if you would be as good as someone who was naturally really good at something and worked hard."

At that point, Charlotte, Maeve, and Isabel had had enough. "Don't worry about it," they groaned. Avery had answered them with one of her now famous *snurps* (a combination of a snort and a burp), "I won't."

Anyway, Avery decided to take the refereeing course last summer. It had taken several weekends to get certified, but, by the end of the course, Avery had secured her first real job. She was a popular referee. Each game she reffed paid thirty dollars, and today she had already reffed two games. But Avery wasn't really in it for the money. She would have done it for free. She loved soccer that much. And she liked to help the younger girls.

All of a sudden, Avery blew a short blast on her whistle and the game came to a halt.

"What just happened?" Katani asked. She had been daydreaming about how fun it would be to design a whole line of cute dog products. She could see it now: the Martywear Collection. Debuted at *Fashion Week* with Marty jogging down the runway in a groovy Martywear ensemble. Paparazzi everywhere—rock stars with their own little chihuahuas.

"Off sides," Charlotte said.

"I think they've called a time out," said Maeve.

"They don't have time out in soccer," answered Isabel.

A woman behind them jumped up. "Come on, let's go!" the woman yelled. She was wearing a red sweatshirt with the words *Megan's Mom* printed across the front.

The girls exchanged a look.

Katani checked her watch. The game was almost over. The score was tied. "I think they have to go into overtime. Because it's the championships, it'll probably be first goal scored wins," Katani predicted.

"Watch this," Charlotte said, taking advantage of the opportunity to try out one of her new tricks. She took one of the gold coins and passed it through her fingers from thumb to pinky and back again, over one, under the next, over and under again until she had done it several times.

"Whoa, I'm impressed. How did you do that?" Katani said, meaning it.

"Pay no attention to the man behind the curtain," Charlotte said in a stage voice, and they all laughed. It was a quote from *The Wizard of Oz*, which Maeve's father had screened for them over the weekend. They all agreed that they loved the movie, they were still afraid of the Wicked Witch of the West, and that "I'll get you, my pretty, and your little dog, too," was one of the all-time great movie lines.

Katani, who claimed she had no acting talent, in fact did an awesome imitation of the Wicked Witch. Donning a witch's mask and hat, Katani had scared them all by bursting into the Tower room one night at Charlotte's as they lay sleeping, and cackling the famous line.

The girls screamed so loud that Marty ran and attacked

the leg of Katani's pants, shaking it back and forth and growling madly. Katani fell to the floor laughing hysterically. The other girls pummeled her with pillows so hard that one of them broke and the feathers burst out and floated throughout the Tower.

Mr. Ramsey, Charlotte's dad, came running up to the room to see what was wrong. When he walked in, a feather fell right on his nose. He just stood there, nodding his head back and forth at the laughing witch on the bed and the feathers in the room. The girls went crazy and laughed even harder.

"Try not to wake up the whole neighborhood," Mr. Ramsey said as he walked out of the Tower. "And ... don't let the bedbugs bite, girls."

Ever since then, all Katani had to do was crouch over and begin to speak in her witch voice and Charlotte, Avery, Maeve, and Isabel would crack up.

CR

CHARLOTTE, THE MAGICIAN

At the soccer game, it was about Charlotte and magic.

"Now you see it, now you don't."

Charlotte made a sweeping motion, and just like that, the old coin was gone.

"Et voilà!" said Charlotte in her best Parisian accent.

"Where did it go?" Katani laughed, checking her teacup.

"How did you do that?" Isabel seemed genuinely interested.

"Nothing up my sleeves," Charlotte said, showing them.

"Hey, that was my coin," Maeve said. She had loaned the coins to Charlotte a week ago.

"You mean this coin?" Charlotte asked, reaching into Maeve's pocket.

"Or this coin?" Charlotte pulled another one from behind Katani's knee.

"Or maybe this one," she said, reaching into Isabel's sleeve. She handed all of the coins back to Maeve. "*Un, deux, trois*," Charlotte counted.

"Hey, I'm rich," Maeve grinned.

"Where *did* you learn that trick?" Isabel was clearly fascinated.

"From my father's friend Jacques in Paris. He used to be a magician before he gave it up to be a lawyer. He said the pay was better for lawyers. But it's also in one of my magic books. I wasn't this good at it before. The first time I practiced it, one of the coins landed in my dad's soup. We were eating dinner at Le Languedoc, this really fancy Paris restaurant in the Bois de Boulogne, for his birthday. The soup splashed all over the tablecloth. The waiter screamed, 'Oh, *mon Dieu*!' ... He was not happy. The French are very serious about their food, you know," Charlotte explained.

"Excellent coin-in-the-soup performance," clapped Maeve.

"Well, I've been practicing a lot since then," Charlotte said. "You know me," she laughed. "I get totally into things."

"That's a sweet trick," Katani said.

"Very cool," Isabel agreed.

"Only a few seconds left," Katani said, turning back as the game started up again.

Maeve handed Charlotte back the coins. "Keep them for a while," she said.

Charlotte was about to put them back in her pocket when Megan's mom popped up again, knocking the coins into the air. Charlotte caught one of them, Katani caught another, but the third one fell under the bleachers.

"No!" Megan's mom yelled toward the field, oblivious to what she'd just done.

One of the Twisters had been running the ball toward the goal when a girl from the Tornadoes suddenly appeared and stole the ball. It was close to the line, but Avery's whistle did not blow.

The whole Twisters' bench stood to watch in horror as the Tornadoes' player dribbled the ball all the way down to the other end of the field and scored the winning goal.

"No way!" Megan's mother was already off the bench and on the field. "That ball was completely out of bounds!"

From where they were sitting, it was difficult to tell who was right and who was wrong. But Avery hadn't called a penalty. And Avery knew what she was doing when it came to soccer.

Charlotte crawled under the bleachers to search for the coin. By the time she found it, there was a big commotion on the field. Megan's mom was arguing with Avery, who was trying her best to stand her ground. And Megan's mom was pretty scary with her yelling and her finger pointing right in Avery's face. Avery looked very little standing next to her. Suddenly, both coaches were on the field and everyone was talking loudly at once.

"What's going on?" Charlotte asked, poking her head out from under the bleachers.

Maeve had been totally focused on what was going on with the argument on the field. "Megan's mom keeps yelling that Avery's call was bad, that the ball was out of bounds, even though nobody says *out of bounds* in soccer."

As Megan's mom continued to shake her finger at Avery, Marty jumped off the bench, and, in a flash, was running toward the field barking his head off.

"Yikes," said Isabel as the girls began to chase after Marty, while poor Charlotte, who was still crawling through the bleachers and hurrying to catch up, caught her pants on the corner of the bleachers and ripped the seat of her jeans. Disaster! Underwear Showing Alert!

Great, another embarrassing moment in the life of Charlotte Ramsey. Why don't we just hold up a sign. Well, no time to think about it now, Charlotte thought. Standing up, she took off her warm, cuddly sweatshirt and wrapped it around her waist. Life was about to get very cold, she realized as she climbed back up on the bleachers to see what was happening and felt the fall wind whipping through her light jersey ... and her pants.

Maeve managed to catch Marty first and was doing her best to hold him still. He barked wildly at Megan's mom, who was barking wildly at Avery.

"You better keep ahold of that vicious dog," Megan's mom yelled over to Maeve.

"Vicious dog! I don't think so," whispered Maeve furiously under her breath, but she did try to shush Marty.

It was easy to tell which girl was Megan. She was the Twister who'd had the ball stolen from her in the final seconds of the game. Even if Charlotte hadn't seen the play, she would have been able to tell from the embarrassed look on the girl's face as she listened to her mother rant on and on about how that ball was out of bounds, and how Avery had failed to make the correct call. Charlotte could tell that Megan wished she was anywhere but on that field.

"I feel really sorry for that little girl," Isabel whispered to Katani. "I would totally die if my mother acted like that."

"I know what you mean," Katani whispered back. "This is one of those things that every kid lives in fear of ... being embarrassed by your mother in front of hundreds of people. It's like every kid's worst nightmare!"

"That ball was clearly out of bounds," Megan's mother screeched. "You need to have your eyes checked. I think you need glasses!"

Uh-oh! The girls could see that Avery was really under some serious pressure here.

"You can't be old enough to be a referee. How old are you?" Megan's mom continued.

"Ma'am," the Twisters' coach said, raising his voice, "You need to calm down and take your seat right now. No parents are allowed on the field during a game."

Megan's mom opened her mouth to say something, but the Tornadoes' coach interrupted her. "Ma'am, the goal was good. You know the rules. The ref calls the play. Please go back to your seat or leave the field," the coach said firmly.

The next thing they knew, Megan's mom turned on him. She apparently couldn't believe what she was hearing. "Well," she sputtered angrily, "the soccer board will be hearing from me." She grabbed Megan's hand and dragged her humiliated daughter off the field.

"What just happened?" Avery asked in a bewildered little voice. "I didn't mean . . ."

"It's okay, Avery," the Twisters' coach said before she could finish. "Some of these parents get really carried away sometimes. It's totally inappropriate behavior ... way out of bounds," he added as he winked at Avery. "Although I wish it were different and we'd won the game, that ball was in. But even if you were wrong, the ref calls the play. That's the way the game goes."

Both coaches shook hands. Then they shook Avery's. "Don't let this discourage you, Avery," the Tornadoes' coach said. "You're a terrific referee, and I will talk to the soccer board about what a great job you did today. If you're worried, have your mother call me, and I'll be glad to talk to her about all of this."

Avery beamed. "That's okay, Coach. I knew that reffing wasn't going to be easy. But I didn't think it would get this crazy."

"Sometimes it takes people a long time to learn how to be a good sport," the Tornadoes' coach said.

Marty didn't stop barking until Megan's mom had driven away.

"You tell her, Mr. Marté," said Maeve as she shook his little furry paw after Megan's mom.

No Dogs Allowed

After the game, Avery wanted to treat her friends to hot chocolates at Montoya's, but first they had to stop at Charlotte's house to drop Marty off and so Charlotte could change her pants. They all felt bad about leaving him. "If we were in Paris," Charlotte said, "Marty could come."

"That's so cool," enthused Avery, who had tucked Marty under her arm. "Let's start a petition here. After all, dogs have rights, too!"

"You've gotta run for office someday, Avery," cheered Maeve.

Avery grinned. "Maybe I will. Somebody's got to save the planet from unfair rules ... it might as well be me!" Then she smushed her face into Marty's face, whereupon he gave her a big slurpy kiss right on her mouth.

"That's so gross, Avery," said Katani as she made a face. Katani was not a fan of slurpy dog kisses. Too undignified.

"Did you hear that, Marty? You have just been insulted,"

Avery said to Marty as she scratched his tummy.

"He'll get over it," added Katani sarcastically.

Charlotte laughed. "Katani, you have to come to Paris. You would not believe how much people love their dogs there. They have better clothes for their dogs than even all those fancy movie stars do."

Katani suddenly seemed interested. "You know, I was thinking of dog outfits at the game. Maybe I should design a few outfits for Mr. Marté here ... maybe a little beret and sweater." Avery looked skeptical, as if the idea of Marty in a designer beret didn't quite sit well with her.

Charlotte, who had lived all over the world before she came home to Brookline, clapped her hands enthusiastically. She had lived in Australia, Africa, and most recently Paris. And even though they wouldn't let dogs into the cafés here, she thought Katani's idea was awesome. "Marty in a French beret and a sweater would bring a little bit of Paris here. I love it."

Charlotte really liked living in Brookline, Massachusetts. The Beacon Street Girls were here, and it felt like home. And it was where she had lived when she was a little girl, when her mother was alive. Sometimes Charlotte and her dad would have breakfast on Newbury Street, Boston's fashion center. Afterwards they would walk around the corner and look up at the apartment they had all lived in when Charlotte's mom was still alive. It seemed to comfort them both.

Avery settled Marty into the colorful little doghouse Isabel had recently painted for him. It had a cut-out door so he could come and go whenever he wanted to, and fancy trompe l'oeil (which means "trick of the eye" in French) painted windows with curtains and a window box and cute little tulips and daffodils.

Avery thought it looked kinda girly for a boy dog, but Marty loved his little house. Over the past few weeks, he had dragged all his toys inside as well as a few other items he fancied, like one of Katani's pillows ... and an empty box of dog cookies.

Still, even though he loved his house, Marty didn't want to stay there today. Determined to come along, he followed them to the door.

"Stay," Avery said firmly. Marty hung his head and looked a little crushed.

"I'll bring you back part of my buñuelo," Isabel promised. Marty licked his lips.

Everyone laughed.

"Sometimes," Isabel said as they turned to go, "I could swear that dog understands what we're talking about."

Avery stayed behind for a minute, tossing Happy Lucky Thingy, Marty's most favorite chew toy, around with the "little dude" until he got tired enough from his favorite game to lie down and take a dog nap.

"There you go," Avery said, putting Happy Lucky under his head like a little pillow. Before Avery reached the door, he was snoring softly.

"I wish I had a camera," Maeve said, looking back through the doorway. "I think we should send this picture to a famous movie producer. He is too adorable for words."

"Can't you just see it? Marty riding in a limo, pulling up to the red carpet for Oscar night. It would be so cool."

"Avery, you're beginning to sound like me," Maeve laughed. Avery joined in. There were no two people who were less alike than Avery and Maeve. Maeve was all pink and flashy, while Avery was the sporty girl. It was amazing they were such good friends. But they were.

ᏅᏬ

Montoya's Bakery was warm and cozy. Steam streaked the windows. The whole place smelled of chocolate and cinnamon. Mouths watered before even ordering.

Avery ordered hot chocolate for her friends. Isabel had gotten everyone hooked on Montoya's buñuelos, so they all chipped in and shared one, saving a tiny piece of it for Marty.

Nick Montoya, whose parents owned the place, brought the hot chocolates over to the table. Nick was so cute. Even if they didn't have a crush on him, girls liked to drool over his big brown eyes, his black hair, and his friendly smile. The BSG felt lucky to get seats because it seemed like there were a zillion kids from Abigail Adams Junior High there.

Charlotte especially liked it when Nick was working. She remembered when Maeve told her that he was the cutest boy in the whole seventh grade. Maeve used to have a major freak-out crush on Nick. Charlotte did think that he had the most amazing eyes and a great smile. He was also really sweet and relatively easy to talk to.

But Charlotte just wasn't sure she was ready for the whole dating thing yet. It seemed a little complicated. Less complicated to worship from afar, she thought. That way there were no totally embarrassing moments or awkward silences when neither of you knew what to say. Although she and Nick usually had a lot to talk about ... you just never knew. Maybe later on the dating thing. But how much later?

"So, who won the game?" Nick asked Avery.

"The Tornadoes," Avery answered. "By one goal in overtime."

"Sounds exciting," Nick said, smiling. "Those fourth-grade

❀ 19 ❀

games can really blow you away." Everyone knew he was joking.

"Actually, it was really exciting," Charlotte said. "One of the soccer moms picked a fight with Avery."

"No way," Nick said.

"She didn't really pick a fight, but she was yelling a ton," Avery admitted.

"The mother kept yelling that the ball was out of bounds," Isabel said.

"Sounds intense!" Nick said.

"It kinda was," Avery nodded.

"I felt so sorry for that little girl," Maeve said.

"Megan," Katani added.

"She was so embarrassed. She looked as if she wanted to hide," Charlotte said, suddenly empathizing that this would have been one of those times when being able to become invisible would have really come in handy.

"Why do parents act like that?" Isabel wanted to know. "It's only a game."

"Parents are so weird sometimes. They make such a big deal over stuff. They should just let the kids handle it," Avery said. "You know what else is funny? Her mother couldn't come to two of the games, and Megan played much better when she wasn't around." Avery took a big gulp of her hot chocolate.

"Big surprise," said Maeve.

"Sounds like the only thing out of bounds was Megan's mom, she probably needs to chill out!" Nick said, as he wiped off the table next to them.

2

The Talent Show

Isabel was running late.

She ran down Beacon Street, turning right on Harvard, and passing Yuri, who was just setting up the fruit stands outside his shop.

"Hey!" she waved, but she didn't stop. Yuri was Charlotte's friend, and lately, she and Isabel often stopped to talk to him together. Sometimes he even gave them a free apple.

"*Hola*, Isabel! What? You don't stop to see your friend Yuri today?"

"I'm so late," Isabel shouted back over her shoulder. "Charlotte and I'll stop by later." Isabel loved Yuri. He acted so grumpy, but he took the time to speak Spanish with her every day. He said he was trying to set an example for Americans, who, he claimed, were "language impaired."

"Maybe Yuri will not be here later. Maybe Yuri will close early and go to the beach!" Yuri was obviously making a joke. Today was even colder than yesterday. "You Americans," he yelled after her, "always rushing, never time to enjoy ..."

Isabel sprinted up the front of Abigail Adams Junior High, her long, black hair whipping around her face as she ran. At the playground just to the side of the school there was the usual cast of young mothers from the neighborhood, sipping their morning coffee and chatting back and forth as they watched their toddlers stumble and fall every few feet in the sandbox. The toddlers looked like fat little cartoon munchkins with their chubby faces and puffy jackets. Normally, Charlotte and Isabel would have stopped to say hi and play with them for a few minutes, but there was no time today. Isabel's alarm clock hadn't gone off this morning, and she was too late to stop.

"You better go, girl!" one of the mothers cheered her on. "The second bell hasn't rung yet!"

As if on cue, the bell sounded.

Isabel sprinted past Mrs. Fields, the school principal, who was standing outside on the school steps talking to two custodians. They were all staring at some disgusting looking brown water that had pooled alongside the building. One of the custodians scratched his head as if he were seriously puzzled about something. Isabel rushed past them, pushing open the big wooden door with all her might.

Too late. The halls were deserted. Certainly, not a good sign. She stopped dead in her tracks, wondering what to do next. Isabel hated moments like this. You only had a split second to make a decision, and what if you were wrong?

If you were late to school, you were supposed to stop in the office and have Mrs. Fields sign a pass so you could get into class. But she was only a minute late. And besides, Mrs. Fields was outside. Isabel didn't want to interrupt her. And she didn't want to be any later than she already was. So, she decided to go for it. She would break the rules, just this once.

PERFORMANCE ANXIETY

When she opened the door to Ms. Ciara's music class, Isabel could hear Henry Yurt singing "Happy Birthday" at the top of his lungs. He didn't sound good; in fact, he sounded really, really terrible, kind of like a nasty old screech owl. The really funny part was that Henry looked so sincere. But was he? Henry was a puzzle. Was he faking or just the worst singer ever known to man?

Isabel wondered whose birthday it was. As she moved into the room, she saw Henry standing by the side of his desk, not singing to anyone. He was looking straight ahead. And no one was singing along. This was a solo performance.

Ms. Ciara saw Isabel standing in the back of the classroom and motioned her to an empty seat next to Charlotte. "You okay?" Charlotte whispered.

"Alarm meltdown. It didn't go off," Isabel whispered back and sat down.

When Henry finished singing, the class just sat there, not knowing what to do. It was such an outrageous performance. Henry couldn't sing a single note on key.

Most of the kids were trying not to laugh, all except for Anna and Joline, who were giggling madly. Trademark Queens of Mean behavior.

"Well, that certainly was an interesting choice, Henry," Ms. Ciara said. "Please tell the class why you picked that particular song."

"I couldn't help it, Ms. C," Henry grinned. "You said to bring in a favorite song, something that means something to you and your family, but my family is so unmusical it's not even funny. The only song we ever sing is 'Happy Birthday,' and even that is pretty rare. We usually go out to restaurants on our birthdays so someone else will sing the song for us."

That did it. The whole class burst into laughter at that one, even Ms. Ciara was smiling. "You may sit down now, Henry," Ms. Ciara said. The boys in the back, led by the Trentini twins, began to chant "Yurt, Yurt, Yurt" as Henry walked back to his seat.

"Settle down," Ms. Ciara said sharply. The boys obeyed immediately because everyone knew that Ms. Ciara was not opposed to sending kids to the principal's office. She was a nice teacher, but you had to really behave in her class. She would have made a good policewoman.

"Clearly, Henry put some ... meaningful thought into his assignment," Ms. Ciara said, struggling for the appropriate words, "and into his performance. Let's see what some of the rest of you came up with."

Naturally, Betsy Fitzgerald's hand shot into the air. Betsy was always the first to raise her hand for everything. She was driven to make a good impression on all of her teachers. Isabel was curious about Betsy and what made a girl try so hard to be the best all the time. At the same time, she had to admit that Betsy was pretty nice. She was never really mean to anyone. It was just that she was ... sooo intense, and so PERFECT!

Isabel felt kind of bad for her when Ms. Ciara looked around and spotted Maeve's hand.

"Maeve, why don't you go next?"

Maeve didn't stand next to her desk, but rather walked confidently to the front of the room where she could face the entire class. While Maeve sometimes struggled with her schoolwork, she was a true performer. All her classes in drama and music had prepared her to stand in front of an audience and not be paralyzed with embarrassment. The only time Maeve remembered feeling anxious on stage was when she won an award for her blanket project. When Maeve saw her parents sitting separately for the first time, she got upset and clammed up like she'd never seen a stage before. Very embarrassing and confidence shredding!

Today was different. Maeve was totally in charge. She didn't even care that the Queens of Mean, Anna and her "I'm so never gonna leave your side" sidekick, Joline, were whispering about her.

"I'm going to sing a song from Ireland," Maeve said.

"And why did you pick this particular song, Maeve?" Ms. Ciara asked, not wanting any more surprises.

Maeve thought for a moment. "I think the real reason I picked it was because I can sing it a cappella."

"Does anyone know what a cappella means?" Ms. Ciara turned to the class.

"It means unaccompanied," Charlotte blurted out. Ooo! she hoped she hadn't sounded like a know-it-all. She looked around quickly to see if anyone was rolling their eyes.

"That's right, Charlotte," said Ms. Ciara.

Maeve taped up a poster collage of Ireland. It was a landscape with gardens and fields and old castle ruins. In one corner, there was a thatched roof cottage. Little green shamrocks were stenciled all around the border.

"I thought I needed a little set decoration," Maeve smiled. Leave it to Maeve. She loved to make things sparkle.

Unfortunately, one end of the poster came undone and started to roll up. Anna and Joline took to snickering at Maeve, who was trying to flatten the corner. Katani glared at them and they made a face at her, but they stopped. Katani had a way of getting people to back off. Maeve flashed her a grateful smile, and Ms. Ciara went to her desk and came back with more pushpins.

Isabel took advantage of the extra time Maeve was using to get herself settled. She reached into her backpack and pulled out a cassette player. Then she found her music notebook and flipped to the page where she had written today's assignment. She hoped she hadn't misunderstood what they were supposed to be doing. She was pretty sure Ms. Ciara hadn't told them they had to sing. She would have remembered that. Isabel didn't mind singing with a group, but getting up and performing by herself was way too terrifying for words. What if she sounded like Henry Yurt? Isabel felt she would just die of embarrassment.

Better check. Whew! Her notes just said to bring in music that represented some kind of family tradition; it didn't say sing. The music Isabel had picked was from her cousin Irma's Quinceanera celebration, which had taken place last summer at their grandparents' home in Mexico City.

In the Mexican community, when a girl turns fifteen, it is cause for a big celebration, one that is often planned years in advance. Isabel's sister's Quinceanera celebration was planned for this coming spring. Relatives and friends would be coming from all over. Even though she hadn't been feeling all that well lately, Isabel's mom was enjoying making plans for Elena Maria's Quince. It gave them all something to look forward to. Hardly a week went by when they didn't plan some detail, from the pink dress that looked like a bridal gown, to the princess tiara, to the selection of the Quinceanera's court, which was the toughest decision so far.

Isabel wasn't all that sure she wanted a Quince. It seemed like an awful lot of planning for just one night. Besides, knowing herself, she would manage to spill paint all over her fancy party dress. In fact, looking down, Isabel could see a splotch of blue paint the size of a quarter on her clean white T-shirt. Great, thought Isabel. *I just hope Ms. Ciara doesn't pick me to go to the front*, she thought.

Isabel looked up from her notes. Maeve was singing a song called "She Moves Through the Fair." It was a traditional Irish ballad with a mournful air. Maeve had a clear, strong voice that could belt out a ballad or switch to rock and roll without missing a beat. Everyone was listening intently.

Elena Maria wanted to sing at her Quince celebration. She was all excited about it. She practiced her scales religiously any time of day or night, which had gotten to be kind of a joke between Isabel and her mother. Elena Maria was not nearly as good a singer as Maeve, but she was so enthusiastic that no one wanted to discourage her. Isabel thought her sister should stick with cooking, which she was really good at. But no, Elena Maria was bound and determined to master singing. And to her sister's credit, Isabel had to admit, she was getting better.

When Maeve finished her song, Ms. Ciara stood still for a long moment. "That was beautiful," Ms. Ciara said.

Isabel caught Dillon looking at Maeve. He was clearly enamored by her singing. She would have to remember to tell Maeve about the look on his face.

When she had finished, Maeve just stood there, punctuating the silence with her breathing. Then, with a big grin plastered across her face, just as the kids were starting to clap, she broke into "The Rattlin' Bog," a wild and lively Irish tune. By the end of the song, everyone was laughing and clapping in time. Amazingly enough, even some of the boys in the back were drumming on their desks. Henry Yurt jumped up and managed a pretty credible Irish jig. Ms. Ciara was enjoying herself so much she let the Yurtmeister continue all around the room.

When the second song was over, Maeve took a bow. Riley shook his head in disbelief as the whole classroom broke into applause. Maeve was so proud she practically flew back to her desk. The thought that she made people happy with her singing made her feel all toasty and warm inside.

When things settled down, Ms. Ciara said, "That was just wonderful, Maeve. I have a feeling we may see you on a real Broadway stage some day." Maeve beamed. This completely made up for the C- she got on the math quiz yesterday.

"I know it was supposed to be one song. But my dad thought that everyone would really like both songs."

"That's perfectly fine," Ms. Ciara said. "Now can you tell us something about the family tradition of singing Irish songs? Such as how it started?"

"How it started?" Maeve looked at her blankly.

"Yes, could you give us some background? Were these songs passed down through the generations, or were they sung on some special occasions, like Henry's song?"

Some of the kids couldn't help giggling at the reference to Henry.

"Um ..." Maeve hesitated. "They sang them all the time. Both my mother and father ... I mean, whenever they felt like singing. They used to do harmonies." Used to. As soon as the words were out of her mouth, Maeve realized she'd said more than she intended. She could feel her face getting red.

Avery and Katani exchanged looks. Clearly, Maeve was uncomfortable. They both hoped that Ms. Ciara wouldn't ask any more questions. Maeve's parents hadn't sung any songs together since they had been separated.

"So these are songs that have been passed down through your family?"

"Yes. I mean, no. Not actually passed down." The truth was she had learned them with her family. "We learned them from my grandparents and from some old Irish movies ... we actually ..." Maeve's voice broke off.

Anna and Joline snickered again.

What was up with these two anyway? thought Isabel, as Ms. Ciara shot them an admonishing look.

A minute ago, Maeve was in her glory. Now she just wished she could sit down.

"That's very interesting. I want you all to think about this because there's a lesson here about traditions and how they get started. For any of you who don't know, Maeve's parents own our local movie theater. So it makes sense that some of their traditions would come from the movies. See, we're not only learning about music here, we're learning about family and cultural traditions and how they develop over the years ... Very nice job, Maeve."

Maeve sat down. Relief spread over her. She loved singing in public, but she didn't want to get into family matters, not now. She couldn't trust what her responses would be if anyone asked about what was going on at home. The only people she felt she could talk to were her best friends.

"Who wants to go next?" Ms. Ciara asked. "I know Maeve is a hard act to follow, but remember, Maeve studies singing and dancing outside of school. I don't expect the rest of you to perform at her level." You could practically hear the collective sigh of relief. Ms. Ciara asked again, "Any volunteers?"

Still, not a single hand went up. Maeve's song had been so good that no one wanted to follow her. Not even Betsy Fitzgerald, whose hands remained folded on her desk.

Walking around the classroom, Ms. Ciara spotted the cassette player on Isabel's desk.

"Isabel," she said. "Why don't you go next?"

Oh, no, *lucky me*, sighed Isabel to herself. I shouldn't have taken out my recorder. There was nothing to do but get up from her desk and walk slowly to the front of the room. Very slowly. Maybe the clocks were wrong and the bell would ring. Isabel put her right hand behind her back and crossed her fingers as she turned to face her classmates.

Following Maeve was the last thing she wanted to do, but she couldn't exactly say no. She took as much time as she could setting up the cassette player.

"This music is from my cousin's Quinceanera."

"Quincey a whata?" Anna whispered so everyone could hear.

Ms. Ciara didn't even say anything this time. She was probably getting sick of dealing with the Queens of Mean, thought Maeve. I mean, how many times a day would you want to tell kids to be quiet, or shape up, or whatever? Meanwhile, Maeve could see Isabel's hand shaking as she slid her tape into the player.

"Quinceanera is a special celebration that happens in the Mexican community when a girl turns fifteen. It's a like a growing-up ceremony. The first part takes place in the church, but that's mainly for the family. Afterwards, there's a huge party, with costumes and dancing and everything." Isabel could feel everyone's eyes on her. Suddenly, in front of all these people, the idea of a Quince seemed very old fashioned.

"Kind of like a Bat Mitzvah?" Maeve offered.

"Yes, kind of. But practically every Mexican girl gets a Quince party. People bring gifts, and usually the party lasts all night."

"I think it would be cool to stay up all night," Avery said.

"The Quinceanera, which is the name for the girl whose party it is, usually wears a tiara and carries a scepter, like a princess. And she has a court of fifteen Damas—which are girls—and Chambelans—the boys. They are the ones who do the dance, which is usually a waltz."

"A waltz?" Anna snorted. "No one does waltzes anymore."

Ms. Ciara shot her a really scary look. Anna better be careful, thought Avery. Ms. Ciara looked like she had had enough. Detention looked about a minute away.

Isabel's face was getting redder and redder, she could feel it.

"Go on," Ms. Ciara said. "This is very interesting."

Isabel took a breath before speaking again. She couldn't wait for this to be over so she could sit down. She reached for some photographs she had brought, hoping that no one would notice her shaky hands as she passed them out. "These pictures are from my cousin's Quince. It was in Mexico City last summer. The ceremony was at the Church of San Juan Bautista, and the party was at my grandparents' house."

Isabel had planned to say more, but, instead, she went right to the music. She pressed the button on the cassette player and the waltz began. It was beautiful. When they got to the last chorus, Isabel's family began to sing along. You could hear their voices blending with the band. Isabel stood waiting while the tape played. Then she picked up the cassette player and headed back to her desk.

"Very nice, Isabel," Ms. Ciara said. "And now we've seen another kind of tradition, also musical ... Very good."

"Thank you," Isabel said, relieved to be back in her seat. As she passed Anna and Joline's desks, she noticed that they were drawing little princesses with tiaras and funny faces all over their notebooks. Isabel wished she had some paint with her now, something she could accidentally spill on their drawings. That was the thing about Anna and Joline. They sometimes made you feel like being mean, too.

"Does anyone have any questions or comments?" Ms. Ciara asked.

As if on cue, there was a knock on the door, and Mrs. Fields walked in. "Sounds like you're all having fun in here today," she said.

"We're discussing musical traditions," Ms. Ciara explained.

"Well, then, I've come at the perfect time," Mrs. Fields said. "I have come to talk about an Abigail Adams school tradition ... the seventh-grade talent show."

Katani looked at Mrs. Fields. It was difficult, sometimes, for Katani to believe that the principal of Abigail Adams Junior High was her own grandmother. Her grandmother had worked hard to get where she was, and Katani was proud of her. It was all about education at Katani's house. But, still, it was pretty weird having your grandmother be the principal, she thought.

"Each year we have a wonderful show. And from what I heard out there in the hall, it sounds like we have quite a few potential performers here. The audition times are posted on the board. The show is voluntary, of course, though I hope each of you will perform in some way, as this is a charitable event. And that is really the part I came here to talk to you about.

"Last year, the proceeds of the talent show funded a field trip along with a sizable contribution to the Peabody Essex Museum. The year before, we held an art show to benefit a local charity. This year it can be anything you want, with one stipulation. The event or cause you choose must be somewhat educational. What do I mean by that? A class trip to the Museum of Science is educational. A trip to Crane's Beach is probably not ..." She thought for a minute. "I take that back. A trip to Crane's Beach could be educational if it included a nature walk ... or a visit to a historic monument ... You get the point. You are all encouraged to submit proposals to the Student Council. This group will make a decision at their next session."

Betsy Fitzgerald's hand shot up.

"Yes, Betsy?" Mrs. Fields said.

"Mrs. Fields, I move that we use the proceeds of the show to hire a college PSAT coach to host vocabulary enhancement training sessions at the school." Betsy looked around. "Any seconds?"

The Trentini twins started banging their heads on their notebooks, pretending that Betsy's vocabulary program would drive them over the edge.

Mrs. Fields was clearly amused. "Don't you think that's a bit premature, Betsy? I mean, for a seventh-grade class."

"It's never too early to build your vocabulary, Mrs. Fields," Betsy said.

"True enough," Mrs. Fields said. "Well, if that's what you would like, I urge you to write it up as a proposal and submit it to the Student Council. One page only."

Betsy started making notes in her notebook even before Mrs. Fields finished what she had to say.

"I will post the audition schedule as well as the proposal guidelines on the bulletin board next to the cafeteria. Please make sure to stop by and take a look at them."

The bell rang and Maeve rushed over to Charlotte, Isabel,

Avery, and Katani, who were on their way out the door.

"Isn't this so cool? A talent show," Maeve enthused. "I went to one at my cousin's high school once. It was super fun."

"Yeah, super fun if you have a talent like yours, Maeve," said Avery. "But I see backstage work in *my* future."

The other BSG cracked up, remembering Avery's voice and dance dyslexia. She could kick a soccer ball like Mia Hamm, but performing on stage was definitely not one of Avery's strong points.

The Beacon Street Girls made their way to the bulletin board. There were lots of kids huddled around, and at the center of the whole crowd were Anna and Joline, talking and whispering with Kiki Underwood. If Anna and Joline were the Queens of Mean, then Kiki was the Empress. She was so unfriendly to everyone none of the BSG could understand why she was so popular. Katani said it was because she looked like a Barbie doll and wielded power like an army general. That seemed like a good enough explanation.

The Beacon Street Girls didn't have much to do with Kiki. With the exception of gym and music, she wasn't in any of their classes, and she never spoke to them. They guessed they weren't cool enough. But that was okay with them. It was too much work to be around someone like Kiki. You never knew what she was up to. She barely spoke to Anna and Joline, and they were supposed to be her friends.

"What are you doing for an act?" Kiki asked Dillon. She was leaning into him as she spoke, pretending she was doing it to get a better look at the announcement on the board.

"Talent shows are not really my thing," Dillon answered. He didn't sound too encouraged.

Maeve jumped into the conversation. "I think I'm going

to do something from *Fame*, it has the best songs and dances," she said, trying to move between them.

"*Fame* is lame," Kiki said, looking at Maeve as if she were some annoying bug.

"We've decided to do something together," Joline proudly pointed to Anna and Kiki.

"How nice for you," Katani said. Katani totally had a way of stopping a conversation flat when she wanted to. It was a handy quality to have in a friend, as long as you were on the right side of it. Katani once told the BSG, "You really need to learn how to get people to stop talking without shouting at them. I mean, like what if you have some totally obnoxious employee and you have to squish him before things get out of hand?" She had a point.

"Would you guys mind moving away from the board so we can look?" Charlotte asked politely. Charlotte was always polite. She said it was from living overseas, where adults got really freaked out if kids weren't polite.

Dillon stepped out of the way, as did Nick.

Dillon bowed, "All yours, girls."

They were really nice guys, but today that seemed to annoy Kiki.

"I thought you Beacon Street whatevers would be doing an act together," Kiki said. "I heard you do everything together."

"Where did you hear that?" Avery said challengingly.

Anna snorted. "No one had to tell us. Everyone can *see* you're attached at the hip."

"So what kind of act are you going to do?" Kiki said, ignoring Anna.

"A great one," Avery said.

"Like what?" Anna challenged.

"We're going to do a magic show," Charlotte blurted out, surprising even herself.

The other BSG tried to look as if they weren't surprised.

"Right, like you know magic," Anna said.

"Charlotte studied magic in Paris," Maeve said. It wasn't exactly a lie, but it was a stretch.

"Yeah, right," Joline said.

"She did so!" said Maeve, this time with attitude.

"So, what, you're like David Copperfield or something?" asked Joline.

"More like Harry Houdini," Charlotte said. "Which reminds me, isn't it time for our vanishing act?"

Attempting an exit with attitude, Charlotte managed to send the bulletin board crashing to the floor as she turned to walk away. So much for being smooth. Katani put the board back in place and shot a glare over her shoulder, silencing the snickers from the Empress and Queens of Mean.

"Do you think Anna and Joline were born that way?" asked Isabel when the Beacon Street Girls had finally made it down the hall.

"No way," answered Avery. "I think they practice after school to see how they can annoy everyone."

"I think they are really going to be sorry when they grow up. If they stay that way through high school, nobody is going to want to see them at our high school reunion," Maeve said vehemently.

Ready to change the subject, Avery turned to Charlotte. "So, did I hear you right? Did you just say we're going to do a magic show?"

"Sorry, it just popped out," Charlotte said.

"I think that's a great idea," Isabel said. "Avery, you should have seen the magic trick that Charlotte did the other day."

"I think it'll be fantastic," Katani said.

"I really want to do it," Charlotte said, just realizing how excited she was.

"I'm in," Maeve said.

"Me too," added Katani.

"Me three," Isabel chimed in.

"There's just one teeny problem, Charlotte," Katani realized.

"What?" the others answered in unison.

"Think about it. Charlotte is the only one who knows magic," she said just a little smugly. "What are the rest of us going to do?"

"Oh, yeah, good point," said Avery with her customary "let's get real here" attitude.

"No problem," Charlotte jumped in to reassure them all. "A magic show has lots of different parts . . . costumes, props, music. Somebody needs to get sawed in half."

"Eww!" Maeve shrilled. "Count me out."

"It's fake," Charlotte explained. "The whole thing is an illusion. That's what magic is all about. Maeve, you could be the girl in the fancy costume, who walks around the stage with funny signs. And Avery, I could make you disappear. We'll all get to do something really fun. Just wait and see."

Avery thought for a minute. "Okay, I'll do it," she said, her eyes sparkling. "But only if I get to pull Marty out of a hat." She began whooping and running down the hall.

In chorus, the Beacon Street Girls groaned and began to chase after her.

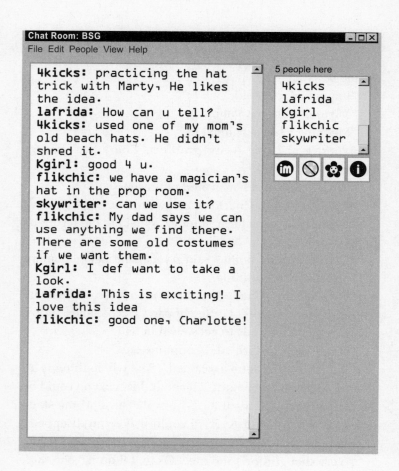

Chat Room: BSG

File Edit People View Help

4kicks: practicing the hat trick with Marty, He likes the idea.
lafrida: How can u tell?
4kicks: used one of my mom's old beach hats. He didn't shred it.
Kgirl: good 4 u.
flikchic: we have a magician's hat in the prop room.
skywriter: can we use it?
flikchic: My dad says we can use anything we find there. There are some old costumes if we want them.
Kgirl: I def want to take a look.
lafrida: This is exciting! I love this idea
flikchic: good one, Charlotte!

5 people here

4kicks
lafrida
Kgirl
flikchic
skywriter

CHAPTER

3

Magic and Old Movies

Dear Diary,
Magic show—am I completely out of my mind? How am
I going to figure all of this out in time for the talent
show? I can see it all now—Charlotte Ramsey, daughter
of renowned travel writer, Richard Ramsey, and a
member of the now famous Beacon Street Girls, has been
arrested for a magic trick gone seriously wrong. As a
result of Ms. Ramsey's ineptitude, a young girl lies in
the hospital with a rather large wound (yuck!) and Ms.
Ramsey faces serious criminal charges for being the
worst magician ever in the history of magicianship. If
convicted, Ms. Ramsey will be sent to prison until she is
at least twenty years old and she will never be able to do
magic tricks again!

Charlotte lay down her pen and leaned back on the big
stuffed pillows, her face creased with worry. Marty leaped
on the bed and laid his head on her stomach.

"Hey, pumpkin, what's the long face for?"

Charlotte started and sat up straight. Her father's friendly, concerned face undid her.

"Oh, Dad, I am in big, huge trouble," Charlotte said in one of those voices that meant she was almost ready to cry.

"Wow! That sounds serious, sweetheart. Good thing I just brought you some tea and cinnamon toast." He walked across the room and set the snacks down on her nightstand.

"Oh, Daddy. That's so nice, but I am really serious. I think I signed up for something I can't do."

"Well, I think we better talk this one through," he said as he popped a piece of the toast that was supposed to be hers into his mouth.

"Hey," Charlotte protested with a big smile on her face.

"I need sugar if I'm going to rescue my desperate daughter," and he popped another piece in his mouth.

Charlotte threw one of her pillows at her dad, and he threw one back at her. The pillow fight was on. Marty got so excited he jumped off the bed and ran for Happy Lucky Thingy, his favorite chew toy. Marty raced around like an animaltronix robot, shaking his toy and growling furiously until Charlotte collapsed onto her bed, laughing hysterically.

"Now, I think we should talk about this *Very Serious Thing* that is happening with you," her dad said as he plopped down on the bed beside her. Marty jumped up between them, Happy Lucky Thingy still in his mouth. He was quite a happy pooch, now that Charlotte *and* her father started to pet him. Charlotte plowed through the whole thing from start to finish, including her promise of the magic act. When Charlotte finished her story, her father fell silent for a minute, rubbing his chin as if he were deep in philosophical thought.

"Daddy," Charlotte poked him in the ribs. "So what am I going to do?"

"How does moving to Fiji sound?"

"That's not funny ... I don't think I can pull this off without some help. And you don't know magic ... who can I get to help me?" Charlotte asked, desperation in her voice. "I don't want to disappoint my friends. They were all really excited about this. And Maeve told Anna and Joline that I was a real magician."

"I've got it, by Jove, I've got it," her dad answered in his best British accent.

Guys, even when they are your dad, just love to joke around, thought Charlotte.

"Well," Charlotte said impatiently.

"Jacques!"

"Omigosh, Dad! Why didn't I think of that ... do you think ... do you think ..." Charlotte sputtered in her excitement. "Do you think he would help us ... me?"

"Let's go find out."

Charlotte and her dad phoned Jacques and woke him up, because it was six hours later in Paris, but he was so excited to find out what Charlotte was doing that he didn't care. Jacques spent an hour giving her all sorts of magician secrets. And he made her promise that she would never reveal them. It was the "Magician's Code of Honor" that you never reveal how a trick is done except to another magician. His advice was so helpful that Charlotte began to think that they were really going to pull it off.

When they met at Maeve's house the next day, Charlotte explained the code to everyone, and Avery and Maeve immediately fell in love with the whole secret magic society thing. They both said it made them feel very honored to be part of such an old tradition. Katani was a little suspicious and wanted to know if there was any money involved. Charlotte assured her that Jacques was not charging them at all. Isabel was so excited—she couldn't wait to find out how real magicians managed to do some of the things they did.

Charlotte loved the idea of the BSG all working together. Everyone could take part, and they would have a super amount of fun. Charlotte was making a list of everyone's talents. "I'm listing everything I can think of," she said. "You never know which one may come in handy." The list sounded impressive, even if some of the girls' talents could be hard to put on stage.

⤷ .... ⤶

Charlotte's list of the amazing talents of the BSG:

1. *Charlotte: Reading, writing, traveling, magic tricks, klutz factor which could provide comic relief.*
2. *Maeve: Singing, dancing, anything on stage, Hollywood-style glamour, impressions, acting very grown-up ... mastery of high heels.*
3. *Isabel: Art, computer art and animation, cartoons.*
4. *Katani: Costumes, business, math.*
5. *Avery: Sports, politics, team building, animal training.*
6. *Marty: Official mascot of the Beacon Street Girls, major cuteness factor.*

The animal training part was something Avery had just scribbled on the list herself. She had spent all yesterday afternoon teaching Marty to jump through a hoop. Bribed by various treats, Marty learned the trick quickly. Then, just as quickly, he learned that it was easier to just walk around the back of the hoop and pick up the treat himself.

"Is swimming a talent?" Isabel asked, munching on a BSG favorite—Chocolate Gag brownies that Maeve had baked for their planning meeting.

"Yeah," Katani said, "but I'm not sure it's something you can do onstage."

"Don't you do ballet?" Avery asked.

"I do water ballet sometimes," Isabel said.

"But you used to do ballet." Avery was sure she'd heard that somewhere.

"Yes, but that was a really long time ago," Isabel said. "And I don't think they put ballerinas in magic acts."

"Isabel, you have to do the scenery," Katani said. "You are such a good artist, I'll bet you could do something really cool."

"Okay," Isabel happily agreed. Scenery she could do.

"I planned on that already," Charlotte laughed. "We'll need a box big enough to crawl into. Something very colorful, with sliding panels and mirrors."

"That sounds kinda complicated. When I did Marty's doghouse, I just bought a doghouse and painted it," Isabel said.

"My dad can help us with that. He's really good at building things," offered Charlotte.

"Perfecto," answered Isabel. "But, I'll do all the painting. He doesn't have to worry about that."

"But we need you to be on stage, too," Avery said.

"We all don't have to be on stage," Isabel said.

"Isabel and I can work behind the scenes. Right, Isabel?" Katani asked.

"Sounds good to me," Isabel replied, looking over Katani's shoulder at the elaborate black-and-gold sequined outfit Katani was sketching for Maeve to wear.

"And Maeve, you will be the magician's assistant. We'll just put you in the box and ..." Charlotte said.

"Excuse me?" Maeve interrupted, dropping her brownie on the floor. "Can't we just do a card trick or something?" she asked.

"No way," Avery said.

"How about that coin trick? That coin thing you did the other day was really good," Maeve suggested hopefully.

"I'm afraid it wouldn't show from the stage," Charlotte said. "Only the front rows could see it."

"We need something mega," Avery said. "Really MEGA!"

"Can we at least go downstairs and check it out?" Maeve pointed in the direction of the movie theater, which had a stage. "I mean, before I volunteer?"

"It's just magic, you know," Avery said.

"I'm sooo relieved," Maeve said with a grin.

"Tell her how it's done," Avery said to Charlotte. Since Charlotte suggested the magic show, Avery had read every one of Charlotte's books on illusionists and magic.

"Relax, it's all done with mirrors," Charlotte said to Maeve as they started down the stairs to the theater in a dash.

The theater was really dark. They all stood in eerie silence as Maeve walked back to flip on the stage lights. Just like in a real performance theater, there was one single bulb, burning center stage. In fact, the Brookline Movie House had been a live theater at one point a long time ago. Maeve swore to her friends that sometimes when she was alone she could practically hear clapping and singing. None of the BSG believed her.

Charlotte stepped on stage and immediately tripped over something. So Charlotte. Avery grabbed her arm and caught her just in time.

"What was that?" Charlotte asked. The klutz of the group, her friends almost expected her to trip for no reason at all, but this time there was something there.

"Orchestra pit," Maeve said. "This used to be a live theater," she said. "Stay put until I get some more lights on."

The group stood still. As the house lights came up, Charlotte saw what she had tripped over. The orchestra pit had been filled in. You could see the platform they built over it. In the top of the platform was a small trapdoor with a ring handle lock that was sticking up slightly.

"I never knew this used to be a live theater," Katani said. She had lived here all her life, but she had never heard anything about it.

"Most people have no idea," Maeve said. "In the beginning, it was a vaudeville house. During the Great Depression, when people were really poor and stuff, they used to do comedy acts here so everyone would feel better. They gave away door prizes, sometimes even food. Then, during World War II, people used to come here to see the newsreels of the troops overseas. Later it was owned by a big Hollywood studio. I heard they even held a premiere here once … I think it was with Doris Day—remember I showed you that movie with Cary Grant?" The girls nodded, but none of them ever remembered the names of the old movie actors. Maeve did. She never forgot one. It was like the stars were her friends. Yup, Hollywood was Maeve's destiny ... someday. The lights, the action, the applause ... Maeve was ready for all of it.

The girls looked around. Usually, the place was dark, so none of the girls had ever noticed what a beautiful building it was. Only from the stage could you see some of the fancy detail ... Beaux Arts, Maeve called it. It was really majestic. It wasn't hard to picture what it must have looked like back in the day. You could almost see the old-time stars walking down the red carpet to their seats with their fur coats draped around them and the flashbulbs blinking at every turn.

MAEVE IN JEOPARDY

It was time to get down to magic show business. The girls sat in the audience while Charlotte tried her coin trick. Everyone agreed it wasn't visible from the stage.

"I still don't want to be put in a box—even if it's only with mirrors," Maeve whined.

"Maybe we can just use her hands," Charlotte said to Avery, who was the only one who knew what she was talking about. "That way the box can be smaller, and there'll be less work for Isabel."

"Let me see your hands," Charlotte said to Maeve.

Maeve reluctantly held them out. Her nails were painted with bright pink polish. Maeve had even glued a rhinestone to every nail, very Hollywood glam, except the polish was chipping around the edges. It was hard to maintain her beauty regime and do her homework, too.

"Now I need to see everyone else's hands," Charlotte said, carefully examining each pair, turning them over.

"Avery, you're the best match for her," Charlotte said. "Your hands are the same size."

Avery pulled back her hands in horror. "I have no nails," she said.

"Fixable," Charlotte said. "Nail polish will do the trick."

"What are you up to?" Katani asked.

"I'll tell you what she's not up to," Avery said. "She's not painting my nails!"

"I don't understand," Isabel said to Charlotte. "What kind of trick is this? It sounds creepy!"

"Oh," Charlotte said gleefully. "We build this little thing. Separate the box into two pieces, and voilà, it looks as if Maeve has been separated from her hands. A few dramatic noises, Maeve's Academy Award performance, and the audience will believe it."

Now that it involved acting ability, Maeve was starting to get interested. "I can scream really well," she said, and she proceeded to give them a preview.

"Fabulous," Katani added with sarcasm. "I don't think you have to do that again until the talent show."

Maeve stuck her tongue out playfully at Katani.

"What about you?" Charlotte turned to Avery.

"Do I have a choice?" Avery asked.

"Not really," Charlotte laughed.

"Is the Marty trick still in the show?" Avery asked.

"Yes," Charlotte said.

"And I want to do a trick with the guinea pigs, too," Avery said, realizing she had some leverage.

"What trick?" This was the first Charlotte had heard of any guinea pig trick.

"I don't know yet. I'll think of something," Avery said.

"Now you're pushing it," Charlotte said.

"That's my final offer," Avery said, putting her hands on her hips. "It's either the guinea pigs or …"

"Okay," Charlotte said. "Okay, okay, okay. Are we all in?"

"I'm in, but this trick is kind of creepy. I don't know if anyone's gonna let us do it," Isabel said doubtfully.

The girls worked until almost dinnertime. By the time they were finished, they had five tricks lined up, including one with the guinea pigs, newly renamed Siegfried and Roy. Avery was delighted. Katani decided she wanted to make an endless scarf that Isabel could pull all the way across the stage. Everyone liked the idea. "I'm not sure yet what material to make it out of," she said.

"Something diaphanous," Maeve suggested.

"What does that mean?" Isabel asked.

"You know, sheer, transparent ... something that seems to glow with its own light," Maeve said dreamily, getting carried away with a vision of herself dancing across the stage.

"Good word," Isabel said. "You must read a lot of books."

"Everyzing I know I've learned from ze movies," she said in her best French accent. "Particularly the old ones," Maeve added in her own voice. "My dad and I love to watch them together. Especially old Katharine Hepburn films."

Dramatically putting her hand to her forehead, she launched into her best Katharine Hepburn imitation: "The calla lilies are in bloom again ..."

Katani smiled.

Isabel looked at her blankly.

"Please don't tell me you haven't seen any Katharine Hepburn movies," Maeve said.

"I saw *My Fair Lady*," Isabel said hopefully.

"That's Audrey Hepburn, not Katharine," Maeve said.

"Sorry," Isabel said.

"Wasn't she in *Chicago*?" Avery asked. She hadn't seen the movie, but she'd heard the name.

"That's Catherine Zeta-Jones," Katani said.

"That's it. Avery ... Isabel ... your movie education is in serious jeopardy. I cannot work under these conditions! We have to have a screening right now," Maeve said, marching off the stage.

"Where are you going?" Isabel asked.

"To talk to my father," Maeve said, and walked out of the theater.

Maeve saw the light on in the office and barged right in. "Dad, Dad, can we screen a Katharine Hepburn film? Can you believe Isabel and Avery don't even know who she is?"

Maeve's father looked up from his desk with an expression on his face that immediately silenced Maeve. Mr. Taylor was not alone. There was someone in the office with him.

"Maeve, I'd like you to meet Mr. Callahan from Citibank of Boston. Mr. Callahan, this is my daughter, Maeve."

Maeve extended her hand with the most movie charm she could muster. With just a hint of a southern accent, she held out her hand and said, "It's a pleasure to meet you, Mr. Callahan."

But something was up, and Maeve knew it. Although Mr. Callahan was clearly amused by the greeting, her dad didn't smile. She must have looked alarmed, because her father explained right away. "Mr. Callahan is here because I have applied for a second mortgage on the theater."

Maeve had no idea what a second mortgage was. She wasn't even all that sure what a first mortgage was.

"Could we talk about Katharine Hepburn later? Mr. Callahan and I have some things to discuss." Maeve's father walked her to the door.

"But Dad," Maeve said. "The BSG just wanted ..."

"We'll talk over dinner," he said, cutting her off. Then, trying to recover, he smiled. "This is my night to make dinner with you and your brother, isn't it?"

Maeve just nodded. Things must be really bad if he had forgotten about tonight. For a week, they had had plans to make their own pizza tonight. They were all looking forward to it. At least Maeve and Sam were.

When she got back to her friends, Maeve's whole demeanor had changed.

"Maeve, are you okay?" Isabel asked.

"Does anybody know what a second mortgage is?" Maeve looked as confused as she felt.

"Sure," said Isabel. Her parents were both accountants. She was familiar with the lingo.

"My dad's trying to get a second mortgage on the theater. Why would he do that?" Maeve asked Isabel.

"My dad says people sometimes get a second mortgage when they want to make improvements on a property, and need to borrow some money to do that," Isabel said. "Or because interest rates are low and their monthly payments would be less." Everyone stared at her. "I know," she laughed. "I sound like an accountant. But my parents think it's important to know this stuff."

"I totally agree," said Katani. "Girls totally need to learn about money." Money and how to manage it was Katani's new passion. Most girls her age were thinking about school, sports, and boys. Not Katani. She thought about business and money and how she could use it to help people.

"Maybe your father wants to do the place over," Charlotte suggested, thinking of what a beautiful theater it would be after some restoration work.

"Or sometimes people do it when they need money to pay bills," Isabel said.

"Oh God, do you think he needs money? I mean, with the two apartments and all, and my mother's only been able to work part time." Maeve was beginning to sound tearful.

"Don't worry," Katani said. "I'm sure it's something positive." Katani knew something about mortgages, too. She wasn't at all sure it was something positive, but she wasn't going to tell Maeve anything that would make her worry. Maeve had enough to worry about lately.

"So I shouldn't worry?" Maeve asked.

"Of course not," Charlotte said.

"No way," said Avery.

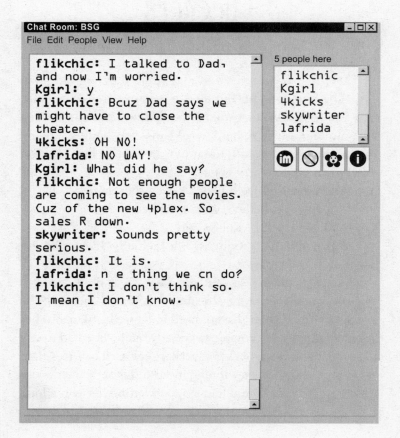

4

Checkers

Katani had promised Kelley that they would play checkers tonight. But after one game, Katani called it quits. She was worried about Maeve, and she wanted to figure out a way to help her. Maeve was having a really tough time lately, and Katani didn't want her to have anything more to worry about.

"You promised we'd play," Kelley complained.

"We *did* play, Kelley," Katani replied.

"Only one game," Kelley said.

Katani felt bad about it. She actually liked playing checkers with her sister.

Even though she was autistic, Kelley was pretty good at the game, and every time she jumped a line of checkers, she howled with laughter. Katani used to let Kelley win, but her sister was really improving, especially lately. She had a way of seeing potential moves on the checker board before Katani saw them, and she was winning more and more games every time they played. Katani had stopped letting her win a long time ago.

"I have some research to do, and you should probably go to bed," Katani said.

"It's not my bedtime yet, Miss Bossy!" Kelley said, looking at the clock.

"Then go downstairs or something," Katani suggested.

"I don't have to go downstairs. This is my room too, you know."

Katani knew that only too well. Aside from being a fashion designer, her other big dream was to have a room of her own. Still, she didn't want to hurt Kelley's feelings. "I'm sorry. I just meant I have to do something, so you should do something else now, okay? So I can concentrate."

"Okay, Miss Bossy." Kelley said. She liked this title for Katani, especially since she could tell that Katani didn't.

Katani searched the Web for movie theaters. What had other old theaters done when they saw their profits dying? One theater she found had become a revival house. It showed nothing but old movies. A theater on the Massachusetts North Shore now hosted a children's show. And still another gave away prizes every night. Isn't that what Maeve had said? That the old theaters used to give away prizes?

They were all things that could help the theater long term, but Mr. Taylor needed help with the taxes right now. And as Katani surfed the Web, she was starting to get an idea that might work right now. It was based on something Maeve had said earlier when she was doing her Katharine Hepburn imitation. What was it Maeve had said? Oh yeah. *Everything I know, I've learned from the movies.* Even if that was stretching it, Katani could make a case for it, and she might be able to help the Movie House.

"Hey Kelley," Katani said, feeling bad about how she had treated her before. "I need your help."

Kelley was sitting on her bed, sulking. But she wasn't really mad. Her mood improved instantly at the thought of doing anything with Katani. "Okay," Kelley said, trying not to sound too eager.

"Tell me one thing that you have learned from going to the movies," Katani said.

"Like what?"

"I don't know. Anything at all. Something that you didn't know before, but that you know now."

Kelley thought about it for a long time before she answered the question. "I learned not to put my feet on the chairs in front of me."

Katani laughed.

"That's not funny," Kelley said, offended. "I also learned not to put popcorn on people's heads." Kelley thought about it for a minute. "That last one might be a little funny."

Katani was trying to hide her smile. "Etiquette," Katani said, suddenly excited. "You learned etiquette."

"Well, I don't know about that!" Kelley said. She wasn't sure what the word meant, but it sounded like an insult.

"Etiquette means manners. You learned good manners from going to the movies!"

Kelley looked proud. "Of course I did. I'm not stupid, you know."

"Yes. And you helped me with my paper."

Kelley was delighted with herself. The hall phone rang. Kelley ran to get it. A minute later she brought the phone back to Katani. "It's my new best friend Charlotte," Kelley said. "She wants to talk to you."

"Tell her I can't talk right now," Katani said.

"Is that good manners?" Kelley asked.

"If you say it in a nice way, it is," Katani said.

"Katani said she doesn't want to talk to you right now," Kelley said in the sweetest voice she could muster.

Now it was Katani who was irritated. That was the thing about Kelley, she always told the truth.

"Tell Charlotte I'm working on a report, and that I'll call her when I'm done."

Kelley got back on the phone, but Charlotte had already heard. "Charlotte says the book report isn't due until next week. She says she needs to talk to you about Maeve's problem." Kelley's face scrunched up with concern. "What's the matter with my friend Maeve?" Maeve was another one of Kelley's favorite people, and Kelley looked really worried.

"Nothing, Kelley, Maeve is fine." Now Katani was getting upset. She had to finish her proposal by tomorrow, or any hopes of helping Maeve would be gone.

"Just tell her I'll call her back, okay?"

Katani's voice sounded annoyed. "Okay," Kelley said. "Charlotte, Katani doesn't want to talk to you right now because I just beat her at checkers and she's really mad. Why don't you come over and play checkers with me? ..."

5

A Secret Plan

Charlotte sat up late in the Tower waiting and waiting, but Katani never called her back. She hoped Katani wasn't mad about something, because Katani always called people back right away. Katani loved to talk on the phone. She said it was easier than talking to people in person, where you got distracted by what they were wearing or what they looked like. You could just concentrate on what your friends were saying, which in the end was the important thing. "The extra bonus," Katani said, "is that you can be in your sweats with funky-looking hair and no one can see you."

But, Charlotte was frustrated. She had something really important to talk to Katani about. She had been thinking all day that the BSG had to do something to help with the Movie House. After all, they took an oath to be loyal to their friends forever. And of all the Beacon Street Girls, Katani was the one with the best business sense. If they were going to come up with a way to help the theater stay open, Katani was going to have to get involved.

Clearly, Maeve needed their help. It wasn't fair that her family had to face a new crisis. But, Charlotte's dad always said that "life wasn't fair" and that if you wasted your time thinking about how things were unfair all time you'd be pretty miserable. And then you couldn't get anything done because you'd always be feeling bad because life was unfair. He had a point.

So, instead of worrying about Maeve and thinking about why Katani hadn't called her back, Charlotte decided to focus on the magic show. Saving the Movie House would have to wait until the BSG got together, she reasoned.

She pulled her notebook out of her backpack and began a list of things they'd need to do for the show.

Materials needed for magic show.

1. *Mirrors for box*
2. *Fabric for costumes*
3. *Hat for Marty to jump out of. Check prop room at Movie House*
4. *Rope for rope trick*
5. *Fabric for endless scarf ... think diaphanous*
6. *Magician's outfits and hats for Avery and me*
7. *Magician's wands*
8. *Lots of spangles and sparkles*
9. *Fog machine? (Maybe we could borrow one)*
10. *Something for guinea pig trick*
11. *Treats for Marty ... make that lots of treats*
12. *Nail polish and makeup for guillotine trick*

Remember: borrow props and take donations. Need money. How??? Sell Chocolate Gag in the cafeteria? Need to have a fund-raising meeting.

Sitting at her desk the next morning, Charlotte was so engrossed in reviewing her list from the night before that she didn't see Katani standing over her.

"Yikes, you scared me. What are you doing here? Didn't you go to school with your grandmother?" asked Charlotte.

"I told her that we needed to do some work on the talent show. She said, 'Fine, just don't be late for school.'

"I'm sorry I didn't call you back last night," Katani continued. "I didn't finish my report until after eleven. I figured you'd understand."

"Oh, I was a little worried. I thought you might be mad or something."

"No, I was busy on my report."

"The research report?" Charlotte asked worriedly. She didn't think their reports for Ms. R were due yet.

"No, this report." Katani held out a paper. "Actually it's more like a proposal. I was going to ask you to proofread it."

Charlotte took the paper and caught sight of the title:

The Movies: An Educational Experience
Why we need to save the Brookline Movie House

"What is this?" Charlotte asked.

"Just read it. I don't know if this will work or if people will think it's stupid. Just read it," Katani said.

Katani stood over Charlotte, watching her as she read.

"You want to use the money from the talent show to save the movie theater?" Charlotte asked when she finished.

"To help them with the taxes at least. They need it now. I have some other ideas too," Katani said.

"This is really brilliant, K. You're amazing. This must have taken so much work," Charlotte said, truly impressed.

Katani actually blushed. She was embarrassed by Charlotte's praise, but she was also totally relieved that her friend liked the idea. "Do you think it will work?"

"I think it might. I mean, I'd vote for this in a minute," said Charlotte.

"But do you think the Student Council will?" Katani looked doubtful.

"Why not? All the kids like to go to the cartoon fests and horror nights at the Movie House. Remember Frankenstein Fest last month? Everybody was there. Kids would really miss the old place if it were gone," Charlotte said. "And Maeve and her parents would miss it most of all."

"That's really why I did this. Maeve would be so sad if the theater went out of business. Plus, where would the BSG go to watch movies and eat free popcorn and candy?"

Charlotte looked up at her with mischief in her eyes. "We better get all the kids behind this proposal 'cause I am used to having my own private screening theater."

"I have another question," Katani said.

"What?"

"Do you think Maeve will mind? I mean, that everyone will know about the theater. Maybe she'll be embarrassed that it needs money?" Katani looked worried.

"I don't know," said Charlotte. She hadn't thought about that possibility.

"I was thinking about it and wondering if I'd mind. I mean, if it were me," Katani said.

"And would you?" Charlotte asked.

"I don't think so," Katani said. "I mean, if the theater does end up closing, everyone's going to know it anyway, right?"

"Maybe we should ask her," Charlotte suggested.

"I don't think so," Katani said.

"Why not?"

"Because I don't want to get her hopes up. We have no idea whether the Student Council will pick this proposal."

Maeve walked in with Avery.

"Hey you two, we were looking for you outside," Avery said, jumping up and down and getting Marty all excited. This was a treat for him to see Avery in the middle of the week. The two of them were acting like goofballs within a couple of minutes.

"Too cold," Katani said.

"How're you doing?" Charlotte asked Maeve.

Maeve forced a smile. "Okay."

Maeve's one-word answer made Charlotte realize that Katani was right. Maeve had enough to deal with right now. "Guess what? My father has a tape of *The African Queen*. He also has *Little Women*, *On Golden Pond*, and *The Philadelphia Story*. And *Bringing up Baby*," Charlotte said. "So we can watch Katharine Hepburn movies on Friday night in the Tower. It won't be the same as the big screen, but it'll still be fun."

"Cool," Maeve said, trying to sound enthusiastic.

CHAPTER
6

Isabel's Great Day

Kiki Underwood, who had already designated herself star of the seventh-grade talent show, was using the gym to practice her dance routine. The BSG watched as she hipped and hopped and gyrated her body, doing a pretty good imitation of a rock star. Kiki's costume was so tight that Avery winced every time she made a major move. Split spandex was not something Avery wanted to see. Neither apparently did Dillon, whom Kiki seemed most anxious to impress. Dillon's cheeks were flushing as he tried to handle Kiki's demands for more lighting.

"You know, I have to hand it to Kiki. Six weeks of hip-hop lessons and she's got kind of a cool dance going," Maeve said.

Charlotte added, "Yeah, she looks pretty good, but who would want to dance with her? Look what she's doing to Anna and Joline."

Anna and Joline were behind Kiki, trying to mimic her moves. Just when they were starting to catch on, Kiki altered her steps. Anna and Joline had a hard time keeping up with her, and Kiki was getting annoyed with them.

"They're even mean to each other," Katani said, shaking her head.

"You know, I'd rather go to a museum every night with my mother than hang out with those girls. It would take up too much energy trying to figure out what they were up to all the time," Avery decided as she popped some trail mix into her mouth.

Avery hardly ever ate candy—she said it made her tired, something that none of the other Beacon Street Girls could understand at all. Maeve loved chocolate and Swedish Fish with a passion, Katani was partial to Twizzlers, and Isabel loved caramels. They loved to tease Avery for eating whole-wheat wraps with avocado, tomatoes, and turkey. But, in fact, ever since they saw a picture of the amount of fat in a fast food meal, the girls secretly admired Avery for being such a healthy eater. It's just that they personally weren't ready to give up their candy!!!

Suddenly, Maeve looked around. "Hey," she asked. "Where's Isabel? I hope she's not late. I heard they give you late slips and it goes on your record; and you get labeled a slacker." Maeve looked very proud of herself for that pronouncement. The problem was that none of it was true.

"Maeve," Katani jumped in. "All that happens is that if you get three late slips in a month, they call your parents to help you get more organized."

"Oh, okay." Maeve sighed. Too bad. She did like a drama.

"Anyway, where is Isabel?" Charlotte asked.

"Remember, she told us her mother was seeing a new doctor, and the whole family wanted to be there," Avery reminded them. "It must be hard to have a mom with multiple sclerosis," she added.

"Oops, here comes Mr. McCarthy, beloved coach of my superstar sisters."

Katani's sisters were famous at Abigail Adams. They were two of the best athletes the school had ever had, and they never let Katani forget it.

On Wednesdays, the whole seventh grade had gym together first period. Kiki had snuck in to use the gym before school started.

As soon as the gym teacher came in, Kiki stopped the routine and sat down. Although the class was coed, Mr. McCarthy liked to have the boys sit on one side of the gym and the girls on the other. That was the way they did it in the last school he taught in, and that was the way he wanted it done here. Nobody really cared, except for Avery, who said it was sexist.

Kiki took a seat, wiping her forehead with a towel. Anna and Joline sat down next to her, copying her every move. "We're looking for another backup dancer," she said to Maeve. "You interested?"

"Sorry, I'm already booked," Maeve said.

"With what? *Fame?*" Kiki snickered. "That's like so out of date."

"Maybe, but I like it. It's fun," Maeve responded, brushing off Kiki's put-down. The one thing Maeve was confident about was her ability to perform. So she wasn't even bothered by Kiki's comments. They were like annoying little mosquitoes buzzing around her head that just needed a bit of swatting. Now math—that was a whole other thing. Maeve dreaded being called to the board to do a problem. That was pure agony as far as she was concerned.

"Maeve's also in the magic show," Katani said.

"Oh, right, the magic show. Lame and lamer," Kiki spat.

"Our number is going to be the show stopper," Joline boasted.

"Think VH1 meets Cirque du Soleil," Anna offered.

"What, you're doing a circus act?" Avery asked.

"More like a rock video," Kiki said. "Multimedia, film, music, computer animation—the works."

"Kiki's father produces music videos," Anna bragged.

Kiki looked as if she'd gotten all of her fashion sense from watching rock videos, Katani thought. But she didn't say it. Her personal rule was that she really tried not to make fun of anyone else's style. She read about this fashion designer once who loved to walk the streets of New York, looking at regular people and their clothes. She said it was very inspiring. The designer had said, "I mean, what if someone had criticized sweatpants the first time they saw them—where would we all be?" Life without sweatpants was too grim even to imagine. Nope, you better keep an open mind when it came to fashion, Katani reasoned. Even for the Kikis of the world.

And then Kiki looked over at Katani. "I would have invited you to join, Katani, 'cause you are so good at sewing and everything, but everyone knows you can't dance …"

The BSG glared at Kiki. She had gone too far. Katani was sensitive about the fact that she wasn't coordinated. Just as Avery, rescuer of all underdogs, was about to jump to Katani's defense, Kiki quickly changed the subject. "My father has a lighting designer flying in from the coast," she said.

"No one's gonna touch this act," Joline said. "We might even have Paula Abdul help us."

"Might," Kiki said. It was true that Kiki's dad had worked with her once, but he hadn't promised anything. The truth was they hadn't even talked about it. Not yet.

"You could be missing a big opportunity," Kiki said to Maeve.

"Big," echoed Anna.

"Totally big," chimed Joline.

"Sorry," Maeve said, not sounding for one minute as if she meant it. "I'm busy that night ..."

"Too bad," Kiki said. "Your friend Dillon seems to be available."

"What?" Maeve didn't see that one coming.

"Dillon's gonna dance hip-hop?" Avery laughed at the thought.

"Dillon wants to work as a techie. He's going to be my best boy."

"Your what?" Charlotte sounded shocked.

"It's like a technical term," Maeve said to Charlotte. "A best boy works on the electronics and stuff."

Kiki smiled. She waved at Dillon across the gym where he was sitting on the benches. He looked totally uncomfortable with Kiki's blatant attention. Kiki didn't seem to get it that seventh-grade boys weren't ready for major flirting. Most twelve-year-old boys were still giving each other noogies and playing wrestling games on the playground.

"Too bad you couldn't join us," Kiki said to Maeve. "We're all meeting at my house this afternoon to discuss our rehearsal schedule."

Maeve realized from her tone that Kiki had been setting her up. Kiki knew all along that Maeve was in two numbers. She'd seen the sign-up sheet.

Kiki popped up from the bench to get some water at the fountain. Anna and Joline followed.

"I thought of a new trick I want you to do in the magic show," Maeve said, as if nothing unusual had just happened.

"What trick?" Charlotte asked.

"I want you to make Kiki Underwood disappear."

"Funny, Maeve, very funny."

PAST, PRESENT, FUTURE

Isabel didn't get to school until after lunch was over. When the other girls arrived at art class, Isabel was already there, talking to the instructor. They were discussing Isabel's art project for the month. Displayed on the wall was Isabel's art. With her teacher's guidance, Isabel had created a multimedia collage in three pieces entitled: *Past, Present, and Future*. It was pretty amazing and *very big*. It had three distinct panels that fit together—a triptych, her teacher called it. Isabel had worked for weeks on it and her teacher wanted to enter it in an art contest that a bank in Boston ran every year for junior high and high school students.

Isabel's work was part painting, part collage. The first piece, the one entitled *Past*, looked like a child painted it, but better. There were images of Michigan, where Isabel was born, and of Mexico City, where her grandparents still lived in the old family house. There were photos of the family eating tamales in the Mercado de Comida, and others of her little cousins, Pedrito and Miguel Angel. In the lower right corner, a tiny ballerina, Isabel, danced her part in a local production of *The Nutcracker*. Little Isabel danced as her father looked on.

The second painting, entitled *Present*, featured a stage on which a ballerina was sitting down with the other ballerinas around her. Off to the side were a pair of crutches and a caption that said: *Dance cancelled ... for now ...*

To the far right of the center painting, a happy Isabel emerged into a different kind of ballet, a water ballet.

The girls knew the story by heart. Isabel had been a serious ballet student, but she had damaged the cartilage in her knee. It would have taken mega surgery before Isabel could dance again, and the doctor said her knee would always be at risk for more damage. So Isabel had to give up on ballet.

She was depressed about losing ballet for a long time. But one day, her mother took her aside and said to her, "Isabel, no more moping. When one door closes, another opens ... So keep your eyes open, sweetheart ... some little bird will fly in and tell you what to do next."

And something did happen. One day her mother and sister took her to see some paintings of the artist Frida Kahlo in Mexico. Isabel could not believe her eyes. Such color, such images. Isabel had never seen paintings like that. They were so alive and colorful ... and a little ugly, too.

For some reason Frida's paintings appealed to Isabel. Maybe, thought Isabel, it was because the paintings reminded her of the world ... sometimes beautiful and filled with color and sometimes downright ugly ... like the nasty power plant a couple of miles from their house back in Michigan. Anyway, she had begged her mother to buy her some paints that day. And now Isabel was never far from her brushes.

She also discovered swimming at the local YMCA. She hadn't wanted to go, but there was a swimming class that Elena Maria wanted to go to because one of the instructors was so cute. She dragged Isabel along with her. Isabel loved floating in the water and kicking her legs. There was no pain, and she felt like she could swim for miles. One day, while Isabel was waiting for her lesson, she sat watching the synchronized swim team. Isabel was hooked—it was ballet in the water. Synchronized swimming seemed perfect. Isabel wanted the painting to reflect that.

The third portion of Isabel's triptych was all about art. Collage, computer graphics, cartoons, Isabel loved them all. The Beacon Street Girls stood in front of the third panel, which featured images of Boston. There was a painting of the tower, not the way it was, exactly, but they way they'd always talked about decorating it. And Isabel had created future images of her new best friends: Maeve, Katani, Charlotte, and Avery. In the picture, the girls walked together, arm in arm, toward the doors of Brookline High. They were happy, confident, and very, very cool.

"This is so cool, Isabel," Charlotte said, as if she were seeing her friend for the first time. "I could never do this."

"Isabel, I think you might end up in a museum or something," Katani said, impressed. And then she offered up a big, wide Katani smile, which always made people feel like they'd just won the lottery, because the smile came straight from the heart. "You made me look soooo good; I love that." Everyone laughed at that, even the teacher.

"Thanks." Isabel smiled. Inside she felt that this was a really good day for her. Her mother was doing well on her new medication. Her art teacher had picked her painting to display. And, best of all, her father had e-mailed her this morning to say that he really was going to visit them soon when his accounting business slowed down a bit. Since they had come east, Isabel's dad had to run their family business all by himself. He had promised to visit, but he had already booked and canceled the trip twice. His e-mail this morning gave Isabel hope that he would be coming soon ... If only she could find a way to make sure it really happened this time.

Isabel really missed her father. Sometimes at night she cried because they weren't all together. But in the morning, how could she "mope" while watching her mother move slowly and sometimes hesitantly through the house. No, she said to herself. Martinez women did not mope about. They got up and got things done!

CR

When Isabel got home from school, Elena Maria was making empanadas (and practicing her scales—thank goodness she was done before Isabel put her coat away) and fire-roasting chilies on the gas burner of the stove. Her sister was a great cook, just like her mother and father. Her mother was sitting at the kitchen table. Even Aunt Lourdes was there. It reminded her of the last time they were in Mexico … the family all together at the Mercado.

Except that her dad should be here too. "Any …" Isabel stopped herself from asking if there had been any word from her father.

"What?" her mother asked.

Isabel thought quickly. "Any … thing I can do to help?"

Elena Maria smiled. "We're all set. You can be on the cleanup crew with Aunt Lourdes."

Cleanup was just fine with Isabel. Since Elena Maria was the cook, Isabel was willing to help with the dishes. "We have a symbiotic relationship, you and I. I cook, you eat and clean. It works for me," Elena Maria told her.

Isabel hated it when Elena used big words, which she did often. She thought it made her sound smart. It was clear that Elena Maria didn't want to be known only as a good cook. But the big words annoyed Isabel to no end.

Isabel went to put her backpack away. When the Beacon Street Girls first saw Isabel and Elena's room, they had been really surprised. It was decorated like an art gallery. The walls were painted navy blue and covered with art posters. Isabel

❁ 69 ❁

had a *Lion King* poster over her bed, the one from the Broadway show. Julie Taymor, the director of the show, was one of her favorite artists. A papier-mâché parrot stood in the corner, posing as inspiration for one of Isabel's bird cartoons. Her room looked like something you would see on *Trading Spaces*.

Katani had been so excited when she saw the room because she could tell that Isabel loved color and design as much as she did, just in a different way. Now that they were such good friends, the two girls would talk on the phone about their different projects. Their favorite topic: Perfect Color of the Week. Charlotte laughed when she heard about their conversations. "Okay," she added. "You can never tease me again about being a word nerd, because you two are *art nerds!*"

Isabel sat down to check her e-mail. There was one from the Brookline Arts Center, her home away from home. When she wasn't at the tower with the Beacon Street Girls or at the pool, Isabel was at the Brookline Arts Center.

She was surprised when she saw an e-mail from Kiki.

She was even more surprised when she read that Kiki had seen her artwork displayed in class and wanted Isabel to create some backdrops for Kiki's hip-hop dance.

From the description Kiki gave her, it was hard to resist. The act included hip-hop, singing, computer animation, and a rock video that Kiki's father had promised to shoot and maybe even sell. But what really intrigued Isabel was that they were looking for another backup dancer. Kiki had apparently seen Isabel's triptych. She hadn't danced in a really long time. It would be so much fun. One night of dancing wouldn't bother her knee that much. It was so tempting. She knew her father would be over the top with happiness to see her dance again. Was Isabel interested?

Isabel hesitated. She already promised she would do

artwork for the BSG magic act, and she would never let her friends down. But Isabel knew her father would do everything he could to come to see her dance. He had never missed one of her performances, not ever. And, as much as Isabel hated being the center of attention now, she figured she could handle being a backup dancer. She could certainly handle it if it meant she would get to see her dad.

Kiki left her phone number for Isabel to call.

"So what do you think?" Kiki asked.

Kiki sounded so friendly on the phone that Isabel not only accepted both jobs, but she told Kiki the reason.

"That's cool," Kiki said. "I wanted to make some fliers to distribute. Maybe we can send one to your dad."

"That would be fun," Isabel said. "I'll start working now."

"I'll see you tomorrow in the auditorium as soon as school ends," Kiki said. "We can show you all the dance steps so you can practice them before the auditions."

"Okay," Isabel said. Boy, she thought, this is going to be so great!

Chat Room: BSG   _ □ ×
File Edit People View Help

> **lafrida:** Hi Dad, r u there?
> **Papatinez:** I'm here. I've been waiting to hear from you. How did it go today? With your mother?
> **lafrida:** It went great.
> **Papatinez:** I talked to her on the phone a little while ago, and she sounded encouraged.

2 people here

lafrida
Papatinez

---

lafrida: The doctor is really happy with the new medication.
Papatinez: I am so glad to hear that.
lafrida: And she's so happy you might be able to come out soon.
Papatinez: I'm trying my best.
lafrida: The school is having a talent show. I'm dancing in it.
Papatinez: Really?
lafrida: I'm also making sets for two of the acts. I was hoping you could come.
Papatinez: When is it?
lafrida: The 28th. It's a Sat night. I'd really like it if you came.
Papatinez: Then I'll come.
lafrida: For sure?
Papatinez: For sure.

2 people here

lafrida
Papatinez

At dinner Isabel told her mother all about her triptych and the talent show. Isabel's happiness was contagious, though her family didn't know the real reason behind it. Isabel was going to keep *it* a secret, just in case it didn't happen.

For some reason, when she went to bed, she couldn't get that silly old Disney song out of her head for the next few hours. "Zippity do dah, Zippidy ai ay. My, oh, my, what a wonderful day." It was driving her crazy. She had to put a pillow over her head and hum to make it go away.

7

The Audition

Kiki sat in the third row with Anna and Joline, watching as Isabel performed the dance combination. Kiki made Isabel audition like they were famous producers or something, and this was some big Broadway show. Isabel could see them whispering back and forth to each other. She wanted to shout out, "Hey, what are you talking about?" but she wasn't that brave. So she just kept on dancing. Gradually, her body remembered how good it felt to dance. She could feel the sweat begin to drip down the side of her face as the music's beat intensified, and Isabel felt exhilarated.

"She's pretty good," Kiki remarked as she watched Isabel execute a particularly difficult move.

"She's not *that* good." Anna said nastily. "She's kinda too ... too stiff. We're supposed to be like music video dancers."

"Maybe we should get her a tutu," laughed Joline. "Tell me again why we need her?" she asked, not really wanting to share the stage with anyone else but the three of them.

"We need her because she's the only one who can paint the sets I want," Kiki replied. "And she knows something about computer animation. She's even going to do the costumes."

"What? Is she like some kind of art genius?" Anna said sarcastically.

"She takes a ton of art classes ... more than you," Kiki answered in her Empress of Cool Kiki voice.

"You're really going to let her design our costumes?" Anna was horrified. Kiki had never mentioned that before.

"Chill, she can *copy* our costumes." Kiki handed Anna a magazine with a dog-eared page.

"Nice," Joline said.

But Anna wasn't so sure. "Couldn't we put her in another color?"

The dress they were looking at came in red and deep blue, almost the same color Isabel had on today. Blue was definitely one of Isabel's colors. "We can put her in whatever we want to," Kiki said.

"I think we should put her in puce," Joline said, laughing.

"I thought she was the designer," Anna said. "Doesn't she get to decide the color?"

"No way," Kiki said. "I tell her what to do and she does it. It's like she works for me. Hey, I just had an idea. Maybe she could make your costumes and I'll buy a really good costume for myself. The star always needs to have the most spectacular look."

"Who sez?" said Anna, suddenly furious inside.

"Excuse me! Beyonce, duh!" said Kiki, tossing her luxurious mane over her shoulder, which managed to hit Joline in the face.

"Ow! You hit me in the eye."

Kiki ignored Joline completely.

"What ... what if she can't sew?" Anna said, growing more horrified by the moment.

"There's always blue jeans and a T-shirt," Kiki responded, looking nonchalantly at Anna. "Besides, maybe she can use it to get a modeling job."

"I doubt if Isabel cares," Anna answered, her teeth clenched.

"Why not, you do." Kiki smiled sweetly as Anna's face turned bright red. Kiki knew that Anna wanted to use this video as a modeling tape, and if she didn't do what Kiki wanted, she would be out of the show. But Anna was growing mad enough just to say, "Forget it!" Kiki could see that, and she really did not want to lose Anna, so in a sweet voice, she said, "Hey, we all have to do our part. I mean, *hello*, who is bringing in the lighting director, and the chore-ographer?"

"Your father?" Anna couldn't help it.

"Me!" Kiki said, getting agitated that anyone might question her control. "So I get to say what color the costumes are, okay?"

"Okay," Joline said.

"I can't understand why Isabel would agree to this anyway. It sounds like way too much work for one person ... Okay, less for us to do," Anna said laughingly.

"Being a set designer is very cool," Joline said, echoing Kiki.

"Oh yeah, set designer of a seventh-grade talent show is going to do a lot for someone's cool factor," Anna huffed.

"You have to start somewhere," Joline said.

Kiki decided to put a stop to things. "The reason she's taking the job is so she can dance."

"What?" Anna asked.

"She thinks that if she dances in the show, her father will come out and visit," Kiki said.

"She told you that?" Anna asked.

"She did." Kiki smiled. "I can be so charming when I need to be."

As soon as the music ended, Kiki went up on stage to congratulate Isabel. She put an arm around her shoulder. She gave her a few pointers. Then they danced together. If Anna hadn't known better, she would have sworn that the two girls were actual friends. But Kiki didn't have friends … not really.

"I want to be Kiki when I grow up," Joline said, impressed by Kiki's ability to manipulate people.

"I thought you wanted to be me when you grew up," Anna said. It was more cutting than she'd meant it to be, and Anna could tell that it hurt Joline's feelings. Too bad. This little threesome was really getting on her nerves. She didn't want to admit it, but she kind of missed it just being herself and Joline. Being with Kiki was not all that it was cracked up to be.

For all Anna cared, Joline, who was supposed to be her follower, and Kiki could do it themselves. She didn't care anymore. And she especially hated the name Kiki had picked for the group: The Hip-Hop Honeys. How boring was that? Anna wanted to call the group ItGirls. That was a way cooler name. Anna consoled herself with that thought for the moment.

"Come on," Kiki said, motioning Anna and Joline to the stage. "Let's practice the combinations together before everyone gets here."

Anna and Joline reluctantly walked to the stage.

All four Hip-Hop Honeys were practicing Kiki's dance routine when the rest of the Beacon Street Girls arrived.

"OOH," Kiki said to Isabel. "Here comes the *seventh-grade magic clique*."

"Clickety, clickety, clack," Joline said disdainfully.

It took Isabel a minute to realize that they were talking about her best friends. She had never thought of the Beacon Street Girls as a clique. In fact, they were anything but. She'd have to straighten Kiki out on that one.

Maeve, Avery, Charlotte, and Katani took seats several rows back. They couldn't help being surprised to see Isabel with Kiki and the Queens of Mean.

"What's going on here?" Maeve whispered to Charlotte.

"After you said no, they asked Isabel to be in their act," Charlotte said.

"And she's actually going to do it?" Maeve couldn't believe her eyes.

"I thought she didn't like to be on stage," Katani said.

"She must have changed her mind," Charlotte said.

"Or maybe she just didn't want to be in *our* act," Avery suggested.

"You know Isabel used to be a dancer," Charlotte said. "We don't have any dancing in our act."

"We could put in a dance," Avery suggested. "Maybe she could do a little dance with Marty."

Lately, Avery was obsessed with the idea of getting Marty into this show. She had convinced herself that he used to be in the circus. Back in his other life. Before they found and adopted him.

Isabel was good at the dance steps, but as Maeve watched,

she could tell that Isabel really didn't like being center stage. It was in her expression, which was just a little reserved. Her dancing was really nice, though. Maeve thought that Isabel definitely had the moves. All that ballet training had paid off.

"Isabel wasn't lying to us," Maeve said. "She just really doesn't like to be the center of attention."

"I really don't think she has to worry about that," Avery said, looking at Anna and Joline, who were already vying for position and trying to steal focus from both Isabel and each other.

"I have a really bad feeling about this," Katani said.

CR

When Isabel told them the reason she had decided to join the Hip-Hop Honeys, she had hoped that her friends would be more supportive about the opportunity to get her father here. She couldn't wait to introduce her friends to her father. But even after she told them the reason, the Beacon Street Girls were not very excited about the whole thing. Isabel was their friend, and the Anna-Joline-Kiki crew was not to be trusted, in their opinion.

"You really don't want to hang around with them," Avery warned. "They could cause you a lot of trouble."

"They're really not nice a lot of the time," Maeve added.

"Just be careful," was Charlotte's advice.

Even Isabel, who usually liked pretty much everybody, had to admit that Anna and Joline were not the nicest girls in Ms. Rodriguez's homeroom. But this Kiki girl seemed genuinely nice. And it really was Kiki's show; she was the one who was calling the shots. With Kiki in charge, even Anna and Joline were being nice enough that Isabel was starting to wonder if people had misjudged them all along.

But, it was so strange to hear Kiki refer to the Beacon Street Girls as a clique. That just wasn't true. They hated cliques. It was against the Tower Rules. The Beacon Street Girls were just good friends who spent a lot of time together. She would have to make Kiki understand that—if she could make Kiki understand anything at all.

TROUBLE IN PARADISE

"I don't see what the problem is," Isabel said when she saw Katani's face. "I like to design scenery, and I like to dance. Plus, we're allowed to be in two acts."

"There's no problem," Katani said. "If that's what you want to do." Isabel had heard Katani use that tone before, back when they first met. It sounded kind of snobbish. She hoped Katani wasn't going to get mad at her again. They had seriously bonded over their "art nerd" thing, and she didn't want to lose that.

"Okay, everyone," Ms. Ciara said. "People, please take your places now."

There was a sudden rush as the kids all grabbed seats next to their friends in the auditorium.

Avery whispered to Maeve, "We should just go sit with other people and start a new trend."

"Cool idea," Maeve whispered back. But, before they had a chance to move, Ms. Ciara clapped her hands to get everyone's attention.

"Settle down, everyone. We understand that you're just beginning to formulate your plans, so we're not going to make you perform now. All we're trying to find out today is what you intend to do: what kind of act, what it entails, and about how long it will be. For example, if you're doing a musical number, we want to know what kind of music … or what kind of dancing. Then we can set up the rough order of the show."

She called their names in the order they had signed up. Betsy Fitzgerald went first. She had decided on something by John Philip Sousa, but there were too many notes to play any of Sousa's tunes as a tuba solo. Each piece she had tried only ended up making her dizzy.

Betsy had done quite a bit of research before deciding which instrument to take up for band. In the end, she'd decided on the tuba the same way she decided on everything else. The tuba was a favored instrument for college admissions. College bands were always looking for people who could play the unwieldy instrument. And, since not many girls actually played it, Betsy figured that the tuba gave her an edge. Betsy was serious about going to an Ivy League school like Harvard or Yale. Everyone in the seventh grade thought she was obsessed … but smart.

"It says here that you're doing a tuba solo, Betsy," Ms. Ciara said. "One of Sousa's marches?" She looked impressed.

"I'd like to change that," Betsy said. "I still want to play something by Sousa," she said, "but I don't want to play a solo." Betsy didn't want to admit the reason, and nobody asked her to. No one seemed excited about a tuba.

"Well, where are your other band members?" Ms. Ciara asked.

"Um. I haven't exactly found them yet," she said. "But we have band practice tomorrow. I'll get some volunteers."

Maeve went next. She had first intended to perform a solo from *Fame*. But then she found a song she liked even better from the musical *Wicked*. Ms. Ciara was familiar with the show, and thought the song was an excellent choice.

"I'm sure you will do a wonderful job," Ms. Ciara said.

Another girl was going to do a gymnastics floor exercise with rings and trailing ribbons. A boy offered a recitation of a poem by Robert Frost, while a third girl was doing a ventriloquism act using an old Cabbage Patch Kid as a dummy. Everyone loved that idea—it was so funny, and the girl who was doing it was a real crackup.

WHERE ARE ALL THE BOYS?

Ms. Ciara looked around the room. Then she looked at her list again. "That's funny," she said, turning to the other teachers. "I only see one boy's name on this list." She showed the list to the other teachers, who seemed equally baffled. "I have to admit that the ratio of girls to boys has always been off at these events," Ms. Ciara said. "But this is the worst turnout for boys yet."

Kiki raised her hand. "I have a boy," Kiki said, as if both the act and Dillon belonged exclusively to her.

Maeve winced.

Ms. Ciara looked relieved. "All right, Kiki, why don't you and your Hip-Hop Honeys go next?"

Pausing momentarily to preen, Kiki got up slowly and walked to the front of the auditorium. Anna and Joline flipped their hair in unison. Dillon and Isabel walked a few feet behind them. They both looked as if they were wondering what they'd gotten themselves into.

Ms. Ciara turned to Dillon and smiled. "Well, I'm glad to see that you are willing to take a risk."

Dillon shrugged. "I'm not exactly *in* the act," he said, as if it were important that she understand. "I'm just helping them out with the lighting."

"Well, whatever you're doing, Dillon, we're certainly happy to have you involved. Tell me, do you know any reason the rest of the seventh-grade boys have chosen not to participate?"

Dillon shrugged again. "Not really." Some boys in the back row started to laugh.

"Why is it," Katani asked the girl next to her, "that boys in the back row always laugh at other people? It's so annoying."

All of a sudden, Kiki started to sneeze. "Sorry, Ms. Ciara," she said and sneezed again. "I must be allergic to something." She held out her hand. Some girl ran over to her and handed her a tissue.

Wow, thought Maeve, Kiki must be related to the Queen of England. She even has handmaidens.

Anna made a face. "What's that smell?"

"What smell?" Joline asked.

"It smells like a wet animal in here," Anna said.

Joline shrugged. Anna was right; it did smell funny up here. But Joline didn't feel like giving Anna the satisfaction of an answer.

Katani looked at Maeve.

"What?" Maeve said.

"I just can't believe that Isabel is up there with them," Katani said in a loud whisper.

"I can't believe Dillon is," Maeve answered.

"Okay," Kiki said, taking center stage. She looked around. She walked the length of the stage, counting her steps.

"What are you doing?" Ms. Ciara asked.

"I was just measuring," Kiki said. "We're going to do a big production number, and I'm just making certain that this stage is big enough." Kiki paced the rest of the stage as if she were a circus performer walking a tightrope.

"Does the school have a good projection system?" Kiki wanted to know.

"It has a projection system, yes," Ms. Ciara said, amused by Kiki's entitlement.

"What kind of sound system do you have? THX would be preferable," Kiki said.

Ms. Ciara smiled. "Kiki, you know we have no such thing."

"Too bad," Kiki said.

Maeve rolled her eyes.

Even Isabel seemed surprised. Kiki sounded like some kind of rock star demanding special privileges for her trailer.

"That's okay," Kiki said finally. "I can probably rent whatever we don't have."

"I hope *she's* paying," muttered Anna to herself.

"Suppose we start with you telling us what kind of act you've got planned," Ms. Ciara said. "Then we can all help you decide what equipment you'll need to rent."

"We're going to do a multimedia, hip-hop routine, with film projection and computer animation."

"That sounds interesting," Ms. Ciara said.

"And ambitious," added Ms. Rodriguez, who had just entered the auditorium.

"Oh, don't worry about that part," Anna said. "Kiki's got it covered." Her tone was slightly sarcastic, but no one seemed to notice.

"Yeah," Joline said, tossing her hair. "Her father produces videos for VH1."

Isabel didn't say anything.

"Isabel is our set designer, and," Kiki went on, "she will be doing the computer animation. And anything else that falls into the category of artistic."

"That sounds very ambitious," Ms. Ciara said. "Are you certain you can handle all this, Isabel? And dancing too? I see that you are already listed in another act."

Isabel nodded. But she was starting to have her doubts. This was the first she'd heard of the computer animation. Was Kiki crazy? Isabel had only taken two animation courses at the Brookline Arts Center. It was just like Kiki to spring things on you in front of everyone. What was she supposed to say now? *I'm sorry, I can't do all of that.* There were too many people watching her.

"Okay girls," Ms. Ciara said. "Let's hear your music."

Kiki walked over to the CD player and slipped in a disk. It was an old ballad that morphed into hip-hop. Kiki demonstrated the moves provocatively, as if Dillon was the audience. She danced up to within inches of him. His face turned bright red. When he looked like he couldn't stand the embarrassment another second, Ms. Ciara stopped the music.

Kiki did her best to look surprised.

"I thought you said that Dillon was not in the act," Ms. Ciara said.

"That was for demonstration only," Kiki said. She was speaking to Ms. Ciara, but she was looking right at Maeve.

Maeve stared back at Dillon. She couldn't believe how badly he was blushing.

"Well, the music is acceptable, although it wouldn't be my first choice. But tone the dancing down," Ms. Ciara said very firmly. "I want you to come back and show us new dance steps in a few days."

Suddenly, Kiki let loose with a huge, very loud *snurp*. There was dead silence, and then the whole auditorium broke into applause, which was followed by a few whoops and cheering from the boys in the back. Henry Yurt got up and did a little Yurt dance.

Kiki shrugged her shoulders and walked off the stage with the Queens of Mean trailing behind.

"Nice finale," Katani said. "You actually have to admire her, nobody seems to make her feel uncool." She was trying to make Maeve smile, but it wasn't working.

"Maybe she's allergic to Dillon," Avery whispered to Maeve.

"I wish he were allergic to her," Maeve sighed.

Kiki, Anna, and Joline took their seats in the front row and waited to see the next entrant.

Ms. Ciara read from the list. "Our next act is the Beacon Street Girls Magic Show."

Isabel didn't go sit with the Hip-Hop Honeys, but stayed on stage to help Charlotte set up.

The stage did smell kind of funny, Charlotte thought as she set up her props. It didn't smell like a wet animal, but it smelled kind of musty. Charlotte pulled a stool from behind the curtain. On it, she set up the magician's hat, the magic wand, and a cardboard mockup of the box they were planning to use for the guillotine trick.

Avery had surprised everyone. In the half hour between the time school ended and the auditions began, Avery sprinted over to Charlotte's house, and abracadabra! Marty's little head was poking out of Avery's sports bag. "Shh," Avery said to him. He leaned forward and nipped her nose. Avery giggled. It was something they did. In her early training sessions with Marty, Avery had tried to get him to give kisses to the Beacon Street Girls. But Marty was too macho for kisses. The closest he had come to kisses was the nose nip, and he only did that to Avery. There were no teeth involved, and in that way it seemed more like a human kiss than a doggy kiss (although Marty didn't really have any lips). Anyway, it was as close to a kiss as Marty would ever offer.

"Quiet," Avery whispered into the sports bag. As if understanding her perfectly, Marty pulled his head back inside the bag. Marty's presence was meant to be a surprise. Not even Charlotte knew he was here.

"We're doing a magic show," Charlotte said, coming to the edge of the stage. "Here is the list of tricks." She handed the list to Ms. Ciara. "Isabel is doing the sets and Katani is making the costumes. Maeve is the assistant and I am the magician."

As Charlotte spoke, Katani began to pull the endless scarf out of her sleeve. It was already almost thirty feet long, and quite elegant. It flowed across the set as Katani backed up first to center stage then to stage right. The look on Katani's face was one of surprise ... as if it were really magic and she had no idea the scarf was that long.

Everyone clapped enthusiastically.

"Very impressive," Ms. Ciara said.

"And it's not even finished yet," Katani admitted.

The bewildered expression on her face made everybody laugh. Everyone, that is, except the Hip-Hop Honeys, who didn't like being upstaged at all. They scowled like the wicked stepsisters when they found out that Cinderella had gone to the ball and met the handsome prince.

Ms. Ciara looked down the list. "Good, good," she said. "This all looks very entertaining ... but what is this guillotine trick?" Ms. Ciara looked concerned as she stared at Charlotte's list of tricks.

Charlotte always chose descriptive words; it was the writer in her. She regretted using the word "guillotine" as soon as she heard Ms. Ciara say it out loud.

"It's not really a guillotine," Charlotte said. "I mean, there are no real blades or anything. It's all done with mirrors," she said, hoping to convince Ms. Ciara the same way she convinced Maeve earlier.

But from a distance, the trick looked a little freaky. As Charlotte demonstrated with Maeve, it really did look as if Maeve's hands were gone. Even when you knew how the trick was done, it still looked real.

The boys in the back, who included the Trentini twins, shouted "Awesome!"

But Kiki Underwood said loudly, "I hate scary things like that!"

Everyone knew that was untrue. Kiki always went to Frankenstein Fest, and *Scream* was her favorite movie. Maeve, who was about to add in her special effects noises, caught sight of the look on Ms. Ciara's face and thought better of it. It was clear that the guillotine trick was heading right for the cutting room floor.

"You don't like it?" Charlotte said, reading the look as well.

"It's a standard magic trick," Avery added. "All the great magicians do it."

There were snickers from the Hip-Hop Honeys.

"The set is going to be really beautiful," Isabel volunteered. She felt bad that she hadn't even started to paint the box. It might have made a difference if the box had been as pretty and fanciful as Isabel imagined it would be when it was done.

"It's not that it isn't a good trick," Ms. Ciara said. "And I think it's impressive the way you have it all figured out. I just think it might be a bit too … *graphic* for some of our younger audience members."

"Audiences have seen the trick before," Avery said. "Millions of times."

"But there will be children in the audience," Ms.

Rodriguez volunteered. "They might actually believe it's true."

"In the end, we put everything back together," Avery volunteered. "So there is a happy ending."

"Yes, but ..." Ms. Rodriguez said.

"You wouldn't want to scare the children," Ms. Ciara said.

Katani thought of Kelley. Ms. Ciara might be right.

"No," Charlotte said.

"But it's a really great trick," Avery insisted.

"I have no doubt that it is," Ms. Ciara said. "Tell you what. Show us some of the other tricks you have planned, and let's all take some time to rethink this one."

Charlotte looked confused. The fact was they didn't have anything else prepared.

Avery stepped forward. "I have a trick I want to demonstrate," she said. "I'm going to pull a rabbit out of a hat!"

"What are you doing?" Charlotte whispered to Avery.

"Don't worry," Avery said, putting the sports bag up on the stool. "Pretend this is a hat," Avery said, pointing to the bag.

"But it isn't a hat, it's a bag," Kiki said. "The hat is over there." She pointed to the magician's hat that Charlotte was holding.

"Suspend your disbelief," Avery said dramatically.

"But ..." Kiki started up again, but Ms. Ciara held up her hand to silence her. "Go ahead, Avery."

Avery reached into the bag and fiddled with something. Then, satisfied, she borrowed Charlotte's magic wand.

"Abracadabra," Avery said, waving the wand over the bag three times. Then she tapped the side of the bag, and, very slowly, two rabbit ears began to protrude. As they emerged from the bag, the audience realized that they were attached to Marty's head.

As soon as she saw the look on Marty's face, Avery realized that she should have practiced the trick more. Over the last few days, she had mastered the trick of pulling Marty out of the bag, but the rabbit ear headband was something she had just added this morning when she found it in an old box of Easter decorations in the coach house.

As soon as he was out of the hat, Marty began spinning in circles, pawing the rabbit ears until he got them off. He jumped on them a few times as if they were an animal he was trying to knock unconscious, then he held them in his teeth and began shaking them. When he was finished, Marty lay down on the floor and ripped the ears apart.

It was mayhem. The whole auditorium was hysterical, even Ms. Ciara. Except Kiki, who was sneezing violently.

"I should have known that there was a dog in here!" Kiki shrieked. Her first sneezes had been genuine. It wasn't that these weren't, but she had certainly taken it up a notch. Kiki rushed forward and grabbed the box of tissues. "I am deathly allergic to canines!" she announced.

It was over the top, and everyone, including the teachers, knew that Kiki was putting it on. Still, even Maeve had to admit that Kiki's eyes were getting red and allergic looking. She'd been sniffling for the last twenty minutes. Something certainly was going on, if not anything nearly as dramatic as she was pretending.

"I CANNOT share the stage with a dog," Kiki said and stormed out of the auditorium.

"Oh dear," Ms. Ciara said. Pulling Marty out of a hat was the trick that Ms. Ciara liked best. Even with the chewing and stomping.

Charlotte was about to mention the guinea pig trick they had planned, but she thought better of it.

Kiki's dramatic performance cut the auditions short. They were almost finished anyway, with the exception of the gymnastic routine and the dramatic reading of Robert Frost's poem. Since none of the teachers would have any objection to that material, Ms. Ciara dismissed the group. They all had their assignments, she said. Everyone should let her know in the next few days what changes were going to be made to their acts.

Avery was told to take Marty home. The rest of the girls followed. No one spoke for a long time.

"Looks like it's back to the drawing board," Charlotte said finally.

"Looks like," said Katani.

Avery was too angry to speak. When she finally said something it was, "My mother is allergic to dogs. But we were sitting way in the back. And Marty was in a bag! It wasn't Marty that she was allergic to. Kiki didn't start sneezing until she went up on the stage!"

"Now what are we going to do?" Isabel asked.

"I don't know," Charlotte said glumly.

Isabel had set aside this afternoon to design the sets for the magic show. If she didn't do it today, she didn't know when she'd have time to fit it in. But she didn't want to say that. Things were bad enough already.

No one felt like talking. The Beacon Street Girls Magic Show was clearly a bust.

When they got outside the building, Dillon was waiting for Maeve. "Can I talk to you?" he asked.

"I guess," she shrugged.

"I mean by yourself?" he said, giving the girls an apologetic look.

Maeve hung back to let her friends go ahead.

"You know, when I signed up for Kiki's act, I thought you were going to be in it," Dillon said.

"I'm not," Maeve said.

"That's the only reason I said yes."

Maeve looked relieved.

"Do you think I want to be the only guy in the show?" he asked.

"Then quit," Maeve said.

"I can't do that. They're counting on me." Dillon meant it. It wasn't like him to break a commitment.

"Kiki lied to you," she said.

"No, she didn't," Dillon said.

"If she said I was going to be in the act, then she lied," Maeve said.

"She said she had asked you ... I figured you would just say yes," Dillon said.

Maeve actually might have been tempted to say yes if she had known that Dillon was in the act. But Kiki hadn't told her that part, and it was hard for Maeve to be phony anyway.

"Never assume," Maeve said. It didn't sound nearly as good when it came out of her mouth as it had in her head. In fact, it sounded kind of mean. But she couldn't exactly take it back now. She mumbled that she was sorry.

They stood there silently for a minute, then Dillon started to walk away. "I gotta go," he said over his shoulder.

Maeve walked slowly to catch up with the others. If she felt bad before, she felt worse now.

"What'd he say?" Isabel asked.

"I don't want to talk about it," Maeve said. She couldn't look at Isabel, so she just looked away.

Avery had to get to soccer practice. Charlotte wanted to

❀ 91 ❀

get home ASAP to start researching some new tricks. Since the Beacon Street Girls didn't have an act yet, Isabel thought she should switch her schedule around and get started on Kiki's video background. Good thing the teachers were cutting back on homework or she would be toast!

That left Maeve and Katani.

"So, do you want to talk about it now?" Katani asked after they'd walked a few blocks.

Maeve told the story to Katani as they walked.

"He was trying to be nice," Maeve said. "And I wasn't very nice at all. I feel really bad about it."

"Maybe you should call him," Katani suggested.

"Maybe," Maeve said. But she knew she wouldn't. It was too awkward and confusing. Besides, Maeve had enough on her mind these days with the possible closing of the theater and all of her parents' problems. Trying to deal with boys right now was just too complicated.

"Let's go to Irving's," Katani suggested when she realized the shop was only a few more blocks away. "I'm having a Twizzler emergency and you can get some Swedish Fish." That sounded good to Maeve.

CHAPTER
8

Good Advice

M aeve liked chatting with Mrs. Weiss. Ever since she was little, Maeve had enjoyed a special relationship with the owner of Irving's Toy and Card Shop—the local kids' hangout near their school.

Maeve and Katani stood at the counter at Irving's, chomping away. By the time they finished the bag, Maeve had told Mrs. Weiss the whole story. First she told her about Dillon.

As they talked, Mrs. Weiss nodded and smiled. "I wouldn't worry too much, Maeve. Just be nice to Donald the next time you see him. He'll forget all about what you said." The girls smiled at each other. Mrs. Weiss didn't get the name right, but her advice was pretty good.

Maeve nodded. She knew Mrs. Weiss was right. Dillon wasn't the kind of boy to hold a grudge.

"So how is your family?" Mrs. Weiss asked. She knew about Maeve's parents' separation and guessed that what was bothering Maeve right now probably had more to do with her home life than with her current crush.

As soon as Mrs. Weiss asked her, the whole story poured

out. She told Mrs. Weiss about the theater and all the financial problems her dad was having. "We're going to have to close down the Movie House if my father doesn't think of something soon," she said.

"Tsk, tsk. It would be such a shame to close it down," Mrs. Weiss said sympathetically.

"That theater has been here forever," Katani said. "My mother and father went there on their first date."

"I didn't know that," Maeve said.

"What about getting the community involved?" Mrs. Weiss suggested. "Maybe holding some kind of fund-raiser."

"What do you mean?" Maeve seemed genuinely interested.

Katani had been trying to come up with a way to tell Maeve about her proposal. Mrs. Weiss had just created the perfect opportunity.

"I have an idea," Katani said, then corrected herself. "I mean, I had it a while ago."

"You have an idea for a fund-raiser?" Mrs. Weiss asked.

"Yes," Katani said. "The talent show." Katani looked directly at Maeve when she spoke.

"The seventh-grade talent show?" Maeve asked.

Katani nodded. "You know how they are looking for something to support? Some community project?"

"Didn't they say it had to be educational?" Maeve didn't exactly understand what Katani was getting at.

"That's just it. I think the movies are educational. Remember the other day, when you told Isabel that everything you ever learned, you learned from the movies?" Katani asked.

"I was just kidding around," Maeve said.

"Well, I think you had a point. I got thinking about what

I'd learned from the movies. And I asked a few other people as well. Pretty soon I had a whole proposal for the Student Council," Katani said.

"You gave a proposal about the movie theater to the Student Council?" Maeve asked.

"That sounds very interesting. I'd say you're thinking outside the box, or at least outside the box office," Mrs. Weiss said, chuckling at her own joke.

"Don't be mad at me," Katani said to Maeve.

"I think it's a wonderful idea," Mrs. Weiss said.

They both looked at Maeve.

"It's fantastic," Maeve said, meaning it.

"But they haven't said yes. Not yet," Katani warned.

"I'll keep my fingers crossed," Mrs. Weiss said.

"Me too," said Maeve. She smiled at her friend.

"If they say yes, I will put a notice in the store for you girls," Mrs. Weiss suggested. "Maybe I can even sell a few tickets. Lots of kids come here after school."

"I know it doesn't solve the whole problem of profits," Katani said. "But it might help pay the taxes, though."

"We should probably tell my father," Maeve said, not absolutely certain that he was going to approve.

"I agree," Katani said.

"Maybe we should wait and see if we get it first," Maeve said.

CR

Kgirl Notes

Ideas to help the Movie House after the talent show:

Kgirl

1. Children's theater. It has a big stage.
2. Concerts, private screenings, big birthday parties for rich people.
3. Children's Saturday matinees. Maybe add an old-fashioned ice cream counter. Yum!
4. Non-Profit: I don't know how to do this, but maybe we could look into it.
5. Community events: One theater hosted an ugliest dog contest. Not sure that Marty would approve.
6. Meetings: There are a lot of big companies around.
7. More film festivals like Frankenstein Fest, Cartoon Fest, Comedy Fest, Stupid Movie Fest.
8. Talent shows for the whole community— people of all ages.
    So fun!

Maeve, Avery, and Charlotte were busy coming up with new magic tricks. They weren't having much luck, but they were IM-ing each other a lot. They were looking for a real big slam-bang trick. Charlotte said magic was boring unless they got people excited with something spectacular. They had agreed that the new trick had to have something to do with Houdini, but, as yet, they hadn't figured out any more than that.

Chat Room: BSG

File Edit People View Help

3 people here

skywriter
4kicks
flikchic

skywriter: Where's Isabel?
4kicks: She's working for Kiki tonight.
skywriter: I thought she was going to work with us tonight.
4kicks: Well she's not online.
flikchic: She changed her schedule because we didn't have the act yet. Plus she had so much to do 4 them.
4kicks: We have to talk to her about them.
skywriter: Let's talk...at the sleepover.
flikchic: I saw her to do list. They're working her way too hard.
4kicks: She should change her name from Isabela to Cinderella.
skywriter: That's kinda mean.
4kicks: Sorry...but it's kinda funny though
skywriter: Does that make Anna and Joline the wicked stepsisters?
flikchic: Yes, and Kiki is the ugly stepmother.
skywriter: Cinderella's in over her head. I think she needs a fairy godmother.
4kicks: I think she needs to quit.

CHAPTER
9

Saving the Theater

So how come none of the boys signed up for the show?" Charlotte asked Nick Montoya, as they sat in homeroom waiting for the bell to ring.

Ms. Ciara had asked the girls to find out.

Nick shrugged. "You know guys, they think it's dorky to be on stage."

"What about you?" Avery asked Henry Yurt.

"Too stupid," Henry said without hesitation.

"It's not stupid. It's fun!" Avery said, too quickly.

"Why do you think it's stupid?" Charlotte really wanted to know.

"Because they want us all to get up there and make idiots of ourselves. For what?"

"What if the money went to help some cause you liked?" Katani asked.

"Like what?" Nick wanted to know.

"Like something that made a difference in your lives. Like something that, if it disappeared, you would really miss."

"Like what?" Henry asked, his curiosity getting the better of him.

"I'm not saying. I'm just asking you if you would sign up if the money went for something you really believed in," Katani said. "Would you be in the show if it was for something good?"

"I don't know," Henry said.

"What about you?" Katani turned to Nick.

"Yeah. I guess so," Nick said.

"So Nick said yes," Katani turned back to Henry. "What about you?"

"Maybe," Henry said.

"What would you do for your talent?" One of his friends teased. "After your last performance, I don't care if I ever hear 'Happy Birthday' again."

"I'd dress up like a cheerleader and do a little cheer," Henry said, and then proceeded to mimic the moves of a cheerleader.

It was hilariously funny to his friends, and they were beside themselves with laughter.

"That's how sure I am that the money won't be going to a cause I want to support," Henry said.

"But if it did," Katani said. "Then you'd dress up as a cheerleader? With pompoms and the whole thing?"

"Yes," Henry said.

The other boys whooped in support of the idea. The Yurtmeister as a cheerleader was something the whole seventh grade would come out to see.

"Hey, I don't know what you're laughing for, you're gonna be right up there with me."

"No, I'm not," Nick said.

"No way," the others agreed.

Anna and Joline sidled in then, breaking the festive mood. "So, how's the magic show coming?" Anna asked Charlotte.

"Yeah, did you figure out any new tricks that don't involve rodents?" Joline asked.

"Marty is not a rodent!" Avery turned on her. "He's a dog."

"That was a dog?" Joline laughed.

Joline handed Avery a copy of the flier Isabel had made last night.

"What's this?" Avery said.

"What's going on?" Maeve asked.

"What's going on is that we're gonna have the most awesome act ever, thanks to your friend Isabel," Joline gloated.

Isabel looked as if she had been up all night working on the brochure. There were dark circles under her eyes.

"I'm gonna say something to her," Avery said to Maeve. And she would have done it, too, except that the bell had already rung and Ms. Rodriguez was motioning for everyone to take their seats.

"Wait until tonight," Charlotte said. "We'll all talk to her together."

"Okay." Avery reluctantly agreed to wait.

"I hope those girls aren't using Isabel," Maeve said.

"My guess is ... YES!" Katani said sarcastically.

Before passing the flier back down the row to Joline, Avery altered it slightly. By the time it got to Charlotte, Kiki's nose had a big wart drawn on it.

"Avery!" Charlotte was shocked. "That's so mean!"

"Well, I'm sorry, I just can't help it." Avery said. "Kiki already acts like a wicked stepmother, and now she looks like one."

Maeve tried not to laugh as she passed the flier back to Joline.

"Very funny," Joline said as she took back the flier. "Maybe you should switch to a comedy routine. Since you don't even have a magic act to begin with."

"We have a magic act," Avery said.

"Yeah? What is it?" Joline challenged Avery.

"We're going to do a trick so good that the whole school is going to remember it, forever."

"Keep dreaming," Joline said and took the flier back to her seat.

Joline was livid about the flier. She thought Anna would be mad too, but instead of getting angry, Anna looked amused.

☙

The girls talked about the magic act all through lunch. They were getting nowhere until Charlotte, tapping herself on the side of the head, said, "Omigosh—a disappearing act, that's what we need to do. People love it when things disappear. Harry Houdini was so great at that."

Avery loved the idea. "I want to be the person who gets to disappear. We could have smoke and everything. It would be so cool."

There was only one problem: Charlotte didn't know how to do the trick. She would have to call Jacques back.

"I hope my dad doesn't mind. Calling Paris is really expensive."

"You have to, Charl," said Katani. "We don't know how to do the trick otherwise."

All of a sudden, the cafeteria was silent.

"It's your grandmother," whispered Isabel to Katani, whose back was facing the door. As Katani turned around, her stomach did a little flip-flop. She knew her grandmother was about to announce the winning proposal.

Mrs. Fields was making her way into the lunchroom, followed by the president of the Student Council. She walked to the front of the room. "Quiet, please," she said, waiting for the room to settle down.

"As you know, this is the day that we announce the winning proposal. But, before I announce the winner, I must tell you that the Student Council received ten outstanding proposals, quite possibly the best Abigail Adams has ever seen. It was quite difficult to choose one among them. So, before the Student Council announces the winner, I'm going to read the names of the students who submitted proposals. As I do, I want each of them to stand. And when I am finished, I want you all to give a big round of applause to the following students: ... Betsy Fitzgerald ... Rachel Gorden ... Anna McMasters and Joline Kaminsky ..."

Charlotte looked over at Katani, who was staring at her hands. Charlotte tried to signal her, but she wouldn't look up. The suspense was killing Charlotte, and Maeve was looking pensive and nibbling on her lower lip. Avery was wriggling in her seat like her snake, Walter.

Then Mrs. Fields called "Charlotte Ramsey." Charlotte couldn't believe it. She must have misheard. So, she didn't move. But, Mrs. Fields looked around the room and called her name again. Avery gave her a little shove in the ribs ... "Get up, Charlotte ... don't be so modest ..."

There was nothing Charlotte could do but get up. But she looked at Katani and shook her head quizzically. As everybody clapped, Charlotte tried to get Katani to look at her, but K refused to meet her glance. There was nothing she could do but stand there and wait for the winner. Katani must have put Charlotte's name on the proposal even though Katani had done all the work.

When Mrs. Fields finished reading the other names, she began to clap, and everyone joined in. Charlotte could hear the Trentinis doing their usual woo-hoos in the back of the cafeteria. How weird is this, thought Charlotte. Here I am standing in front of the whole seventh grade taking credit for something I didn't even do. She felt really bad. And what if the teachers found out? Charlotte could feel her cheeks begin to flush.

Mrs. Fields asked everyone to sit, and then she turned the floor over to the Student Council president. "I want to ..." Suddenly, Mrs. Fields interrupted. "I wanted to let you all know that I was not part of the judging committee this year. Ms. Ciara stood in for me." Then she told the council president to go ahead and make the announcement.

Charlotte looked over to Katani, who had a shocked expression on her face. Charlotte gulped. Of course ... Katani had put Charlotte's name on the proposal to save her grandmother from having to be in an awkward position. It all made sense. Mrs. Fields must have forgotten to tell Katani that she had taken herself off the committee. Now Katani wouldn't get credit for her idea, and they would have to keep the secret from everyone. What a horrendous mess. Charlotte almost felt like crying.

And then it got worse ... or better, depending on how you thought about it. The council president announced: "Thanks to a winning proposal by Charlotte Ramsey, the Student Council has voted unanimously to use the proceeds of the show to save the Brookline Movie House. This historical landmark may be forced to close because of serious competition from all the big cinema chains. But the Movie

House is unique in the kinds of movies it offers the community, and it has been here for our grandparents and great-grandparents during the Great Depression and during both World Wars. We felt that we just couldn't let this Brookline landmark disappear from Coolidge Corner."

There was some applause, as well as some sounds of surprise.

"I didn't know the Movie House needed saving," Joline said loud enough for Maeve to hear. Maeve totally ignored her. This was not the time for pride. The theater needed saving, and that was that.

"Saving the movie theater," Katani said to the boys at the next table. "Is that a good enough cause for you?"

The boys had to admit it was. They were total horror movie nuts. They never missed the Frankenstein Fest.

"So you'll be in the show?" Katani said.

"Oh, man," said Nick.

Henry Yurt slouched in his seat.

Katani raised her hand. "I'd like to make an announcement, too," she said.

Mrs. Fields looked surprised. "Yes, Katani?"

"Because they really want to support the cause you chose, the seventh-grade boys have agreed to be in the show."

"Oh, man," Nick said again. But this time he said it under his breath.

The bell rang and everyone began to disperse. The girls had to race to their classes, but Charlotte had seen Katani head to the girls' room. She followed her in. Katani was splashing water in her eyes. Charlotte walked up to her and patted her on the back. "Katani Summers, you are the most amazing girl." Then she turned and walked out the door.

Late that afternoon, Maeve and Katani met with Maeve's dad.

"So this proposal might not help with your long-term profits," Katani said. "But it might help you with back taxes."

"I don't know what to say," Mr. Taylor said. "I'm completely flabbergasted."

"Say yes," Maeve suggested.

"Well, yes. Of course, yes." Mr. Taylor smiled.

"I have some other ideas," Katani offered a little tentatively. She didn't want to sound too pushy.

"I'd like to hear any ideas you have, Katani," Mr. Taylor said. "You seem to have a real head for business."

"That's what she wants to do," Maeve said proudly. "She wants to have a fashion and advice empire. And teach ladies how to make and manage their money, all while they feel beautiful doing so."

"Well, I'd say she's on the right track." Mr. Taylor sounded genuinely impressed. "And I guess that makes me your first client."

Katani beamed.

SETTING THE RECORD STRAIGHT

Charlotte knocked on Mrs. Fields' door.

"Come on in," she answered.

Charlotte straightened her shoulders and said, "Mrs. Fields, I have something to tell you."

CR

Chat Room: BSG

File Edit People View Help

yurtmeister: yo you girls owe us big time
skywriter: sorry but u promised!
4kicks: yeah, chill ... u want the theater to stay, right?
montoya33: yeah but i can never show up there again after i'm a CHEERLEADER
Kgirl: haha i can't wait
lafrida: what are your colors, boys?
yurtmeister: why not pink & white?
montoya33: yurt, that's not funny
4kicks: i think it's HILARIOUS
flikchic: lol me too ... anyway, thanx guys ... you're the best!
yurtmeister: yeah we know

7 people here

yurtmeister
skywriter
4kicks
montoya33
Kgirl
lafrida
flikchic

Just before supper, Charlotte decided she couldn't wait any longer for her father to come home. Perhaps Miss Pierce knew something about magic.

Charlotte went downstairs and knocked lightly on the door. Over the months, she and Miss Pierce had become friends, but she was always careful not to intrude on her reclusive landlady's privacy.

"Come in, Charlotte," Miss Pierce said as if she had been expecting her. "Sit down."

Charlotte sank into the overstuffed couch.

"What can I do for you?" Miss Pierce wanted to know.

"Do you know anything about Houdini?" Charlotte asked.

"Harry Houdini?" Miss Pierce said the name as if he were a longtime friend.

Charlotte nodded.

"What do you want to know?"

Charlotte pulled the Houdini books out of her backpack. "I've read these biographies," Charlotte said. "I was wondering if you know anything about the tricks he performed ... the escapes and things. I thought maybe you knew how he did them."

"What makes you think I am familiar with Houdini?"

"I saw some books when I was here before," Charlotte said. In fact, she had seen several books on Houdini, a whole shelf of them. Right next to the more scientific astronomy journals. Somehow, it seemed to suit Miss Pierce to have both. Maybe it was because she lived in a house with a secret Tower room and seemed like a bit of an escape artist herself. Or maybe it was just a hunch. "I need a really good trick for the talent show. I was hoping you could help me."

"As a matter of fact, Charlotte, I do know a few of his tricks," Miss Pierce said, pulling her chair closer to the couch. "The key to Houdini's magic was that he was an incredible athlete ... and a great escape artist."

Charlotte leaned forward with excitement. Miss Pierce, went over to her bookshelf and took out a dusty old volume with a leather cover. It was an illustrated biography of Houdini, one that Charlotte had never seen before.

CR

When Katani opened the door to home, all the lights in the house were out. Strange, she thought, everybody's car is here. She pushed open the door to the kitchen.

"Surprise!" her family shouted. Katani dropped her book bag. Kelley and Patrice held a banner that said, "We are proud of you!" while her parents and grandmother stood in front of a big chocolate cake from Party Favors, which, in pink frosting, told the world the truth. "To the girl with the best proposal ... ever!"

I'll have to talk to that Charlotte, thought Katani.

10

Marty's New Trick

Saturday night, Charlotte and her father were down in the basement when the doorbell rang.

"Oh, Dad, that must be everybody."

"That's okay, honey, you go ahead. I'll finish up down here."

Charlotte started to run upstairs and then she ran back down again.

"Thanks so much, Dad, I couldn't have done this without you."

"No problem ... hammer and nails I can do. Just don't ask me to pick any colors for the box. They would boo you girls off the stage."

"That's okay, we've got Isabel. She can paint anything."

The doorbell rang again ... and again ... and again.

"Gotta go, Dad. Avery is doing her, 'Open this door right now' routine."

Charlotte ran to get the doorbell before Avery had a heart attack. Marty was so excited to see all the girls that he was jumping up in the air and doing backflips. Just as

Charlotte opened the door to let everyone in, the phone rang. And then the pizza man came.

"I feel like I'm on roller skates today," Charlotte said, as she bolted up the front hall stairs. She and her father lived on the second floor, and Miss Pierce, their landlady, lived on the first.

She was out of breath when she got there, so she let out a big whoosh of air when she answered the phone. She sounded like Betsy Fitzgerald did after playing the tuba!

"Is this the Ramsey residence?" the voice on the other end asked hesitantly.

"It's me, Isabel," Charlotte answered breathlessly. "I just ran up two flights of stairs. Are you coming?"

"Go ahead and start the Katharine Hepburn movie without me, I'm going to be late."

On Golden Pond turned out to be a really cool movie, and it had a totally cute boy their age in it. They ate popcorn, snarfed down the pizza, and ate a bag of candy from the Movie House, compliments of Mr. Taylor. At the end of the movie, everyone wanted to see all the old films with Katharine Hepburn in them and everything with both Henry and Jane Fonda. Avery wanted to go out and practice her backflip like Jane did in the movie, but she was going to have to wait until next summer to perfect it because Jane did it off a diving board.

Where Is Isabel?

Miss Pierce had loaned Charlotte some things for the act: a Chinese finger puzzle, a magic cape, and the design for the Houdini Box that they had taken from the book. When the movie was over, Charlotte's dad carried up the box they had been working on for the talent show. She demonstrated everything for Avery, Maeve, and Katani. Lifting up the false back and sliding the secret panel out of the way, Charlotte showed them how the box was supposed to work. "And this is how you escape," she said to Avery.

"But won't people see that?" Maeve asked.

"You're supposed to create a diversion, something to lead their eyes elsewhere," Charlotte said.

"Smoke and mirrors," Avery said.

"We really need a camouflage curtain of some kind," Katani said, thinking of something she could make.

"Too bad the school auditorium doesn't have an orchestra pit," Maeve said. "Like the theater does. That door Charlotte tripped over would have made a perfect escape hatch."

They all thought as hard as they could, and then made a list. They agreed that each of them would come up with at least one diversionary tactic by Monday.

"Of course, Isabel will have the final say on the box design," Charlotte said.

"If she ever gets here," Avery said. "Where is she?"

"Did you see her in the computer lab Friday afternoon?" Katani asked. "I didn't leave school 'til four o'clock, and Isabel was still there trying to figure out some animation thing that Kiki ordered her to do. Something with film images of Kiki. Kind of *A Chorus Line* thing to make it look like there are hundreds of Kikis dancing."

"That's a scary thought," Maeve said.

"It kind of defeats the purpose of having backup dancers, doesn't it?" Avery asked.

"I think that's the point," Katani said.

"I think Ms. Ciara should stop this. It's too much work for Isabel," Maeve said.

Charlotte was trying not to say anything. But she kept

looking at the clock. She was really starting to get worried about her friend.

An hour later all four girls were worried. "Wasn't their rehearsal only supposed to last until seven o'clock?" Avery wanted to know.

"That's right," Charlotte said.

"What time is it now?"

"Almost seven thirty," Charlotte said.

They all looked at each other.

"I'm going to ask my dad to take us down there," Charlotte said.

"Let's wait a little while longer and then go," said Katani. "We don't want to interrupt them. You know how obnoxious Kiki gets."

They all agreed that that was a good idea.

Everyone was quiet and tense. Avery decided to show them the new trick she was working on with Marty.

She pretended to hypnotize him. "You are getting sleepy," she said, waving a pocket watch she had borrowed from her grandfather. Marty's eyes followed the swinging watch.

"You are completely under my power," Avery said. Marty looked at her expectantly.

"Play dead," Avery said, giving him his first command.

Marty fell to the ground in a heap.

The girls started to clap, but Avery held up a hand to silence them. The trick wasn't over. Then she reached under Marty and picked him up. He was as stiff as a board, his four legs in the air.

The girls became hysterical with laughter. The longer Marty stayed that way, the more they laughed, until Marty lifted one eyelid and looked at Avery as if to ask, "How long are you planning to make me stay like this?"

"When I snap my fingers, you will wake up," Avery said. She snapped her fingers. Marty came back to life and jumped down.

The girls clapped.

Marty moved from Maeve, to Katani, to Charlotte, expecting treats from each one.

"That's the bad part," Avery said. "If you clap, he expects a treat from you."

But no one minded. They were only too glad to give Marty a treat. Marty had saved the party.

"Marty's got to be allowed in the show," Maeve said, patting his head.

"Oh, he will be," Avery said. "One way or another."

"I don't know what that means," Katani said.

"I don't want to know," Charlotte laughed.

When Isabel wasn't there by eight p.m., Charlotte got her father to take them down to the school.

The school was still open and the janitor was washing the floors. He was still cleaning up from the Abigail Adams Eighth-Grade Art Night. The girls headed for the auditorium, but when they got there, all the lights were out.

"They're gone," Charlotte said.

"Maybe she went home," Katani suggested.

"She wouldn't just go home. She would have at least called us or something," Maeve said.

As they turned the corner, they ran into Isabel's favorite art teacher.

"We're looking for Isabel Martinez. Have you seen her?" Avery asked.

"I just left her in the computer lab," he said, as he stooped down to get a drink of water. "I told her that we are going to close the building in twenty minutes and she needs to leave by then."

The girls and Mr. Ramsey hurried down the hallway toward the computer lab. Sitting in front of the large monitor was a lonely figure ... Isabel. Even stranger was that hundreds of Kikis stared back at her from the screen. Suddenly, Isabel slammed her hand down on the desk. The thousand and one Kikis had turned blue and stopped dancing. Isabel shook her head in frustration.

"Hi, Isabel," said Charlotte.

Isabel looked up, surprised and a little freaked out to see them. "What time is it?"

"Almost eight thirty," Charlotte's father said. "You shouldn't be here this late."

"I'm sorry," Isabel said. "I meant to come by, I really did. I just lost track of the time."

"It's okay," Charlotte said, feeling really bad for her friend. "We decided to come get you."

Everyone wanted to say something. About how she shouldn't let Kiki take advantage of her like that. About how she should quit the stupid act. But they all knew getting her father here was the most important thing in Isabel's life right now.

Finally, Maeve, who couldn't take the silence anymore, said. "I think Kiki looks good blue."

That broke the ice. They all giggled about the vision of a thousand and one blue Kikis on talent night.

"It could work," Katani said in a light tone, hoping to make Isabel feel better.

But Isabel didn't even smile. Too overwhelmed to see the humor of Kiki in blue, she shut down the computer. As

Isabel left the lab with Maeve and Avery, Katani whispered to Charlotte, "We're going to have to talk to her. She is pushing herself too hard."

When they returned to the Tower, the BSG made Isabel sit on the couch. They had a lot to talk to her about, but first they wanted her to see Charlotte's magician's box and Marty's trick.

Isabel nodded politely and said, "Cool." The other girls stared at each other. This quiet girl was not the Isabel they knew. Surely, Avery's trick would lift her spirits.

Marty repeated the trick flawlessly, and, at the end of his performance, he made the rounds. Just as before, Marty went to everyone who applauded for him, expecting treats. He went to everyone except for Isabel. She was the only one not applauding. Not because she didn't like Marty's act, but because she had missed the whole thing. Isabel was fast asleep on top of her sleeping bag.

11

Game Two

Avery's Blog
Possibilities for Marty's Future

1. Dog shows—I mean the big ones. Like you see on TV. I know the dogs are usually purebreds, but that is SO NOT FAIR. Marty is smarter and way handsomer than all of them.
2. Late night TV—sometimes I watch Leno & Letterman with Scott when we're on vacation. They always have animals on there doing crazy tricks. But I've never seen any dog play dead as well as Marty does. I'm serious.
3. Hollywood—with his super canine charm and major good looks, Marty's a star. He and Maeve can walk the red carpet together. Dog and girl ... Oscar superstars.

All the BSG, including Marty, went to see Avery referee the Twisters vs. the Tornadoes in the second game of the fourth-grade girls' soccer tournament. After the last game, no one wanted to leave Avery to face the wrath of Megan's mom alone. Nope, they had to be there in full BSG force.

No one in the stands had jackets on today. It was hot. New England weather again. Go figure. The girls had on tank tops and shorts. Of course, Katani sported an adorable tank that Isabel had painted little bumblebees on. All the fourth graders in their row wanted to know where she'd bought it.

"Maybe after the talent show we could have a little business selling tank tops," Katani said to Isabel.

"You could call it T time ... get it?" said Maeve.

"I love it," said Katani. "Okay, Maeve, you get to write all our advertising copy."

"Me write? It's me, Maeve ... me and the writing thing are not like the best combination."

"That's okay. Charlotte will fix the grammar and you can come up with all the slogans and stuff," Katani remarked, looking over at Isabel.

Isabel just nodded. Maeve, Charlotte, and Katani exchanged worried glances. It was like somebody had turned off Isabel's light.

Suddenly they heard it. Megan's mom was yelling again. She was the only parent in the stands who was yelling instructions to Megan, who was trying to ignore her mother and listen to the real coach. Charlotte thought that life with Megan's mom couldn't be easy.

"I can't believe she is still yelling like that," Katani said.

The Beacon Street Girls sat as far away from Megan's mom as they could get, moving all the way to the top of the bleachers, where they were less likely to hear her.

"Maybe we should sit on the other side," Isabel suggested.

"No way. We have to root for Megan. I think she needs us," Maeve said.

"Wake up! What are you doing out there?" Megan's mom yelled.

"Was that kick illegal?" Charlotte asked.

"You're asking me? The girl who can't kick a soccer ball two feet without stumbling over her own feet?" Katani replied.

"Actually, it is," Isabel said. "But I'm not going to be the one to try to tell her."

"Me either," Charlotte said. "I'm going to take Marty for a walk down behind the bleachers."

Hearing his name, Marty poked his head out of the sports bag and barked at Megan's mom.

Isabel patted his head. "You are the cutest little dude there is."

Marty nuzzled her.

"I swear he understands us," Charlotte said, as she clipped his leash on and took him under her arm and made her way down the stairs. All the way down, kids reached out to pat Marty on the head. Marty was very pleased to reward each one of them with a slurp on their hands.

At the bottom of the stairs, Charlotte put Marty down on the ground. Before she could contain him, he was off and running across the field as fast as his legs could go, his leash trailing behind him. He had seen something in the distance ... something very pink. Oh, no, panicked Charlotte. If he runs into traffic, he could get squished. Charlotte sprinted after him, afraid that Marty's days would be numbered.

Lucky for Charlotte, the very pink thing in the distance that Marty had spotted was a *dog*. As Charlotte got closer, she could see that it was an elegant-looking, very large pink poodle, accompanied by a young woman about twenty-five ... also a vision in pink. Charlotte wanted to stare. The young woman was wearing pink capri pants, pink sneakers, a pink tank top, pink hoop earrings, pink sunglasses, and to top it off, she had dyed her hair a dark raspberry. The effect was quite startling, but she could also see that the woman seemed a bit exasperated with Marty's attention to her very fancy poodle.

Breathless, Charlotte finally reached the trio and grabbed Marty's leash and began to apologize.

"Oh ..." Charlotte was stumped. Should she say Ms., or Ma'am, or Miss? It was so confusing trying to decide what to call people. She decided to just blunder ahead.

"I'm so sorry, Miss. Marty just took off. I ... I don't think he has ever seen a pink dog before. Actually, come to think of it, neither have I," said Charlotte as she tried to pull Marty away from the poodle and sneak a closer look at this very pink young woman.

But Marty was having none of that. He was leaping and spinning circles in front of the poodle. She, on the other hand, simply stood there staring at him as if she had never seen anything quite like Marty either. Suddenly, she lowered her aristocratic nose and slurped Marty on his nose ... a very elegant slurp, but a slurp, nonetheless. Overcome, Marty instantly lay down in front of her and stared up at her with rapturous doggy eyes.

"I think your little dog is in love with my La Fanny," the woman sighed as she told La Fanny to sit quietly next to her. "It happens all the time. Every day at the park, La Fanny is surrounded by admirers. But ...," she paused.

"I've never seen her 'slurp' another dog before. She always avoids them. You know," she added conspiratorially, "most dogs are so rough. She doesn't care for that. Do you, La Fanny?" She bent down to caress her very pink dog. La Fanny preened and stretched her neck as her mistress scratched her fuzzy pink ears.

Charlotte was speechless. She had never seen anyone dressed like this, much less anyone dressed like this *and* accompanied by a pink French poodle named La Fanny. Only at the Cannes Film Festival would you see something this outlandish. Even passersby were staring and smiling. One elderly gentleman tipped his Red Sox cap toward the pink pair.

"Are you from France?" Charlotte thought to ask the pink lady.

"Oh, no, but I am very flattered that you asked. I admire the French so much. What a country! Such food, clothes, design ... it's so elegant there. Of course, everything is so *très cher*—expensive—and that is why I came back home to live ... and start my little shop.

"What is *your* name ... little ... Miss?" she asked Charlotte.

Good, thought Charlotte. I'm not the only one who can't figure out what to call people.

"My name is Charlotte."

"I love that name," the woman said enthusiastically. "It's very elegant."

"What's your name?" Charlotte politely asked in return.

"Razzberry Pink."

"Excuse me?" Charlotte thought she must have misheard.

The young woman smiled. "Yes, you heard correctly. My name is Razzberry Pink. That's Razzberry with two Zs. I named myself that when I was eighteen. I was walking along the Charles River and it was springtime. Gardeners were planting hundreds of pink flowers along the river bank. The vision of all that glorious pink made me so happy that right then and there, I decided to change my name.

"I vowed that I would devote my life forever to the color pink. I mean, you could do worse things in life. Pink makes people, especially girls, very happy. And really, could you see me in an office?" She didn't wait for an answer. "They are far too drab. And if I had to sit at a desk and look at a computer all day, I would turn into a prune. No, it had to be a pink store. There was no other choice."

Charlotte couldn't resist asking, "What was your name when you were born?"

"It's a secret," she whispered, a definite twinkle in her eye.

Since they had been talking, the sky had clouded over. And it looked like it was going to rain, and probably soon. Ms. Razzberry Pink looked at her watch and tugged at her dog's leash.

"La Fanny, come along. We don't want any nasty old rain to ruin your beautiful pink fur now, do we? ... besides, Ms. Strawberry will want her break now."

"Ms. Strawberry?" Charlotte said quizzically. Charlotte thought there couldn't possibly be more of them.

Razzberry laughed. "Everyone who works in the store takes on a pink name for the day ... you know, like Ms. Rose, Ms. Fuchsia. People love it. It's very good for business."

Charlotte got it. Ms. Pink might look a little flaky, but she was really a smart businesswoman. Because all Charlotte now wanted to do was race back and tell everyone she knew about Ms. Pink's store.

Suddenly, Charlotte felt a drop of pink ... oops ... a drop of rain on her nose and heard a big cheer from the crowd. Yikes, she had forgotten about the game.

"Marty and I have to run; my friends will be looking for me!"

Charlotte tugged on Marty's leash, but the little guy planted his feet firmly in the ground. No way, no how, was he leaving without La Fanny.

Charlotte bent down to pick him up.

"Sorry, little guy, gotta go."

Before Charlotte could grab Marty, La Fanny left her adoring fan with another delicate slurp on the nose. Overcome, Marty flipped in the air for La Fanny. It actually didn't turn out so well, as he fell on his back. But, La Fanny seemed not to notice anyway.

"Here is my card, Charlotte. Please, bring your friends to my store sometime. It's a total pink fest. I even have pink dog biscuits. Everybody loves the place. It's so silly, and that seems to make my customers really happy. Once the Mayor of Boston came in to buy his wife a pink sweater. Valentine's Day is my biggest day, of course."

As Razzberry walked away, Charlotte looked down at her card.

"Would you like to come to a magic show at the Abigail Adams school?" Charlotte called after her.

Ms. Razzberry Pink turned her head. "I'd love to ... I went to Abigail Adams when I was little." Charlotte watched her walk away, waving to people who beeped their horns as she passed by. It's not every day you get to see someone like Ms. Razzberry Pink.

"Marty," Charlotte said to her little buddy, who was looking very bummed out at being torn from his new crush. "Nobody is ever going to believe this one!"

CR

Avery thought Megan was doing really well in this game, even with it starting to rain and her mother yelling ... at least her mom hadn't come on the field this time. And the game was really almost over. Avery had her fingers crossed that they wouldn't call it for bad weather ... just ten more minutes.

As Charlotte raced up the bleachers with Marty, Maeve asked, "Where have you been, Charlotte? You were gone forever."

"You are not going to believe this story."

Suddenly, a cheering round of applause erupted from the Twisters' bench. Megan's mom looked as proud as if she herself had been voted MVP ... Megan had scored her third goal—the game was now tied. It was mayhem on the bench and in the stands.

When Marty heard the applause, he began running from person to person to get treats, assuming that the applause was for him. The girls scrambled after him, managing to capture him before he and Megan's mom had another confrontation. Nobody wanted to go through that again. The BSG agreed that they would have to talk to Avery about Marty's training.

There must be another way to train him that didn't involve treats. Besides, Marty was starting to look a little pudgy. And they needed him in top form for the talent show.

All of a sudden, they heard it—thunder overhead. The coach waved his arm and pointed at Avery to blow her whistle. The Twisters and Tornadoes would have to meet again.

After they left the field, the girls headed over to Charlotte's to work on the scenery. Along the way, Charlotte told them all about Ms. Pink and her store. Katani was beside herself with excitement. She had never been there ... all the girls couldn't wait to go there. None of them had ever seen a store entirely devoted to pink. Avery, of course, couldn't wait to meet Marty's girlfriend. Although she was a little concerned that Marty would be so taken with a pink poodle. She wondered if Marty might be a tad superficial. The sentiment was so Avery that the BSG just rolled their eyes.

TEAM EFFORT

The girls decided that they were all going to help Isabel paint. They could see that the whole Kiki extravaganza had overwhelmed her. Katani told Isabel that she could just tell them where to paint and what color to use and it would all be fine. And if it wasn't perfect, nobody would notice because they were on stage and smoke would be blowing around.

Isabel had laid out an amazing set design. She painted large silver stars to represent the constellations Orion, Capricorn, and Sagittarius. She had even mapped out the Dog Star, Sirius, for Marty. In the center of the stars she had placed plastic glow-in-the-dark stars.

"I think we should do the constellations as a backdrop, too," Isabel suggested. "As sort of a camouflage thing."

"I absolutely love this," said Charlotte.

"The stars as camouflage will be awesome. It will distract everyone," Katani said.

Maeve was excited because when you turned out the lights, the effect was dramatic! She could imagine that she was on a Broadway stage. Avery fantasized how Marty would be so famous after the show that maybe Kiki's father might use him in one of his videos. "It could happen," she protested when the girls rolled their eyes at her hopefulness.

If they had been planning to talk to Isabel about how overbooked and tired she was, everyone forgot. Today Isabel seemed so happy. She had slept all night and had woken up feeling fine. And she kept talking about how her father was coming out for a visit. He had already gotten his tickets, she'd said. He had told Elena Maria that he was coming. But they had decided to surprise their mother. He hadn't been here since he helped move them in with Aunt Lourdes, almost three months before.

∞

On Monday, Isabel didn't leave school with the rest of the girls. She had a rehearsal at four p.m., and it was already three thirty, so she decided to stay.

"Maeve, do you think you could stay for a minute and help me with something?" Isabel asked.

"Sure," Maeve said, motioning for the other girls to go ahead.

"It's my harmony ... for the song. I've got a rehearsal now, and I'm having a lot of trouble with it." Isabel looked worried.

"That's a tough song to harmonize to," Maeve said, as she unfolded her umbrella.

"I thought it was just me," Isabel said, relieved.

"Sing it for me," Maeve said.

Isabel looked embarrassed at the thought of singing alone, so Maeve sang the melody softly while Isabel sang the harmony she was supposed to be learning.

Isabel was right; she was having trouble with it. "Let's do it again," Maeve said, "only this time you sing the melody and I'll try to pick up the harmony."

Isabel sang the song softly, afraid that people on the street would hear her. Maeve, unconcerned about anyone listening, sang a few bars of harmony, and then stopped again. "I know what the problem is," Maeve said.

"What?"

"You should be singing the melody," Maeve said. "Isabel, you have a really nice voice."

Isabel blushed. "No way," she said.

"I mean it," Maeve said. "I've taken a lot of singing lessons, and your voice is better for the melody. You should try to get them to switch it around."

Even if Isabel had wanted to sing the lead, which she didn't, there was no way it was going to happen. "Kiki is singing the melody," Isabel said.

"That figures," Maeve said.

They worked for half an hour, until Isabel was getting more confident that she had learned her part.

"Thank you so much," Isabel said.

"Anytime," Maeve answered.

Maeve left before the rest of the Hip-Hop Honeys arrived. She didn't want to run into Kiki. She walked down the street toward the movie theater.

Maeve made it inside just as the big storm hit. The rain began pelting down on Harvard Street, and thunder and lightning lit up the sky.

CHAPTER
12

Rain, Rain, Go Away

It rained for the rest of the day. And it rained all the next day. The streets of Brookline were flooded.

Kristy B. reported a cold front coming in, which would explain the intermittent thunderstorms. Katani had counted three different storms so far, none of them knocking the lights out, but strong enough so that her mother told her to unplug her computer.

"I'm scared," Kelley said. For someone who said she was scared, Kelley seemed brave enough. Every flash of lightning made her eyes go wide, but every peal of thunder made her giggle. Katani couldn't tell if Kelley was really scared and it was nervous laughter, or whether her sister was enjoying the drama of the storm.

"Here, let's count," Katani said at the next flash of lightning.

They counted together, "One one thousand, two one thousand, three one thousand, four one thousand ..."

They got to six before the thunder caught up. "I think that means that the storm is six miles away," Katani said. It was something everyone did—the counting—although she didn't know how scientific it was.

"It's six thousand miles away," Kelley said vehemently. There was no arguing with Kelley once she set her mind to something. Katani's mom said it was part of Kelley's autism. She could get pretty rigid about things.

Katani didn't want to argue the logic with her sister, especially since she didn't even know if her own logic was correct to begin with. "Anyway," Katani said. "The thunderstorm is far enough away, so we don't have to be scared of it."

"I'm not scared of a thunderstorm," Kelley said out the window. "I'm not scared of a silly old thunder-stupid-storm that's six stupid thousand miles away. Ha!"

Katani had to laugh. Sometimes Kelley was the funniest person. As much as she wanted her own room, she knew she might miss the comfort of having her sister nearby ... especially at times like these.

"Kelley," whispered Katani.

"What?" Kelley whispered back.

"I love you."

"I love you too, Miss Bossy," and then for good measure Kelley added a big "Ha!"

CHAPTER

13

Rained Out

When they got to school on Wednesday morning, there were fire trucks outside Abigail Adams Junior High. Of course, Henry Yurt and the Trentini twins were all over the scene. They were excited to see the firefighters—rugged uniforms, exciting equipment, anything to give them a break from school—their least favorite activity.

"Those dudes are so awesome, I think I want to be a firefighter when I'm older," said Billy Trentini earnestly. He was particularly impressed with state-of-the-art ladder truck.

"Dude, we're in trouble if you're with the fire department," the Yurtmeister responded with a big grin.

Billy grabbed Henry playfully by the neck and gave him a Trentini special—a super noogie with a Three Stooges flick to the head. Ms. R had to break them up.

Charlotte, Avery, Isabel, and Maeve stood to the side watching the action.

Maeve looked worried. "I hope it's not really a fire. I wouldn't want the school to burn down ... especially ..." she said.

Katani, who had just appeared, rushed to assure her.

"No, it's not a fire. My grandmother said it was just a big leak that had gotten out of control."

This was serious. No one was allowed inside the building. The leak they had seen outside a couple of mornings ago had turned into a small lake, one that extended all the way into the auditorium.

"That's what the smell was," Charlotte said. "It was mildew from the water."

When the building had been thoroughly checked, the classrooms were finally opened. But the wing that housed the auditorium was off limits.

By the time they got to class, it was already second period. They had missed math, for which Isabel was grateful. The truth was, she hadn't entirely finished her homework. On Sunday night, Kiki had called Isabel at home with yet another in the long list of Kiki requests. She liked the film of herself, she said, but there were a number of details she wanted changed.

Isabel had done all the math problems, but there hadn't been any time to check them. And Isabel always found mistakes when she checked her work. She hated doing it, but it always seemed to pay off in the end. Isabel had never received less than a B in math. She wasn't an A student, but her father said B meant that you understood most of what the teachers were presenting.

At lunchtime, Mrs. Fields came into the cafeteria to make an announcement. "I'm very sorry, but I have some bad news," Mrs. Fields said.

"I hope they're sending us all home for the day," Henry Yurt speculated. He wouldn't consider that bad news at all.

"The leak in the auditorium roof is quite extensive," Mrs. Fields said. "So extensive, in fact, that I'm afraid we're going to have to cancel the talent show."

The students were shocked. There was a collective groan and a chorus of "OH NOs!" Not having the talent show would be a huge disappointment, especially since Henry Yurt had finally agreed to dress up as a cheerleader. The student body of Abigail Adams was expecting an evening of hilarity, magic, and dancing. This just couldn't be happening.

"You mean postpone it," someone said.

"I'm afraid I mean cancel," Mrs. Fields said. "Even if we could get the roof repaired in time for the show, I'm afraid that leak has been going on for a while. I am told that we will have to close down that whole wing of the school until further notice."

The Beacon Street Girls stared at each other. They were completely shocked.

Betsy Fitzgerald actually put her head down on the table. She had just found her mini brass band.

Anna and Joline looked stricken, and Kiki looked outraged.

The Beacon Street Girls turned in unison to Maeve. If they were upset about the show, how much worse was Maeve going to feel? And what would happen to the theater?

"Oh, Maeve," Charlotte said.

"The show is cancelled?" Maeve asked, as if she were just starting to understand the implications. "Totally?"

"I'm ... I'm so sorry, students. Things don't always go as planned. It's one of life's hardest lessons." Mrs. Fields said the words to the whole class, but she was looking directly at Maeve.

Isabel M.

It was raining cats ... nasty cats

Part Two
Taking Charge

14

Dream Denied

On Sunday afternoon, the scene in the Tower was not a happy one. Katani sat in the Lime Swivel, tapping her toes and spinning slowly as she looked at the ceiling. Isabel was near tears because she was afraid that her dad wouldn't come once he learned that the show was cancelled. Maeve chewed on her fingernails. Thoughts of losing the theater loomed large and heavy. And Charlotte stared out the window toward the Charles River, wishing she was sailing on one of the boats bobbing up and down on the water. Their disappointment over the show's cancellation had set them all on edge. But the one who seemed the most upset was Avery. It had to do with Marty.

Somehow, Avery had become completely convinced that Marty had been a circus performer in his past life. It had been a fun game they'd played when they first brought Marty to the Tower. Every girl put together a story about Marty's history. And each story was more fanciful than the last. But when the girls started the magic show, Avery really started to believe that her story about Marty was the correct one.

Marty had an unmistakable talent for show business. He loved to be in the limelight and enjoyed practicing tricks for treats.

Ever since the show got cancelled, Avery swore that Marty was depressed. "His self-esteem just isn't what it used to be," Avery complained to Charlotte.

Charlotte told Avery that she thought Marty's moping had more to do with the fact that he hadn't seen his new crush, La Fanny, the pink poodle they had met in the park, in a long time.

"He's a dog. Dogs don't get crushes, Charlotte."

"You didn't see him, Ave. I did, and I am telling you he was in love."

"Marty is not a love-at-first-sight kind of dog."

"What, you read dog minds now?" Charlotte answered sharply.

"Maybe she can," said Isabel in an annoyed tone. "They do have dog psychics, you know."

"Stop it, you guys. You don't even sound like yourself, Charlotte," an exasperated Katani said.

"This arguing isn't going to help anything," a frustrated Maeve said in between picking at her sore nail.

That did it. Everyone sat up straight. There was Maeve and her commonsensical advice again.

They all agreed to stop snapping at each other. They had put so much energy into their acts. The bad news had completely taken the wind out of their sails. But, sitting around moping wasn't helping either.

They sat in silence for a few more minutes, watching Marty shake his favorite toy, Happy Lucky Thingy. When even that didn't lift their spirits, Avery announced, "This is getting really grim and boring. I'm going home. I don't even want to think about this anymore." She stood up, grabbed her coat, and walked out, just as Charlotte was about to say ...

"I have an idea."

"Do you think she's really mad?" Isabel asked worriedly.

"No," said Katani. "You know Avery, she just gets totally frustrated sometimes when things aren't happening the way she thinks they should."

"Avery never gets really mad, Isabel," said Maeve. "Now Katani, that's another story." Katani laughed and threw a pillow at Maeve's head. Maeve ducked and the pillow bounced off Marty, who pounced on it like it was a squirrel. The rip-and-shred game was on.

The timing was perfect. Watching Marty race around the room at warp speed was just what they needed to lift the gloom.

Suddenly, Charlotte had new inspiration.

"Why don't we make a poster for Avery to cheer her up? We can think of what Marty would say if he could talk. Like his rules for life. She'd love it."

Maeve thought that sounded hard, but then she came up with the first rule and they were off and running:

Marty's Rule #1: Always do your doggone best.

Then Maeve said she had to leave because she had to go get her brother Sam at his friend's house. Katani wanted to leave, too, because she was hoping her mother would take her to the fabric store for some material to make another poncho.

That left Isabel and Charlotte. They worked on the poster all afternoon, in between making popcorn, wondering what Miss Pierce was up to, and discussing the Trentini twins and how goofy they were. Isabel thought that maybe the boys

would grow up to be like the two characters in *Dumb &
Dumber*.

"So how are you doing, with the show being cancelled
and everything?" Charlotte asked Isabel as they worked.
"Your dad must be really disappointed."

Isabel hesitated for just a minute before answering.
"Actually, I haven't told him yet," she said.

Charlotte didn't know what to say. "It's not like he's not
going to find out."

"I keep thinking something is going to happen," Isabel
said.

Charlotte hoped so, too. Now that they'd come so far,
she couldn't picture not doing the magic show. But she
didn't know what could possibly happen to change things.

The girls breezed through most of the Marty List, but
when they got to the tenth rule, they were stumped.

MARTY THE DOG'S GUIDE TO LIFE AND HAPPINESS

Having lived in a garbage can for a while, I have
learned self-esteem through life experience. Here
are my tips:

1. Always do your doggone best.
2. Treat other puppies the way you would like
   to be treated.
3. You won't get the treat if you don't do the trick.
4. Act as if you've already gotten the treat.
   See how success feels. Then do the trick!
5. Every dog is beautiful.
6. Preparation & opportunity = luck ...
   Luck = treats.

7. Forgive other dogs when they make messes. Forgive yourself too.
8. Every time you think about a mess you've made, think of three times you got the ball.
9. Get the ball!
10. If you come to an obstacle, jump over it. If it's too high, dig under it. If that still doesn't work ...

Charlotte stopped. "I'm stuck," she said to Isabel.

"Let me see it," Isabel said.

Charlotte watched Isabel read the list.

Isabel smiled. "This is really cool," she said.

"Except for the last one. I can't seem to get it," Charlotte said, frowning.

"Let me see," Isabel said. She started sketching little Marty dogs jumping and digging. She even drew Marty getting the treat.

Charlotte chewed her pencil.

"What's that song about the ant?" Charlotte asked.

"What song? The ants go marching one by one? That song?"

"No, you remember." Charlotte started to sing. "Once there was a little old ant, thought he could move a rubber tree plant ..." They sang the chorus together. "Anyone knows an ant can ... move a rubber tree plant." They sang the chorus. "High hopes ... high hopes ..."

"Move the obstacle," Isabel said, and Charlotte nodded.

"I got it." Charlotte started to write:

10. If you come to an obstacle, jump over it. If it's too high, dig under it. If that still doesn't work ... MOVE IT!

Isabel started sketching Marty moving the obstacle. She did two sketches, one with Marty pulling it and the other with him butting his head against it, like the ram did in the next chorus of the same song.

"That is so cute!" Charlotte laughed. "We have to move it!" she said suddenly.

"Move what?" Isabel said.

"We have to *move* the obstacle! We have to move the talent show."

"What? Where?" Isabel was hopeful.

"We have to move it to the only place it can go—the Movie House!" Charlotte exclaimed.

Charlotte and Isabel exchanged looks, as they cheered and high-fived each other.

Charlotte and Isabel called Katani on her cell phone. They were so excited, they could barely explain the plan.

"I'll get Avery and meet you in the Tower as soon as I get home from the store," Katani said.

❦

Mr. Taylor looked surprised when all the BSG marched into his office. "Is everything all right?" he couldn't help asking.

"It's better than all right, Dad," Maeve said.

"It's great," Avery said.

Mr. Taylor listened to the entire plan before he said a word. Finally, he stood up. "I don't know why we didn't think of it before," Mr. Taylor said.

"It's a perfect location for the show, and it really shows off the theater," Katani said.

"You girls are something else," Mr. Taylor said.

"So we have your permission?" Charlotte asked.

"If the school approves the plan, it's fine with me," Mr. Taylor grinned.

"They'll approve it," Charlotte said.

"They have to," Isabel agreed.

"Don't get too excited, yet," Katani said. "We have to convince my grandmother first."

"What would convince her?" Avery asked.

Katani thought about it for a while. She had an idea, but it would take a team effort and a lot of work.

The girls got special permission to spend the night in the Tower to really figure out a plan. The first thing they did was make signs: *The Show Must Go On. Save the Movie House. Save the Seventh-Grade Talent Show.*

Then they started an e-mail campaign to each of the cast members who, in turn, promised to forward it to three friends. The letter explained what they were going to do. At three o'clock on Monday, the group would congregate in the main hall. Carrying the signs they made to show their support for their cause, they would march to the principal's office.

1-2-3 MARCH

By the time they got to school on Monday, everyone was talking about the plan to move the show.

"Do you think Mrs. Fields will go for it?" Anna and Joline asked Katani.

How strange to be working on a common cause with Anna and Joline, Katani thought. Even if they were totally out for themselves, Katani could tell that they would do just about anything to make this show happen.

By the time they were ready to start the march, even Kiki had shown up. She and several other seventh graders in her homeroom had made their own signs.

As they began to march, Katani started to get nervous. Maybe they should have just asked her grandmother. Why hadn't she thought of that before? Oh, well, she hoped her grandmother wouldn't be too mad, because there was no stopping the Save the Theater movement now. Instead, she hoped her grandmother would be proud that all the kids stood up for something they believed in. When they were young, Mrs. Fields and Miss Pierce had organized a civil rights march down these very same halls. Katani kept her fingers crossed.

As the group rounded the corner of the corridor on the last lap toward the principal's office, they were met by the cheerleaders.

Fully costumed, pompoms flying, these cheerleaders seemed a little awkward and out of sync.

Charlotte started to giggle as she recognized Henry Yurt.

"Go team!" Henry cheered. He was wearing a red wig. His fellow cheerleaders fell into the end of the line.

It was just what Katani needed to give her confidence. If Henry Yurt could show up in a red wig, and the Red Sox could win the World Series, you had to believe that anything was possible.

By the time they got to Mrs. Fields's office, there were at least forty kids, all carrying banners and marching together. They stopped at the door of the office, just as planned.

Katani went into the office first. "May we speak with Mrs. Fields?" Katani asked.

"Sure, Katani, you know you can. Go right in," her grandmother's assistant said.

"Do you think we could speak with her in the hallway, please?" Katani opened the door and showed the group behind her.

Ms. Sahni looked at Katani strangely. "Okay," she said and went to get Mrs. Fields.

"I'll wait outside," Katani said. She sure hoped she was right and that her grandmother would appreciate the group effort. The look on Ms. Sahni's face made Katani start to doubt herself again. She was beginning to wonder if she had made a big mistake in approaching things this way and not just going to speak with her grandmother alone.

It seemed like a long time before Mrs. Fields came to the door.

"What's going on here?" Mrs. Fields said as she saw the group. "Katani?"

But it was Charlotte who stepped forward, just as planned.

"We want to move the talent show to the Movie House," Charlotte announced.

"So it appears," Mrs. Fields said.

"So can we?" Avery asked a bit too eagerly.

"My father loves the idea," Maeve said. "You know, the Movie House used to be a real theater. It would be a perfect place to have the talent show. Think about all those theater ghosts cheering us on," enthused Maeve.

"You've got a point, Maeve," Mrs. Fields said, bemused.

"Please," Avery said. She hadn't meant to say anything more, it just popped out.

"It's an interesting idea," Mrs. Fields admitted.

As if on cue, the group cheered and raised their signs high.

"Let me look into it," Mrs. Fields said.

It wasn't exactly a yes. But it wasn't a no, either.

感

Katani didn't get home until right before dinner. When she did, her family was in the kitchen, even her sister

Candice, who was home for a few days from college. They were all working together to make a salad, with everyone doing her part. Kelley was hard at work making garlic bread—her favorite. She didn't even look up at Katani.

"Hey Kgirl," Candice said. "Just in time to chop some lettuce!" Candice threw a head of iceberg lettuce to Patrice, who did a jump shot and threw it to Katani.

Luckily, Katani caught it before it hit the floor. She didn't mind helping with dinner, but she wished her older sisters didn't have to always make everything into an athletic event.

"Pass the knife," Katani's mother said. Patrice smiled and handed it to Katani.

Grandma Ruby didn't mention the demonstration they'd held that afternoon at school, or the proposal. Katani's grandmother had a way of separating work and family, and Katani was relieved. She was particularly glad that her grandmother hadn't mentioned the whole thing to Kelley. If Kelley had known about the march, she would never have stopped talking about it.

They ate dinner as usual. Still, her grandmother didn't say a word. It was starting to get to Katani a little. She realized she needed to talk about what had happened.

After dinner, when all the dishes were cleaned up, and she couldn't stand waiting another minute, Katani spoke up. "May I talk to you?" she asked her grandmother.

"Certainly," Mrs. Fields said, making no move to leave the group. "Go ahead."

"In private?" Katani said weakly. She was starting to understand how her grandmother must have felt when she put her on the spot this afternoon.

They walked silently to the den. When Grandma Ruby

closed the door, Katani spoke. "I'm sorry," she said. "I put you on the spot."

"I assumed that was the idea," she said.

"No. That wasn't the idea. I was trying to show support. You know … the whole solidarity thing. I thought you'd be more likely to agree with our plan if you knew the whole seventh grade was behind the idea."

Katani's grandmother thought about it. "I would have preferred that you ask me alone first. Or even if you'd had the students sign some kind of petition. Not that I don't think this is a good idea. But what if I have to say no?"

"Do you?" Katani asked.

"I'm not certain at this point," her grandmother said.

"I'm sorry," Katani said again. A petition would have been the way to go. She honestly hadn't thought of it.

"No," Grandma Ruby said firmly. "I'm not saying you should be sorry. While I might have preferred a different method of communication, it took a lot of effort to organize those students. It was impressive leadership, Katani. How did you manage it so quickly?"

"We used the Internet, but if it put you on the spot ..." Katani said.

"It's all right," her grandmother said. "Sometimes you have to do what you believe in, even if it puts someone on the spot." She smiled at Katani.

"If we do this," she said, "and that's still a big IF–but if we are able to change the location of the show to the Movie House, this is going to be a big job. Perhaps Ms. Ciara can help you organize things. Are you sure you kids are ready for such a responsibility?"

Katani thought about it before she answered. "I think so. We all want to try ..."

"All right, then," Grandma Ruby said. "First things first. Why don't you get your friend Maeve to set up a meeting with Mr. Taylor tomorrow afternoon. Tell him I will be bringing along the school attorney and our insurance advisors, as well as the parent sponsors."

"I'll get right on it," Katani said and headed for the phone. She took a deep breath and crossed her fingers. "Please let this work out," she said out loud. Then she dialed Mr. Taylor's number.

15

Moving the Obstacle

The meeting was scheduled for three o'clock. Maeve had made Chocolate Gag. She'd told Katani that she'd read somewhere that chocolate made people think better, and that it improved their mood. Charlotte had filled a big pitcher of water and added some lemon slices.

Katani was all dressed up in a skirt and a blazer. She really wanted to look smart for the meeting. She didn't want the grown-ups to think moving the talent show to the Movie House was just a silly kid idea.

"I didn't even know you had a business suit," Avery said.

It was an original Kgirl design. She had taken one of her mother's blazers, cut the sleeves to three-quarters, and paired it with her plaid skirt. She looked at least five years older and very confident.

Before the meeting started, Mrs. Fields, the business people, and the parent sponsors walked around the theater. With the exception of Katani and Maeve, the other girls were not allowed to join the tour but hung back behind the screen, trying to listen to the conversation by using an old megaphone they had found backstage.

"What are they saying?" Avery wanted to know.

"I can't tell, there's too much of an echo," Charlotte said.

When the group finished the tour, they went into Mr. Taylor's office, which the girls had transformed into a makeshift conference room. They had carried down the kitchen table from upstairs, but because the kitchen chairs looked too homey to use, they had replaced them with some sturdy-looking ones from the prop room.

Mr. Taylor's office looked like a real conference room complete with little pads of paper and pencils on the table in front of every seat, something Katani had seen in a movie. It really was funny, when she thought about it, how much the girls really had learned from the movies. They hadn't learned everything, the way Maeve had joked that day with Isabel, but what they had learned was significant. Knowing that just strengthened their resolve. They just had to save the Movie House! The plan had to work.

The adults and Maeve and Katani were in the conference room for a long time. The door was thick, so no matter how hard the other BSGs pressed their ears against the door, they couldn't hear a thing. Avery even tried lying on the floor and listening through the crack, but to no avail. Charlotte finally put the megaphone down. "Let's wait upstairs," Charlotte said. "I can't stand the suspense. I have to find something else to do with myself."

The girls went upstairs to Maeve's room to play with Siegfried and Roy. The guinea pigs were running round and round when they got there. Isabel opened the cage, and the guineas scampered out. Avery lay down on the floor and let them run over her.

Downstairs in the conference room, the adults had been

discussing the project for almost an hour.

"So, what do you think?" Mrs. Fields finally asked.

One of the parent sponsors spoke up. "I think it's do-able. The place has clearly functioned as a live theater before."

"In some ways, it's better than the junior high stage," one of the other parents said.

"It certainly is better than the junior high stage right now," Mrs. Fields smiled.

"I say let's do it," the first parent said.

"Hold on a minute," the insurance agent said. For the last several minutes, he'd been poring over the theater's insurance policies.

"What's wrong?" Mr. Taylor asked.

"You're covered for general liability," the insurance man said. "You're even covered if someone falls out of his chair. But you're not covered for live performances," he said. "We can do this, but only if we have a binder."

Katani had no idea that things were so complicated. She knew that there were concerns, that was the word her grandmother had used. She just thought that those concerns had more to do with parental permission than insurance. And what the heck was an insurance binder anyway?

As if reading her mind, Mrs. Fields spoke up. "What would it cost for a one-night liability policy? The kind they get for parties? Or concerts? I know such things exist."

The insurance man calculated. "Five hundred at least. Maybe a thousand."

"Dollars?" Katani was shocked.

Mrs. Fields looked at the others. "How much are the tickets?"

"We were going to charge six dollars," Katani said.

"And what is the seating capacity of the theater?" Mrs. Fields asked.

We need to raise $6,000 to cover the cost of the taxes and one night of insurance.

x = ticket price.

There are 723 seats in the theater.

$$x * 723 = 6,000$$

$$x = \frac{6,000}{723}$$

$$x \approx 8.30$$

The tickets should be at least $8.30 each.

"Seven hundred twenty-three," Mr. Taylor said.

"How much are the taxes you owe on the theater?" Mrs. Fields asked.

Mr. Taylor looked awkward. "What?"

"I'm sorry we're being nosy, but if this benefit is supposed to pay the taxes, I think we need to work backward from that number," Mrs. Fields said.

Everyone agreed.

"The taxes on the theater are almost five thousand dollars," Mr. Taylor said.

Katani realized that the numbers didn't work.

"Do you think we could get ten dollars per ticket?" Mrs. Fields asked Katani.

Katani thought about it. "I think so."

"I know so," said Maeve. "Everybody wants this to work."

Her father looked over at her with a proud smile and winked.

"Do you think we could sell out the theater?" one of the parents asked.

"I think we really could, especially if we really work at it." Katani thought about it. There were ninety kids in the seventh grade. They would each need to sell eight tickets to fill 720 seats, with three seats left open. Maybe they could give some kind of prizes to the kids who sold the most. This was going to be a challenge. Not that many kids had big families, and most of their friends would already be coming to the show.

"You'll have to make a commitment," Mrs. Fields said.

Katani thought about it. Avery had told stories about her mother's fund-raising efforts. Mrs. Madden spent a lot of time doing things for charities. Katani made a note to call Mrs. Madden and talk to her about it. Maybe if they treated the whole event like a super fund-raiser, they'd be able to raise enough money. It seemed like a good idea.

"Do you think you kids can handle this?" one of the parents asked Katani, as if everything depended on her answer.

"Yes," Katani said. She didn't know how they were going to handle it, but they were. As she answered the question, Katani realized that saving the theater had become very important to her. Not just for Maeve and her family, but for the whole town. People's grandparents had come to this theater. It was important to save memories. It was like saving history.

"Yes, we can," she said again. "I know we can!" Already

she was having a million ideas. "You know, we could send an announcement out to famous people who came from Brookline, like Conan O'Brien and Theo Epstein, the general manager of the Red Sox."

"Okay," Mrs. Fields said, smiling.

"Let's do it," Mr. Taylor said.

Everyone shook Katani and Maeve's hands and wished them good luck as they walked out the door.

Katani and Maeve hugged each other. They had done it. But this was only Step One. Now, Katani hoped her grandmother was right, and that the seventh grade could come through and help pull this off together.

The Kgirl Empire: Lessons Learned From My First Business Meeting

1. *Dress it up—my Kgirl business suit was a big hit. It made me confident, and the adults took me seriously!*
2. *Organization is key—think about what questions can come up, and have the answers ready before hand ... it makes you look extra smart!*
3. *Be flexible—things can get really complicated in the business world.*
4. *Don't get so caught up in the big picture that you forget the smaller details ... or the reverse.*
5. *It's really hard to make money, but it's so much fun to try.*

K

CHAPTER

16

Poster Party

They met at Isabel's that night to make the posters. Isabel's mother met them at the door. She was a beautiful woman with dark, flowing hair and a lovely smile. She was merely an older version of Isabel. It was amazing how much they looked like each other.

She welcomed them warmly. "Isabel is upstairs," Mrs. Martinez gestured to a long flight of stairs with tiny white lights lining the stairway, the kind you see on Christmas trees or outside in the regular trees in the southwest. Soft music drifted down the stairway.

"Who is that singing?" Charlotte asked.

"That's Isabel," Mrs. Martinez smiled. "And Elena Maria."

"It sounds pretty," Katani said shyly.

"I didn't know Isabel could sing," Avery said, not shyly.

The girls paused on the stairs to listen to the two soft voices singing to a strummed guitar. They waited until the song was over before they entered the room.

"That was so nice," Katani said as they came inside.

Elena Maria beamed. She had been practicing for so, so long. Isabel quickly put down the guitar.

"You play, too," Avery remarked.

"Not really. I mean, just a little," Isabel said.

"Will you teach me that song?" Maeve asked. "I love it."

"Sure," Isabel said shyly.

"It was really nice, Isabel," Charlotte said. "You too, Elena Maria," she added. None of the BSG really knew Isabel's sister. Charlotte, who didn't have any brothers and sisters of her own, felt a little shy. Elena Maria, who looked really cool, with her long hair, tight jeans, and multicolored peasant top, was super friendly and gestured for them all to come into the room.

Elena Maria asked, "Are you all hungry? I made some cookies."

"We're always hungry for cookies," Avery declared.

"You should have come earlier," Isabel said. "Elena Maria made the most amazing dinner. She wants to be a chef."

"I'll test all your recipes," Avery volunteered.

Elena Maria laughed and went downstairs to get a plate of her famous cookies.

"Is your Aunt Lourdes here?" Maeve asked.

"She's doing a late shift at the hospital," Isabel said. "She'll be at the talent show. And Elena Maria wants to do a Mexican-style brunch for everyone the morning after the show."

"That's so nice!" Maeve said.

"Should we make something to bring to the party?" asked Charlotte.

"You can bring your families. I want you all to meet my father, and he wants to meet you. I've told him all about the Beacon Street Girls," Isabel said with a grin.

"He's still coming," Charlotte said, relieved. "It was good you didn't tell him the show was cancelled."

Isabel smiled.

"So, we'd better get started if we're going to get all the posters done," Katani said.

The word *poster* was Isabel's cue. She walked to her desk and picked up the rolled-up poster of Marty that she and Charlotte had made together. Isabel handed it to Charlotte, who handed it to Avery.

"What's this?" Avery asked.

"It's a present from Isabel and me," Charlotte explained. "We made it for you back when we thought there wasn't going to be a show, and you were so upset."

Avery slowly unrolled the poster of Marty. Katani and Maeve crowded around her. They had left before Isabel and Charlotte had finished the poster.

"Remember when you said you thought Marty's self-esteem was suffering because the show got cancelled?" Charlotte smiled.

A grin spread slowly over Avery's face as she read the poster. "You did this for me?"

"And for Marty," Charlotte said.

"Who, no doubt, can read the words himself," Katani said, and all the girls laughed. If any dog could read, Marty could.

"It's awesome," Maeve said.

"It already inspired us," Charlotte said, pointing to rule #10. "That's how we figured out we had to move the show to the Movie House."

"You guys!" Avery smiled. "Thanks so much. I have to frame this and put it on my wall."

"You're welcome," Charlotte said.

"Piece of cake," said Isabel.

"We better get started; it's getting kind of late." Katani didn't like to push, but they were running out of time.

Isabel sat at her drawing table, and the rest of them stationed themselves around her room. Charlotte was at the desk. Katani and Maeve sat on the floor, and Avery spread her supplies out on Isabel's bed. Avery was relegated to painting the base color black because it required no talent at all.

If they needed artistic inspiration, there was no better place to work than Isabel's room with its bold paint and poster-covered walls. Charlotte stared at one of Frida Kahlo's posters.

Isabel loved Frida's paintings, even though some of them were strange. Especially her self-portrait, which Isabel had posted on the ceiling over her bed. A lot of people thought Frida wasn't very pretty, with eyebrows that went straight across her head. But Isabel didn't care. She thought Frida looked interesting, and to Isabel, that seemed more important. Plus, she was Mexican, and it filled Isabel with pride that such a great artist came from Mexico.

As Charlotte looked around the room, she noticed that Isabel had put an arrow sign that read "Queen of Puppets" and pointed it toward her poster of *The Lion King*. Julie Taymor's puppets had mesmerized Isabel when she had seen the show with her family in Boston. She had, in fact, thought that it would be really fun to make a Beacon Street Girls puppet show with rock music and flashing lights. But that would have to come much later ... after she finished with Kiki and the Hip-Hop Honeys ... which might take her the rest of her life if Kiki didn't stop escalating her demands.

"Isn't Julie Taymor from Boston?" Charlotte asked Isabel.

"Are you serious?" Isabel asked. Boston was getting better all the time. The thought of running into Julie Taymor on the streets of Boston was totally exciting.

"I think she lives in New York now, though," Maeve said, "or maybe L.A."

෦෨

They worked on the posters for almost two hours. Isabel drew a funny logo that featured a cartoon of the Movie House. Everyone agreed that it was really cute. Avery thought it was good enough for Mr. Taylor to use all the time. But Isabel disagreed.

"No way! This is okay for a kid poster, but it isn't good enough for a real poster. But, maybe your dad could take it and have some grown-up artist fix it. I wouldn't mind at all," Isabel said.

The girls loved the funny little drawing of the Movie House and begged Isabel to put it on all the posters that day.

"Do you think people will pay ten dollars for a ticket?" Avery asked. "That's pretty expensive."

"We have to make sure they do," Katani said. "Otherwise, the whole thing will be a total bust." She said it with such certainty that no one dared question her.

"How many tickets do we each have to sell, again?" Isabel asked

"Eight," Katani said. "But it would be much better if each of us sold twelve."

Charlotte wasn't sure she knew twelve people to sell the tickets to. There was her dad. And her grandparents, who didn't even live in Brookline, but they would probably buy the tickets anyway. Or maybe some of the other professors at the college where Dad taught might buy tickets. She could ask him to pass the word. Maybe Charlotte could even talk Yuri into buying a ticket. She knew he liked to go to the movies. And definitely Ms. Razzberry Pink, she had said that she liked magic. Also, lately, Charlotte had been thinking that she wanted to get a ticket for Miss Pierce, even though the odds were high that she wouldn't go. Sapphire Pierce hardly ever left the house. She was what they called a recluse. The boundaries of her life were literal—four walls and a roof.

Well, Miss Pierce probably wouldn't come, and Charlotte didn't want to ask her to buy a ten-dollar ticket. Still, Charlotte knew that Miss Pierce was interested in their magic act. She had really helped with the planning of the Houdini trick. If Charlotte wanted Miss Pierce to come to the show, or to even consider the invitation, maybe Charlotte should buy the ticket herself. And Avery was right; ten dollars was a lot of money for a kids' talent show. But, maybe when people realized that their money was going to save what her father called a "cultural institution," perhaps they wouldn't mind so much. Gosh, Charlotte thought, this was getting nerve-wracking. No wonder grown-ups were so tired all the time, if these were the kinds of things that they had to worry about.

Isabel's I.M. was pinging, and then her cell phone. It was like Grand Central Station in New York City.

"Who's calling you so late?" Katani looked surprised.

"Who d'ya think?" Isabel answered, looking at the messages. They were all from the Hip-Hop Honeys, most from Kiki herself. "Well, it was peaceful while it lasted," Isabel said. There were at least seven full e-mails, all with more to-do lists for Isabel.

"Geesh," said Avery. "She's stalking you."

Avery read the e-mails with her. Kiki was not at all happy with the computer animation, and she had no trouble telling Isabel so. Kiki was getting out of hand.

Avery couldn't contain herself any longer. She had to speak up. It might have been the Marty poster; it might have been the harassment by the ugly stepsisters, but Avery couldn't keep quiet for another minute. "They're taking advantage of you," she said.

"It's true," Maeve said. "We've all been meaning to say something about it."

"But then we decided not to ..." Charlotte said, "because the show got cancelled and it didn't matter anymore."

Isabel looked shocked by all of their concern.

"We're just looking out for you, that's all," Katani said.

"Be careful," Charlotte said.

"She's totally out of bounds on all of this, Isabel. It's like she doesn't even care how much work you are doing," Katani said.

"I can handle this," Isabel said, sounding a little annoyed with her friends.

There it was again ... *out of bounds*, Charlotte said to herself. She was going to have to look up the word *boundary*. People seemed to get so upset about stuff that was out of bounds.

CR

Charlotte's Diary

Dear Diary:

My dad says that if you want to be a writer you have to love words. You have to collect them like some people collect butterflies. So, diary, I'm doing my word collector nerd thing. It's a good thing I have some time to myself, because I wouldn't want to inflict the vocab thing on anyone else. I mean, suppose you were a bug collector (yuck!). You wouldn't expect your friends to go hunting black widow spiders with you in the jungles of Mexico where they have mosquitoes the size of hummingbirds, would you? No, tonight it's just me, Marty, and the dictionary.

Word up! "Boundaries." I've heard that word at least three times today.

Random Charlotte thought: Sometimes I wish there were no boundaries, and we could just time travel to wherever we wanted to go. Like right now, I'd go to Paris and see my friend Sophie. The two of us could go to Madame Bette's Café and have café au lait and fresh, warm croissants with butter and jam. Yum ... I can smell the French coffee now. Maybe we could even go on a hunt to find Orangina ... I miss that little orange fuzzball. Sorry, Marty.

Back to WORD OF THE DAY: I'm sitting in the Tower looking at the night sky. When you look up at the stars, there don't seem to be any boundaries at all. Sophie and I are sitting in different continents, but we're looking up at the same moon. I love that. There was a song, I think ... "Somewhere Out There." Cool song.

If this were school, we would have to use boundaries in a sentence.

Here goes ...

1. *Isabel needs to establish boundaries, so Kiki and the Queens of Mean won't take advantage of her.*
   Mmm — maybe boundaries are like rules that protect you from things that aren't good for you. I guess everybody needs to set their own boundaries from time to time.

Or ...

2. *I think Miss Pierce needs fewer boundaries. So she will leave the house once in a while and not miss all the great things that are out there in this city and in this world.*

What about me?

3. Do I have too few boundaries or too many? What do I know? The more I think about the word, the less it makes sense. "Boundaries." I just said this out loud with a French accent and Marty gave me a very strange look.

4. In sports you need boundaries. Without boundaries the game of soccer would be a total mess. Avery would be out of a job. And Megan's mom wouldn't have anything to yell about (which might not be such a bad thing when you think about it) ... just kidding.

Okay, now I'm getting really sick of the word boundaries, which I have now used at least ten times. Enough already!

These are the kinds of things I think about when it's late at night and I should be sleeping. Good thing I plan to be a writer, because I could probably win the Word Nerd of the Week award. Okay, one more thing. Isn't it weird when you say a word really fast about fifteen times? It doesn't sound like a real word anymore. It sounds like gobbledygook. (now that is a very cool word)

Go to sleep, Charlotte. Does anybody else out there think about weird things?

Ooo! I just saw the most incredible shooting star. It was so beautiful. Now that would be something for Miss Pierce to go out to see. She'd like that. She wouldn't even have to leave the house to do it. No boundaries adjustment necessary. Be quiet, Charlotte.

I'm definitely going to bed now. Good thing, huh?

Marty is licking my toes and it really tickles.

CHAPTER
17

Eyes on the Prize

At the next rehearsal, Henry Yurt as head cheerleader was something to see. Backed by the rest of the boys, the act was more comedy than gymnastics. Even Ms. Ciara and Ms. R were beside themselves with laughter. Henry's rendition of "We are the Warriors, the mighty, mighty Warriors," the high school football cheer, was something out of a goofy sports movie. And when his wig flew off at the end as he bowed, Ms. Ciara laughed so hard she had to sit down.

"I don't know, Maeve, you may have a little competition," Avery said.

Since he made a commitment to participate in the show, Henry Yurt had taken "commitment" to a new level. He even tried to wear his red wig around school. One day, he wore it into homeroom, and Ms. R made him put it in his backpack, saying it was a distraction to the rest of the class.

"I'm trying to get into character," Henry protested.

"Henry, if you think I believe *that* for one minute, you are living in a sitcom. Now, march," Ms. R said firmly.

Ever since he had dumped the water on Anna's head in

science class, Henry Yurt had taken on legendary status at Abigail Adams. Anna still hated him, even though he hadn't meant to do it. The experiment had been to demonstrate surface tension, but Henry had messed it up. Instead of staying in the bottle, the water had soaked Anna.

Anna was furious, but the rest of the class found the whole thing hilarious. And since Anna was so mean, no one felt too bad for her. After all, it was only water ... no need to make such a big deal about it.

But something had happened that day—the incident had transformed Henry from Class A nerd to Class Clown. Just thinking of Henry as "head cheerleader" would make people laugh. The red wig would put them over the edge.

Wig or no wig, Henry was serious about the show. He had started watching cheerleading competitions on cable, and he had even rented movies on the subject. At today's rehearsal, he was trying to coach the other boys to do splits and lifts like the girls.

"Yo, Yurt. Guys don't bend like that," Nick Montoya said, laughing. Nick was very athletic, and the lifts were no problem for him. But the splits were another thing altogether.

This wasn't an official dress rehearsal, but some of the kids had come in costume. Betsy and her tuba band were wearing their marching outfits. Charlotte had a cape and a top hat she had pulled out of the theater's prop room.

Seeing people in costume stirred up Kiki's competitive spirit.

"Why didn't you call me back last night?" Kiki asked Isabel. Kiki's voice had a threatening edge that Isabel didn't like.

"I was busy," Isabel said. "Making posters for the show."

"Let somebody else make the stupid posters," Kiki said.

"We need our costumes. My father has a camera crew. They're going to film us next Tuesday."

"You want me to make the costumes?" Isabel was shocked.

"*Yes*, I want you to make the costumes," Kiki said, as if this were something that they had discussed a million times before.

"But Kiki, I don't know how to sew," Isabel said.

"When were you going to tell me that?" Kiki looked disgusted.

"You never asked me," Isabel said.

"Yes, I did. It was the same conversation where you told me how good you were at computer animation," Kiki said.

Isabel was stunned. They never talked about sewing. She would have remembered that. Or would she have? Isabel was becoming so overwhelmed that she was forgetting whom she was supposed to do what for and when.

Kiki turned her wrath on Anna and Joline. "I thought you told me she could sew?"

"I think you've got me confused with Katani. She's the clothes designer," Isabel said. "Katani can sew up anything."

"I don't care who sews as long as someone does," Kiki said, handing the magazine design to Isabel. "This is what I want," Kiki declared.

Isabel stared at the dress. "You want me to ask Katani to make these dresses?" she asked in disbelief. There was no way that was going to happen.

"I don't care who you get to do it," Kiki said. "I just want it done." She flipped her hair over her shoulder and walked away—a super diva in action.

Isabel stood there gaping after her. Neither Anna nor Joline said a word.

Since it was their first rehearsal at the Movie House, Maeve, in her glory, showed people around the theater, the prop room, and the secret backstage stairwells.

Everyone felt it was a better place to perform than the junior high had been. From back in the day when it was a live theater, the Movie House even had a greenroom, where the actors could hang out until their calls. The student performers made themselves right at home. Someone brought in juice. And they dragged in a big couch from the old prop room, which was now a junk room full of old movie cans and lenses, but still had some of the props from old vaudeville routines. The greenroom was a go!

Mr. Taylor told the kids to help themselves to anything they needed. Little by little, the old props had been finding their way into the skits. Charlotte found her cape in an old costume trunk. Henry Yurt helped himself to the megaphone. Avery dug up a pair of black tuxedo pants with the stripe down the sides. The jacket that went with them was long gone, but the pants fit, once Katani took them in a little and took up the hem. Even Dillon managed to pick up some old tools found in an old locker.

"These belong to Jerry Carbone," Maeve said.

Jerry Carbone was a famous lighting director for theater. He had worked on Broadway, and then moved to Boston. Maeve's father had him over for dinner once, and he told them all about how lighting could make or break a show. Maeve realized as soon as she said it that Dillon didn't have a clue whom she was talking about.

"These belong to someone else?" He started to put the tools back.

"No, I mean they did once, but you can use them now," Maeve said awkwardly. This is so not cool, she thought to herself. A few weeks ago, she and Dillon were friends and maybe a little more, but now everything felt really awkward between them.

It was obvious that they both wanted to say something, but it was hard to get over the awkwardness that had started over Kiki and her act. Plus, Kiki kept watching Dillon from the corner. She wouldn't take her eyes off him. She was waiting for him to set up the lights for their number, and every time he spoke to Maeve, Kiki grew more annoyed until she finally turned her back in a huff.

"I didn't know this was such a serious rehearsal," Katani said to Isabel.

"Kiki's father is going to do a video of us," Isabel said. "He's bringing in a film crew." There was no way Isabel was going to tell Katani about the costume request.

There had been a lot of changes since Kiki had first asked Isabel to participate in the act. Isabel found herself wondering if the filming would even happen. Most of the stuff that Kiki had promised hadn't happened yet. Like Paula Abdul helping them. Everyone was aware that Kiki was doing all the choreography. Not that it was bad or anything, but Kiki was so totally the star of the Hip-Hop Honeys, everybody wondered what Anna and Joline were thinking.

Betsy and her band rehearsed their number first. They played a Sousa march, and it was pretty good. Betsy's part was the longest, and, by the end of it, everyone could tell she was a little dizzy because she staggered backwards after she finished.

"Maybe you should consider sitting down for this number, Betsy," Ms. Ciara said. "The stage is really too small to march very far, and I think all that movement is a bit distracting for the audience."

Betsy nodded. She was grateful for the suggestion. She didn't want to fall on the night of the show. Her parents would be so embarrassed and her brother, the one who went to Harvard, was coming too, and so she wanted to impress them all.

Katani took the opportunity between acts to make an announcement. "I have the posters for the show." She held one of them up. "We have to place them in busy areas around town so everybody sees them. Here is a list of suggested locations. If each of you could take two of them, we could get this done. If you look down the list, you can find your name and where you need to put the posters." And then she sat down, a little overwhelmed that she had just told everybody in the class what to do. Even for Katani, that was a lot of taking charge, and she was afraid that maybe kids would resent it.

But Ms. Ciara said, "Great idea, Katani. Let me see a show of hands of those who can't do it." She looked around the theater quickly. Not one student raised their hand.

"Okay, we are good to go on the posters. Katani, why don't you give them to Ms. R, and she will hand two to everyone who leaves the theater. And now, let's get going, people. Time's running out ... and Katani, I would like to see you for a few minutes after rehearsal."

"Get it done!" Henry Yurt cheered as Katani walked back to hand the posters and lists to Ms. R.

"Do we have any publicity yet?" Joline asked.

"No, but I'm working on it," Katani said.

"We might need some kind of angle," Avery said, "something to get the attention of the TV people."

"Like a real live publicity stunt?" Maeve was thinking old-school Hollywood, the things people did to get noticed. She was thinking of Lucy and Ethel from *I Love Lucy*. They had the wackiest stunts that always seemed to attract a lot of attention.

"Yeah, something really cool that looks good on TV," Avery said.

"I think Avery's right," Katani said. "We need something to call attention not to the show but to the cause. This place."

"What if we all got together and did a group hug?" Henry Yurt was kidding, but it struck a chord.

"Of each other?" Avery asked, appalled.

"Of the Movie House," Henry suggested.

"Like hugging a tree or something?" Nick asked.

"Only with the theater instead," Katani said, starting to understand.

It wasn't a bad idea.

"What do you think?" Katani asked Ms. Ciara.

"I think it's a great idea," Ms. Ciara said. "Providing your father approves. It certainly would attract some attention."

"Yeah, we might all get on TV," Dillon said.

"I think we should take our banners and go in costume," Betsy said.

Everyone looked at Henry Yurt. He threw his wig up in the air and yelled, "Woo-hoo!"

CR

After a short break, the rehearsal resumed. The Beacon Street Girls' Magic Show went on next. Avery was thrilled to find that Marty was listed as a member of the act. "Marty made the cut," she said, beaming.

"He's in the show under the following conditions," Ms. Ciara said. "You're going to have to keep him tied up and away from Kiki. Her mother says it was the mold that was the reason for her allergies, but we need to keep him away from Kiki."

"No problem," Avery said. Avoiding contact with Kiki was something Avery was already an expert at.

The girls didn't do a run-through of the magic act; they were still at the approval stage. Charlotte set up the magic box. The teachers inspected it. They actually put Avery in it. "She goes in here and then, abracadabra, she escapes. Just like that," Charlotte said. But when Charlotte opened the door, Avery was still inside the box.

"I can't believe it," Anna said. "You still haven't figured out how to do that trick? You're going to look so stupid and ruin the show."

Kelley, who had come to meet Katani after her art program had ended, heard Anna's comment, and came to the girls' defense. "They do so know how to do the trick."

"Sure they do," Anna said.

"You're so silly, Anna Banana, even I know how to do that trick," Kelley said.

"Oh yeah? How?" Anna turned to Kelley.

"Abracadabra," Kelley said. "It's magic, that's how."

"Right, it's magic … and I'm the Easter Bunny," Anna said.

Katani shot Anna a warning look. No one was going to mess with Kelley, not even Anna.

Kelley looked at Anna, considering. "Now I know you're just plain silly. You're not the Easter Bunny, you're Anna Banana," Kelley laughed.

Anna huffed off to join Kiki and Joline.

"Well, they're no competition," Anna said loud enough for them to hear. "They don't even have an act."

Kiki and Joline were deep in discussion with Isabel.

"You can say anything you like," Isabel said to Kiki. "But I'm not doing the costumes. And I'm not asking Katani to do them either."

"What's going on?" Anna wanted to know.

"Isabel has decided not to be a team player," Kiki said.

"That's so not fair," Isabel said.

"We talked about this," Kiki said.

"No, we didn't," Isabel said. "I would have remembered."

"So what are we going to do now?" Joline asked.

"I don't know what *you're* going to do now," Kiki said. "But I want this dress." She pointed to the magazine picture.

"That's a $400 dress," Anna said.

Kiki shrugged. "I'm wearing this dress. I'm not going to let some non team player ruin my shot at a music video. I'm ordering the dress."

"What are we supposed to do?" Joline said. "I can't get my parents to buy me some $400 dress to wear as a costume."

"Then I suggest you all go shopping," Kiki said. "Get anything you want. Only stay away from red because that's my color." She walked off.

"Stay away from red because that's my color," Anna's voice imitated Kiki's, in her sing-song way.

Isabel and Joline both turned to look at Anna, but she was walking away.

ᏟᎡ

According to the schedule, the Hip-Hop Honeys were supposed to rehearse their entire number. It was going to be their official run-through. But Kiki kept changing the steps, and Anna kept bickering with her about the changes. Finally, Ms. Ciara stopped them. "This is not productive," she said.

"You can do the entire number at dress rehearsal," she said. "That will give you enough time to make any changes you want between now and then. And Kiki, decide on the routine and stick to it. It is not fair for Isabel, and Anna, and Joline. It gets too confusing. Do you understand me?" Kiki nodded, but anyone could see that she was not happy.

Katani and Maeve looked at each other.

"Anna's really mad at Kiki," Maeve whispered.

Anna almost quit right then, but she didn't. *Eyes on the prize*, she told herself. The prize was herself on video. Now that she knew Kiki's father worked with a lot of famous people, there was no way she could drop out. And Anna figured that once she got the video in her hands, she could have it edited down to just her parts. Her mother told her that she could. It would be good for getting modeling jobs.

No, there was no way Anna was going to quit now. She had come too far and put up with too much of Kiki and Joline's worship of Kiki to quit before the show.

∞

The Beacon Street Girls stayed behind after the rehearsal to wait for Katani. They could see Katani's head nodding back and forth, following Ms. Ciara's gestures closely. They wondered whether Katani had overstepped her bounds by organizing the poster list. Some teachers were funny that way. They didn't like you taking charge unless they gave you the formal okay.

Finally, Ms. Ciara turned to leave, and Katani walked back toward her friends.

"Was she mad, Katani?" Maeve asked sympathetically.

"No, she wants me to assist her with the show. She said that it was a really big job with lots of responsibility. I have to help manage the acts backstage, and if things aren't working, I have to help her figure out what to do."

"Wow," said Avery. "That is a really big job. I mean, what if the Hip-Hop Honeys decide to get in a fight or something on opening night?"

"You can handle it, Katani," Isabel said. "Look how you took charge of getting us organized to make posters."

"That's different," Katani laughed. "We all like each other."

"We better practice our trick before they kick us out of here," said Charlotte. Katani's new job was set aside as the girls focused on their biggest problem: How to get Avery to disappear!

The girls had already pulled a fast one on the other performers ... They had all agreed: It was better to *look* as if they didn't know the trick than to have Kiki and Queens of Mean try to sabotage their act. Only after they were sure Kiki was safely out of the building did they practice the *real* Houdini trick.

Then the girls got into action. They dragged an old mattress out of the prop room.

"Oh, goody," Kelley said. "Are we having a sleepover?"

"Not today, Kel," Charlotte said.

Kelley looked disappointed then intrigued as she watched Avery unlatch the door to the orchestra pit. Once the latch was undone, the trapdoor opened inward, which was just what was needed for this trick. Then they rolled the mattress into a tube and shoved it down the hole. It popped out of sight.

Kelley started to clap, thinking this was the real trick. "Good one!" She laughed.

Avery bowed.

Charlotte was examining the trapdoor. There was a little

metal loop on the latch. "Be careful not to trip over the latch," Charlotte warned.

They closed and relatched the trapdoor, then dragged the magic box on top of it.

"Okay, Kelley, are you ready for the real trick?" Avery asked.

Kelley clapped her hands together in delight.

Charlotte looped scarves around Avery.

"Remember to put your fists together *like this*." Charlotte clenched her fists to demonstrate, and Avery did the same. "It makes them bigger and then the scarf is looser when you relax your hands again."

Charlotte turned Avery around full circle and put her in the box.

"Now you have to be able to scooch down really little and open the latch. *Like this*." Charlotte tried to demonstrate, and fell on top of Avery. "All right, maybe not like that."

Kelley was laughing hard. "Good one, Charlotte!"

Charlotte giggled and closed the lid on the box, waved her wand and opened the lid. Avery had disappeared completely.

"Yay!" Kelley jumped to her feet. Then when Avery didn't come back, she started to worry. "Where did Avery go?" Kelley's eyes went wide.

Everybody waited … and waited.

Finally, Kelley ran to the stage and looked down the hole.

"Where did she go?" Kelley said urgently. "Avery, you better come back here right now!"

"She's all right," Katani whispered. "It's just a magic trick."

There was a long silence, then some crashing around backstage. Finally, a very dusty Avery made her way through the curtains to the front of the stage and took a bow!

"Magic!" Kelley clapped. "Magic!"

"What happened?" Charlotte said.

"We need to remember to clean the pit, and to put on a light or something backstage," Avery coughed. "It's awfully dark back there."

Katani made a note on her clipboard.

Except for the dust and lack of lighting, Avery had performed the trick perfectly.

"You really are like a mini Houdini," Maeve said.

Avery bowed again.

"Let's run through it again," Katani suggested.

Maeve went backstage and turned on a lamp.

This time Charlotte talked as she helped Avery into the box. She talked about Houdini and how he was a great escape artist. She talked about how Avery was a long-lost relative of Houdini, with all the same talents. Charlotte talked for almost a minute. Then she waved her magic wand and said the magic word: "Abracadabra!" When she opened the box, Avery was gone.

Charlotte feigned surprise as she looked into the box. She waved her wand and took a bow, as Maeve gasped and looked around dramatically.

A minute later, Avery broke through the curtains and took a deep bow.

"Perfect!" Isabel said, clapping.

Kelley was clapping and laughing as if she was just seeing the trick for the first time.

Everyone applauded.

"And they said we didn't have a trick!" Avery said. "We have a trick they're going to talk about for years to come!"

Avery didn't know how right she was about that prediction.

To: Sophie
From: Charlotte
Subject: Magic!

Dear Sophie,

Ma cherie, I'm sorry it's been so long since
I've written! I miss you lots and lots. Things
are busy at school because the talent show is
coming up. Katani, Avery, Maeve, Isabel, Marty,
and I are doing a magic show ... and I'm the
magician! Remember when Philippe stole my fake
coins and tried to buy his lunch with them?

How are Philippe and Alain and everyone else? I
hope you like the pink Red Sox shirt, all the
girls and I bought the same ones when we went to
a game at Fenway Park (except for Avery, she
says you're not a true fan unless you wear an
old blue Red Sox shirt). I CAN'T WAIT for you to
meet the Beacon Street Girls and Marty and Miss
Pierce and see the Tower and all of my favorite
places in Brookline and Boston. Any sign of
Orangina? I can't help hoping he'll find his way
back someday ... he's a pretty smart cat! Lots
of hugs! Write back soon and tell me everything!
Au revoir,
Charlotte

18

Boundaries

The next morning, Charlotte and her father decided to have breakfast together at a small French sidewalk café they'd discovered in Brookline. Although it was getting cool again, the owner hadn't yet taken the tables in for the winter, so they sat outside, pretending they were on the Left Bank, eating crepes and almond croissants with marzipan inside.

"Dad, these croissants are really good. They taste as good as the ones we used to get at Madame Bette's."

"Good thing she can't hear you say that. Remember how she used to complain about the way Americans eat," said her dad.

"I know, she called anyone who wanted ketchup with their *oeufs* (eggs) McIdiots."

"Madame could be quite rude," Mr. Ramsey laughed.

"Yes, but she also gave me extra of her homemade jam," Charlotte said. "I miss Paris," she went on, then immediately wished she hadn't. "I mean to visit, not to live." Charlotte loved living in Brookline. Before he took the teaching job, Mr. Ramsey's job as a travel writer had father and daughter living in many different places. Charlotte had wonderful memories, but now she wouldn't leave Brookline for anything. But that was not to say that she didn't love a great vacation somewhere. As long as you knew you had somewhere to come home to, traveling was so exciting. Like the time in Africa when an angry rhino chased the jeep she and her father were riding in, and they had to zigzag across the Serengeti to escape. Charlotte reminded her father of the story, and they both chuckled at the memory of the nervous Dutch lady, who kept wringing her hands, whispering, "goot got." Neither Charlotte nor her father knew what it meant, but whenever things got difficult, one of them would joke, "goot got."

"You've caught the travel bug," her father smiled. "It must be genetic." He considered for a minute.

"What?" Charlotte asked.

"How about Christmas in Fiji?" Charlotte's father asked. "We'll stay on one of the smaller islands in the Yasawas and sleep in a bure."

"Is that anything like a hotel?" Charlotte asked. She was smiling because she already knew it wasn't.

"It's a traditional hut with a thatched roof," he said. "Picture it. Cassava root and mud crab for Christmas dinner."

"Sounds exotic," she said.

"Plus, it's full summer there—no snow, no ice." He knew this one would get her.

The minute he said Fiji, Charlotte had wanted to go. She was only holding out so that he would tell her more of the details. She loved how animated her father got when he talked about travel. "Are you going to write a travel book about Fiji?" Charlotte asked.

"Just an article. *Christmas in Fiji*," he gestured as if the printed title hung in the air right in front of him.

"I'm in," she said.

"Good," he said, "I already made the reservations."

Charlotte laughed. It didn't surprise her a bit.

Mr. Ramsey ordered another café au lait.

"How's the talent show coming?" he asked. Charlotte hadn't told him much about it lately.

"It's coming along," she said. "Avery makes a perfect Harry Houdini."

"What about the hedgehogs? Are they in the show?"

"They're not hedgehogs, they're guinea pigs. They didn't make the cut," Charlotte said. "But Marty did."

"Our little Marty?" Mr. Ramsey asked.

"Our little Marty is about to become a gigantic star," Charlotte said.

Her father laughed.

"I'm serious. Wait 'til you see him. Avery's pulling him out of a hat. Plus, he's doing another trick that is just so cute! I really think Marty may steal the show."

Mr. Ramsey laughed. Then he got serious for a minute. "I'm glad you're doing so well here, Charlotte."

"I am too, Dad."

"How is your new friend Isabel adjusting?" he asked.

"Pretty well. Oh, that reminds me. Isabel's dad is coming out for the show. Her sister wants to host a breakfast for us the morning after the talent show. Can we go?"

"I wouldn't miss it," he declared.

"I was hoping you'd say that," Charlotte smiled.

"By the way," Mr. Ramsey said, "I've sold a few tickets for you at the college. I've got a couple of students who do magic for kids' parties, and they loved the idea of the talent show. Of course, I did brag about my daughter, the amazing, multitalented magician."

"Dad, thanks, but what if I am terrible?" Charlotte pondered. "We could both be really embarrassed."

"Not me, kiddo, you never embarrass me," he assured her, and he smiled.

"Dad, I want to give a ticket to Miss Pierce. Not sell her one, give it to her. Since she helped with the Houdini trick and everything. Do you think she'd come?"

"I doubt it," Mr. Ramsey said. "I'm not trying to be negative, but she doesn't really leave the house, Charlotte."

"Ever?" Even though Charlotte knew this, she was still having trouble believing it.

"Well, I've not seen her go out since we've been here," her father said.

"How is that even possible?" Charlotte asked.

Mr. Ramsey shrugged. "That's just the way it is with some people," he said.

Aren't people strange? Charlotte thought. And so very different and interesting all at the same time.

◌

Isabel went shopping after school with Anna and Joline, looking for costumes. After trying four different stores, they ended up at Filene's Basement in the fancy dress department, where they found three dresses that matched. They were a nice shade of green, flared out at the bottom, but they had a super dorky red bow around the neck. They even had sequins like Kiki's.

"They're not so bad," Joline said.

"Not so bad? Are you kidding me? We're going to look like a bunch of stupid Christmas trees," fumed Anna.

It was probably true, Isabel thought. She almost suggested that they change the name of their act from the Hip-Hop Honeys to Kiki and the Dancing Christmas Trees, but she stopped short of saying it out loud. These were not the Beacon Street Girls. Somehow she had a feeling that Anna and Joline would not find the suggestion humorous.

"I think the dresses are fine," Isabel said. She wasn't being totally truthful. She was trying to break the tie. They had looked everywhere with no luck. In most of the places they'd shopped, even if they *had* found a dress they liked, the store would only have one per size. Since Anna and Joline were close in size, it made things even more difficult than they already were. What made things worse was that Anna and Joline didn't agree on anything, not anymore.

"I'm not so sure," Joline said, looking at her reflection in the mirror. "They are really kind of ugly."

"What do you expect? Who wears these kinds of dresses to dance in anyway?" Anna huffed.

"What is that supposed to mean?" Joline asked defensively. She thought Anna might have been insulting her mother's suggestion to come to the basement store.

Finally, the girls settled on the green sequined dresses. They were short enough to dance in, the skirts would flare, and maybe they could cut the dorky bows off. They went to the cashier to pay.

"I still think it would have been better if you had *made* the dresses the way you promised," Joline said as she pulled out her money.

"I didn't promise anything. I told you, I can't sew," Isabel said. "Don't you *ever* listen?"

"*Don't you listen?*" mimicked Anna.

Isabel was tired and mad and really annoyed with herself.

If she had been with Avery, Katani, Maeve, and Charlotte, they all would have been laughing and making jokes by now. Instead, she was with the two cranky, spoiled Queens of Mean. How had she allowed herself to get into this mess?

Joline's mother, the chauffeur of the shopping expedition, hadn't been able to find a parking space anywhere near Filene's. So she just kept circling the block, which was getting more and more difficult as rush hour approached. The streets were crowded and tempers were short on all sides.

"Where is she?" Anna asked Joline as they watched for the car. "I have to get home by five thirty or I'll be grounded for life."

"She's circling," Joline said defensively. Isabel thought almost fondly of the time, not so long ago, when Anna and Joline had been best friends. They had been annoying then, and mean, too, but they were much worse now. Or maybe they were always like this. Who could tell? It was clear that Kiki and the show were taking their toll on everyone.

Joline called her mother on her cell phone. "Hi Mom," she said. "We're waiting outside. Where are you?" She listened, then turned to relay the message. "She's just a couple of blocks away."

When Joline's mother still wasn't there ten minutes later, Anna thrust her dress at Isabel. "You take this," she said. "I can't wait any longer, I'm taking the T."

"She's right around the corner," Joline said, but Anna just gave her a look.

"What's up with her?" Isabel asked when Anna was safely out of sight.

"What isn't?" Joline said.

CR

They didn't get home until almost six o'clock. Isabel resisted the urge to call one of her friends and tell them that there was trouble in the ranks of the Queens of Mean. She knew they'd be interested. But it was gossip, and Isabel didn't really feel comfortable gossiping about anyone, not even about Anna and Joline.

To: Charlotte
From: Sophie
Re: Magic!

Charlotte, ma cherie,

You are so busy, busy, busy! You know me, Charlotte, I like to sit and sip hot chocolate at Madame Bette's, that is magic to me. No sign of Orangina yet, I'm sorry, but I promise I will keep checking for him. Thanks for the Boston Red Sox shirt, I'm glad you sent the pink! I miss you very much, please send me a tape of your talent show-good luck, I know you'll be a fantastique magician!
Love,
Sophie

Video Divas

So much for a full camera crew and entourage. Instead, Kiki's father arrived on Tuesday as promised with one small hand-held video camera, and he planned to do the taping himself. Mr. Taylor showed him where he could set up.

"You should be happy to have my father at all," Kiki said when Anna questioned the setup. "Do you have any idea who he is?"

Anna knew exactly who Kiki's father was; Kiki had only told them a hundred times. And Kiki's dad, who produced music videos for a living and won awards for them, was the closest she'd ever come to a professional. Anna had dreamed of becoming a model for so long she didn't want to ruin her chances by making Kiki mad. Even though she thought Kiki was the meanest girl she had ever met.

Maeve's father had allowed them to set up their equipment on the stage. But they had to be out by six so he could get ready for a seven o'clock movie screening. That was the deal.

Kiki was full of complaints. The set just wasn't right. The problem was that there was a lot of black and white in it, and black and white did not play well on video.

"It strobes," Kiki said. "You're a visual artist, I'm surprised you don't know that."

But Isabel hadn't known that. She'd never been involved in making videos. Kiki should have told her that before.

Isabel was having a bad day. She'd just discovered that her dress had a huge hole in it. How had she missed it when she'd tried it on? And how had no one else seen it?

Kiki's father saw the look on Isabel's face. "Don't worry about the black and white. I can shoot around it."

Isabel tried her best to smile. If Kiki were mean, which Isabel was coming to realize might be true, the meanness didn't come from her father. He was very nice and patient as the girls got ready. In fact, he told Isabel that he was going to volunteer his services to tape the entire show, and if the class wanted to sell copies of the video as part of the fund-raiser, he'd be happy to donate the tapes. Isabel knew that Mrs. Fields would be thrilled with that news.

"It's a very nice set, Isabel," he said to her. "You are quite talented."

"Thanks," Isabel said.

Dillon agreed with him. "It's really cool, Isabel," he said.

Maeve took Isabel upstairs to try to fix her dress. They were able to find matching green thread in the sewing box, but they both had to admit that they had no idea how to fix the hole. And even if they could figure it out, the dress was layered with sequins, and the hole had taken out a whole patch of them.

Both girls were really relieved when Katani arrived.

"Let me see it," Katani said. She looked at the dress and then at the hem. "I think I can take some sequins from there," she said. "This is a bad hole, though."

"I can't believe I didn't see it when we bought the dresses," Isabel said. "Or that no one else did." Suddenly, she wondered if there was more to "the hole."

Maeve and Katani exchanged looks.

Katani patched the hole, then started sewing the sequins on by hand. It was detailed work, and so it took quite some time. Even for Katani it was a hard job. She had been nervous that she wouldn't get it right and that the hole would show, or the sequins would unravel. Isabel and Maeve practically held their breath until she was finished.

Then Kiki began yelling up the stairs for Isabel. "Two minutes!" Kiki yelled. "Come on! If you want to be a Hip-Hop Honey, Isabel, you'd better get down here."

"Hip-Hop Meanies, if you ask me," Maeve said under her breath, as she started toward the stairs to give Kiki a piece of her mind.

Katani grabbed Maeve's arm. "Oh no, you don't," she said.

The look on Katani's face was so stern and motherly that Isabel started to laugh.

Isabel scrambled into the dress. "Thanks, guys," she smiled. "I don't know what I would have done if you hadn't been here."

Katani looked at her. "From here, you can't even see the hole. It won't show on camera."

Maeve looked at her friend. "You look really good, Isabel."

"I hope your father appreciates all you're going through to get him here," Katani said.

"Oh, he will. I can't wait for you guys to meet him." A warm glow spread over Isabel's face. That was the Isabel Maeve hadn't seen for quite a while.

Kiki yelled up the stairs again. "Isabel, I mean it. One more minute and you're out of the show."

"Who told her she could come into my kitchen?" Maeve said, starting for the stairs again.

But Isabel rushed down the steps before Maeve had a chance to say anything.

"Are you okay?" Katani asked Maeve.

"Hold me back, hold me back," Maeve said, doing an impression of the lion in *The Wizard of Oz*. They both started to laugh, both at Maeve's mimicking and at the ridiculousness of Kiki's new role as Ice Queen of the talent show.

Only when the house lights were dimmed did Maeve and Katani sneak into the projection booth to watch the taping. There was a small glass window in front and two square holes for the projectors. They didn't turn on any lights, but stood with their faces in front of the projector holes.

First the Hip-Hop Honeys did a run-through. Although they hated to admit it, both Katani and Maeve agreed that all the rehearsal time had paid off. And, though Kiki was clearly the star of the show, and really good, it was difficult to ignore Isabel. Even with her patched dress and backup dancer status, Isabel stood out. She really was like Cinderella, Katani thought. A little bit, anyway.

"She's a really good dancer," Maeve said.

"I don't think she can dance a lot though," Katani said, "something about her knees."

"Isabel told me that she loved to dance, but she didn't like being on stage all that much. Personally, I don't really get that," Maeve said in an exaggerated fashion. Katani gave her a playful shove. It was so clear. Maeve was a performer through and through.

The girls had to admit that Kiki's idea for the video was really cool. The video would be edited then projected onto the screen that Isabel had designed, giving the act the illusion of a big production number with a lot of dancers.

And Kiki's father was an artist with the camera. By the end of the run-through, he had learned the blocking well enough to move with the dancers without getting in their way.

They were doing a hip-hop version of an old ballad, starting slow and then speeding to double time and breaking into a hip-hop rhythm. Their green skirts swirled furiously as they danced, and the effect was nothing short of totally cool.

Kiki's father shot the whole number once. Then he went back to get some close-ups. "Take five," he said.

Dillon took the opportunity to adjust one of the lights. Then he turned and headed toward the projection room.

"Oh no," Maeve said. "I forgot that this was also the lighting booth."

When Dillon flipped the lights on in the booth, he jumped a mile. "Man," he said. "You scared me!"

"Sorry," Maeve said.

"I have to adjust the lights again," Dillon said, bringing the house lights up, then down again.

"We should go," Maeve said to Katani.

"No, it's okay," Dillon said. "Stay."

Maeve stood awkwardly off to the side. Finally, not knowing where else to go, she moved over to where Katani had been standing, and they both watched out of the same hole.

The house lights went down and the number started again.

It went just as smoothly with Kiki's dad getting a close-up of each of the dancers in turn. They kept stopping and starting, repeating the sequence until Kiki's father felt he had gotten a good shot of three of the four of them.

Then it was Isabel's turn. Kiki's father moved in, adjusting the view finder. The music started and the girls started to move again.

Kiki's father moved in closer. He was able to capture some great close-ups of Isabel. Then suddenly, there was a loud thumping sound, and Isabel disappeared completely from the frame.

"What happened?" Kiki's father put down the camera and looked at Isabel, who was sitting on stage, her face twisted into a grimace, wincing in pain.

"I fell," Isabel said. She was holding her ankle.

Maeve was out of the booth and up on stage as quickly as a stage mother. So quickly, in fact, that for a moment, no one realized she hadn't been there all along. "They pushed her, that's what happened," Maeve pointed at Anna and Joline.

"We did not," exclaimed Anna and Joline, who for a moment actually looked really scared.

"That's a pretty serious accusation," Kiki's father said.

"I saw them," Maeve insisted.

"Is that true, Isabel?" Kiki's father asked.

Now Katani and Dillon caught up with Maeve.

"What's going on?" Dillon said. "Isabel, are you okay?"

"I don't know," Isabel stammered, trying to stand up. She was trying to be a trooper, but her leg clearly hurt.

"You should have watched where you were going," Maeve said angrily to Anna and Joline. "You tripped her."

Anna and Joline could see that Isabel was really hurt. They had honestly not meant to hurt her. It was just that Kiki had changed the steps so many times Anna had forgotten and had reverted back to an earlier version. She moved left when she should have slid right. But Maeve was really annoying her now, accusing her of something she hadn't really meant to do.

"This is none of your business, Maeve. You were spying on us," Anna said in an aggressive tone.

"You hurt my friend," Maeve retorted.

"Stop it, girls." Kiki's father said firmly. "Isabel's hurt and we need to deal with this now."

Kiki's father turned to Dillon and Katani. "Did you see what happened?" he asked.

It had all happened so quickly that Katani hadn't seen a thing. And as much as Katani believed Maeve, she had to be honest. "I didn't see how she fell," Katani said.

"What about you, young man?" Kiki's father asked.

Dillon shrugged. "I didn't see it. I was looking at one of the lights."

Kiki walked over to Isabel. She looked around, spotting the loop latch on the floor. It was supposed to lie flat, but it was sticking up slightly. She pointed to the latch. "That's what she tripped over."

"That's not true. She wasn't anywhere near that part of the stage," Maeve said.

But no one could back her up. There was so much going on that no one had been paying much attention to where Isabel had been.

"I hope your father has at least paid up his insurance," Kiki said. "He's gonna need it."

Kiki's father shot her a look. "Enough," he said, turning back to Isabel. "Let's get you some ice."

"I'm all right," Isabel said.

"You'd better sit down," Kiki said. "Dad, I think we should call the paramedics." She couldn't help herself. She was tired of the Beacon Street Girls, especially Maeve. What was she *doing* here anyway? She understood why Katani had to be here, but not Maeve. Even though it was her dad's theater, she had clearly snuck in, and now everybody was all upset about Isabel and her leg. *She's probably faking*, thought Kiki.

Isabel took a few limping steps on her foot.

"Maybe you *should* sit down," Katani said. "You might hurt your leg more."

"Isabel, I ... I'm sorry," Anna blurted out. This was a first, an apology from a Queen of Mean.

"I ... I'm all right!" Isabel could not hide the frustration in her voice.

Everyone had been so busy arguing with each other that they really hadn't been paying all that much attention to how Isabel felt about the whole thing. But her tone had gotten their attention. Now everyone turned and stared.

"I'm all right," she said again. And, as if to prove it, Isabel walked down the stage steps all the way to the back of the theater and right out the door.

CHAPTER

20

On the Town

The next morning, Isabel sat in the doctor's office. Her leg felt fine, but Aunt Lourdes had insisted she see a doctor, just to be sure. Her aunt set up an appointment with an orthopedic surgeon she knew from the hospital where she worked.

Dr. Takasugi stood looking at the X-rays.

"I'm fine," Isabel said for the twentieth time that morning.

"Is she?" Aunt Lourdes wanted to know.

"Well, there's nothing broken, and there's just a bit of swelling," the doctor said, coming back over and examining Isabel's leg one more time. "I don't think there's anything to worry about."

"I told you," Isabel said to Aunt Lourdes.

"So she can dance in the show?" her aunt asked.

"As long as there's no pain, she should be all right," Dr. Takasugi said.

"Thank you!" Isabel jumped up from her chair.

"Feel free to call me if you notice any other symptoms, but I'd say you're in pretty good shape." Dr. Takasugi walked them to the door.

"Thank you for fitting her in," Aunt Lourdes said.

"Glad to do it," Dr. Takasugi said. The doctor was clearly a friend. "It was nice to meet you, Isabel," Dr. Takasugi said. "Your aunt talks about you and your sister a lot."

Isabel smiled. It was interesting to think of Aunt Lourdes talking about her.

"Come on, Izzi," Aunt Lourdes said. "I promised to show you around the hospital."

They toured the wards and the grounds. This was a teaching hospital, and, every once in a while, teams of interns would follow their instructors from room to room. Isabel told Aunt Lourdes she thought they looked like ducklings following their mother.

"This is where your mother's doctor is," Aunt Lourdes said.

Isabel recognized the wing where they treated multiple sclerosis. She had visited it only a few days ago to meet her mother's new doctor.

Isabel couldn't wait for her father to see how well her mother was doing. The new medication was working wonders for her mother's MS. She wasn't dizzy anymore. And there were none of the side effects of the other drugs she had been on for the last year and a half.

It had been a tough decision to move to Boston for treatment. But it had been the right one. As difficult as it was for the family not to be together, they all agreed that they would do whatever it took to make her mother better. If that meant being separated for a while, then that was just what they had to do. But the Martinez family was really tight-knit, and to have a split like this was painful for everyone. And Isabel knew in her heart that it was hardest on her mother. It was her mother who felt bad for being the cause of the family being separated. It couldn't be helped, of course, but Isabel had heard her mother tell Aunt Lourdes that she "felt guilty for all that she was putting her family through." Isabel was glad when Aunt Lourdes told her to "shush." Nobody blamed her mother. They just wanted her well.

But, until today, Isabel had never considered that their living situation might be tough on Aunt Lourdes as well. They had all been so concentrated on helping Isabel's mother that no one had even considered how much their move would interrupt her aunt's life, or that she even had a life to interrupt.

Isabel could see signs of her aunt all around this hospital. Every place they went, Aunt Lourdes ran into friends. These were not just people who happened to work together; they were real friends. And everyone Aunt Lourdes introduced to Isabel seemed to already know a lot about her. They knew about her painting and her swimming. They even knew she was going to dance in the school talent show if Dr. Takasugi gave her the thumbs-up.

"So you're going to be able to do the show?" a young nurse asked her.

"Dr. Takasugi said I could," Isabel said.

"Well, if Dr. Takasugi said so, I guess you can," the nurse said. "She's the best."

Isabel smiled.

"I'm excited to see you in the show," the nurse said.

It turned out that Aunt Lourdes had sold tickets to a lot of the hospital staff, particularly the ones who lived in Brookline. Isabel exceeded her quota of eight tickets because her aunt had sold fifteen to her hospital friends.

"Everyone is coming to see you dance," Aunt Lourdes remarked. "But they're also coming to see the beautiful sets you created."

"I hear you're not only a dancer but a very talented artist," the nurse said, "... a real Renaissance woman."

Isabel felt proud that Aunt Lourdes thought so much of her.

"She's really enjoying having you stay with her," the nurse said.

"Me, too," Isabel said, only realizing as she said it how true it really was. If they had to be anywhere but home, it was fun to live with Aunt Lourdes. She had made it so easy for them that Isabel hadn't thought too much about it. From giving up her guest room, to sharing a bedroom with Isabel's mom, to encouraging Isabel to decorate the room she shared with Elena Maria, Aunt Lourdes had made them all feel at home.

Thinking about it made Isabel realize that Aunt Lourdes was talented, but in a different way. She had a talent for making people feel comfortable and secure, a skill that made her a great nurse, Isabel realized.

They ate lunch at the hospital cafeteria. It was actually pretty good, getting salads from the salad bar and splitting a chicken sandwich. After they finished, Aunt Lourdes looked at her watch.

"I don't have to be back here until tonight," Aunt Lourdes said. "And by the time we got you back to school, classes would be almost over. What do you say we go over to the Museum of Fine Arts? They're running a show on the Impressionists. Do you want to go?"

"Are you kidding?" Isabel couldn't believe her ears. "Of course I want to go." The show had been sold out for months. Evidently, her aunt had some connections.

"Good," Aunt Lourdes said.

⠶

For the next two hours, Isabel and Aunt Lourdes lost themselves in the lives of the French Impressionists. Isabel found herself staring at one of Monet's light studies. She watched as the same landscape became five different paintings when viewed from the same perspective at different times of day. Isabel could not figure out how he had done that. Imagine being such an artist that people are still in awe of your paintings years later, she wondered.

They toured the museum until closing. Isabel was thrilled to find out that there were all these discounts if you showed your student ID. Yup, Isabel thought, Boston had a lot going for it. She wouldn't mind if they stayed here for a long time—her dad would have to move, of course.

When Aunt Lourdes suggested tea in the café, Isabel readily agreed. As they sat there sipping oolong from delicate porcelain cups, Aunt Lourdes began talking about the weekend.

"Your dad will be here Friday night. Are you getting excited?"

"Really, really excited." Isabel grinned. "Do you think Mom suspects anything?" They had all been trying to keep his visit a secret. First, because they were afraid that something might happen, and he might not come. He'd made plans twice before, and then had to cancel at the last minute when there was too much work. This time, they decided to keep the visit a secret, just in case.

"She knows something is up," Aunt Lourdes said, "especially with Elena Maria planning the brunch and decorating the house and everything. But she just thinks all the excitement is because of the talent show. She has no idea your father is coming out."

"Where are we going now?" asked Isabel.

"I am taking you to one of my favorite parts of the city. It's called the North End. It feels like another world."

Aunt Lourdes was right. After splurging on a cab ride that took them through the winding streets of old Boston, Isabel and her aunt stepped into the world of Italy. The narrow streets and windows of the North End of Boston were filled with Italian pottery and leather goods, and restaurants, so many restaurants filled with incredible smells.

Isabel could feel her stomach growling, she was so hungry. They stopped at a little café and ordered spaghetti and meatballs, garlic bread, and for dessert, real Italian gelato. Isabel ate so much she thought she would burst. When she scooped her last mouthful of chocolate Amaretto gelato at the Café Paradiso, she said to her aunt, "This has been one of the best days of my life. Thank you so much. I will never forget it."

As they left the restaurant, Aunt Lourdes reached over and put her arm through Isabel's, and they walked down Hanover Street to the T station.

By the time they got home, it was ten o'clock, late for a school night, but Isabel didn't care. Her day with Aunt Lourdes had been too much fun to worry about getting up for school. This day was worth however tired she was in the morning.

Both her mother and Elena Maria were already in bed, so they were as quiet as could be when they came in.

"Thanks again for a wonderful day," Isabel said, meaning it.

"And thank you for the wonderful company," Aunt Lourdes said. Then she looked at the calendar on the wall, and at her watch. "Two more days, Izzi. Forty-eight hours from now, your father will be stepping off the plane."

Isabel was too superstitious to think about it. Her dad had cancelled before. But the third time was always a charm, and, besides, she had something else going for her this time. It was a point of pride with her dad that he had never missed one of her dance performances. She was about as certain as she could ever be that he would show up this time.

She hoped the weather would clear up, though. It had been raining since early afternoon, and Kristy B. was predicting a three-day nor'easter.

Avery's Blog
Wednesday

Whoa! What else can go wrong? Charlotte and I went out to post fliers for the group hug at the Movie House. We got five or six put up, then we lost the whole pile of them. It figures! Charlotte thought I had them, and I thought she did. We found the fliers just where we'd left them (on the park bench outside of school). As we ran to get them, the wind picked up and the fliers went airborne. The fliers became flyers! It would have been funny except that right then it started to rain really hard, and by the time we were able to gather all the fliers, they were a runny mess! We had to go back to Isabel's house to get the original, then go to the copy store to have 20 more made on neon green paper like the ones we'd just lost.

When we went to pay for them, I realized I had left my wallet back at Isabel's. Since Charlotte's house was closer, she went home to get some money while I waited at the copy store so they'd know we weren't trying to rip them off or anything. On Charlotte's way out the door, she slipped on some wet leaves and fell right into the entire

Abigail Adams football team who were coming from a late practice. It was awesome. Once again, Charlotte scored a 10! And boy, did she turn bright red. I think one of the boys was trying to talk to her, but she kept going, running up the street and slipping again on some more leaves. The boys were clapping and calling to her, but Charlotte didn't even turn around, she was mega embarrassed.

We finally got the money paid and we went out to put up the rest of the fliers. But by then, it had started to really pour. We got totally soaked. You could tell that the store owners didn't want us dripping in their stores, but they took the fliers and put them up anyway because it was for a good cause.

When we handed out the last group hug flier and headed out of the store, the clerk looked out the window. "This thing is tomorrow night?" he asked.

"Seven p.m." I answered.

"I hope you have a rain date on your poster," he said. "This storm is a nor'easter, you know."

"It's rain or shine," I said, pointing to the fine print on the flier.

Charlotte had no idea what a nor'easter was. She hasn't lived here long enough to experience one. I could tell she was curious, but I didn't want to talk about it. The flier said rain or shine. But if the rain didn't let up by tomorrow night, we'd just have to change the event from a group hug to a group swim.

But I really hope the man in the store was wrong and the weather clears up. Katani told us that the tickets for the talent show are only about 80 percent sold, which Mom said would be good for a normal event, but not for this one. We're going to have to sell out if we want to save *the theater. One of the reasons we're doing the group hug thing is so that we can get TV coverage and sell more tickets. We're hoping to get a TV crew out there, and everyone knows that they're much more likely to come out if it's not raining on their heads.*

Which brings me to the final thing that happened. Because of the rain, they cancelled today's championship soccer game. The final one between the Tornadoes and the Twisters. It better not get postponed to Sunday, that's the Mexican brunch that Elena Maria is planning, and that I really want to go to. Plus, I was going to use the money I made reffing today's game to go in on a talent show ticket with Charlotte. We decided to get one for Miss Pierce as a thank-you for helping us with the Houdini trick. Hope she comes.

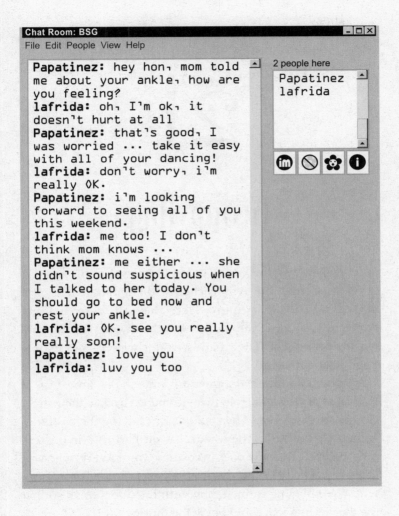

Chat Room: BSG

File Edit People View Help

Papatinez: hey hon, mom told me about your ankle, how are you feeling?
lafrida: oh, I'm ok, it doesn't hurt at all
Papatinez: that's good, I was worried ... take it easy with all of your dancing!
lafrida: don't worry, i'm really OK.
Papatinez: i'm looking forward to seeing all of you this weekend.
lafrida: me too! I don't think mom knows ...
Papatinez: me either ... she didn't sound suspicious when I talked to her today. You should go to bed now and rest your ankle.
lafrida: OK. see you really really soon!
Papatinez: love you
lafrida: luv you too

2 people here
Papatinez
lafrida

CHAPTER
21

Group Hug

If it gets any wetter, we're going to have to build an ark,"
Mr. McCarthy, the gym teacher, said laughingly. Except it
wasn't really that funny. Here they all were, holding
hands, surrounding the theater, but they were freezing cold
and dripping wet. Their hands were slippery, and people
kept having to let go.

The whole cast had agreed to come in costume, but, at
the last minute, Katani told them to change back to their street
clothes and rain gear. She couldn't risk having the costumes
ruined by the rain. They hadn't even had the final dress
rehearsal yet. The only ones in costume were Avery, who was
in the ticket booth with Marty, and Betsy's Sousa Brass Band,
who were playing in the lobby with the doors open so that
the theater huggers could enjoy the music.

Katani had contacted every news station in the city. But,
so far, no one had come. She was beginning to think that all
her efforts were a bust. Great manager, she thought. I bet
everybody is really mad at me for asking them all to come
out in this storm. She was about to throw in the towel and

send everyone home, when Maeve yelled over to her.

"Omigosh, Katani, someone's here."

Finally ... Katani breathed a heavy sigh of relief. The camera crew from Channel Five had come—it was almost eight. Everyone was tired, ready to go home and take hot showers to warm themselves up. But when Mr. Taylor stood in the pouring rain and told everyone how grateful he was for their support, not one theater hugger gave up. Instead, they all rallied and began singing, "The sun will come out tomorrow," until they were all laughing at the absurdity of the situation. Plus, the TV cameras were here! No one wanted to bail out now.

It took the crew about ten minutes to set up. When they finished, the newscaster approached Katani, who was standing, armed with some prepared materials about the Movie House, why it needed saving, and how the proceeds from the talent show would help save the theater from going bankrupt.

The newscaster scanned the sheet quickly and told Katani to look at him, not the camera, when she was being interviewed. Katani's knees started to shake. She hadn't realized that she would be on camera. This can't be happening, she panicked. She thought that Mr. Taylor or one of the teachers would do the talking. But the newsman said that a kid talking about why they wanted to save the theater was much more interesting. The spotlight was on her.

Katani saw Maeve give her a thumbs-up from the sideline. Katani blinked. No way could she let Maeve and her family down.

If this whole thing fails, please don't let it be because I got scared, she scolded herself. Suddenly, Maeve's tip about how not to get scared when you have to speak in front of the class popped into her mind. "Breathe," Maeve said, "Just breathe. You can't be afraid when you breathe."

"Okay, young lady. It's showtime!" And with that announcement, the peppy newscaster turned to face the camera.

"You might want to ask why forty kids and their teachers from the Abigail Adams Junior High are hugging the Movie House theater in downtown Brookline in the middle of a nor'easter? Well, apparently, these kids are historical preservationists. That's right. The old Movie House is about to go bankrupt due to intense competition from cinema multiplexes. And these pretty terrific kids have decided to do something about that …

"Katani, why is the Movie House so important to the people of Brookline?"

Katani remembered to look directly at the newscaster. "Saving the Movie House is important for a lot of reasons," she answered. "There aren't many of these old community theaters left, and this one goes all the way back to vaudeville, when it was a legitimate theater. Even the movie part goes back generations. My mother and father came to the Movie House on their first date."

"So, in essence, if that date hadn't gone well, they might not have gotten married, and you might not be here right now."

Katani laughed. "Yeah, I guess that's right."

"I understand this theater is an historical landmark," the newscaster said.

"Yes, the building was designed in the Beaux Arts style, and there aren't many of these buildings left." Katani turned back to all the theater huggers and asked, "We all want the Movie House to continue in this community, don't we, guys?" The Beacon Street Girls started the cheer, and everyone else joined in. Katani smiled and talked louder. "The theater is really educational. We learn lots of things from the movies. Things we don't necessarily learn other places."

"Some people would argue that kids learn things they shouldn't at the movies," the newscaster said. "Violence, sex ... the list goes on and on."

Katani was ready with her response. "Maybe some kids do. But Mr. Taylor doesn't show those kinds of films. The lessons we've learned at the movies are valuable ones."

"Like what?" the newscaster wanted to know.

"Literature, sociology, manners, history," Katani said.

"History? As in what kind of history?" the newscaster asked, interested.

"When we were studying the Revolutionary War, Mr. Taylor showed us *1776*, a musical about the signing of the Declaration of Independence, and *April Morning*, a really awesome movie about the Battle of Lexington."

"You have a point," the newscaster said, smiling. "Well, I think you are all exceptional kids, both in your educational choices and your community service," he said. "For that, I expect we can thank your parents, Abigail Adams Junior High, and, it appears, the Brookline Movie House, at least in part." He turned back to the camera. "Remember, if you want to help these kids save the Movie House, you don't have to come down here tonight in the rain. There are still tickets available to the seventh-grade talent show playing Saturday—all the proceeds will go to saving the Movie House theater!"

Right on cue, Betsy's Band began another Sousa march.

"So, where do I buy a ticket?" the newscaster asked.

Katani marched him to the ticket booth, where the

reporter pulled out his money and gave it not to Avery, but to Marty, who took it and ran across the counter and gave it to Avery.

"How can anyone resist!" the newscaster said.

Avery put the money in the drawer and gave Marty a ticket. He ran across the counter again and pushed the ticket through the little window.

"Wow!" the newscaster said. "With entertainment like this, I don't see how anyone can stay home. Kids, dogs, magic, hip-hop, and a brass band. This show promises to have something for everyone. Definitely, my Special Pick of the Week: The Abigail Adams Seventh-Grade Talent Show at the Brookline Movie House ... See it this weekend. And if you're lucky, you may get to meet Marty, the Magic Dog."

The group huggers let go to give Marty and the newscaster a cheering round of applause.

The camera stopped rolling, and the newscaster turned to Katani.

"Good work," he said when the camera went off. "Thank you for a great interview." He shook Katani's hand. Katani's face glowed with pride.

"Thank you for coming," Katani said.

"Good luck with the Movie House," he said as he was leaving. "How many tickets do you have left to sell?"

"A hundred and eighty," Katani said.

"A hundred and seventy-nine now," Avery said.

"Well, I hope this helps you all," the newscaster said.

They all thanked him.

Nick walked up to Charlotte and whispered something. Charlotte turned to the group and announced: "Montoya's is serving free hot chocolate for the next hour. To help the cause ... If anyone wants to go in and warm up. It's free."

"Well, let's all go over to Montoya's," the newscaster said.

The huggers marched in a team toward Beacon Street. Avery closed the box office and grabbed Marty.

"No dogs allowed," Avery said. "I'll have to drop you off at home, little guy." Marty barked and slurped her face.

CHAPTER
22

Dress Rehearsal

By the day of the dress rehearsal, the seventh grade had sold ninety more tickets, Maeve informed everyone. Ethel Weiss had sold a ton at Irving's, probably because she gave everyone a handful of Swedish Fish for every ticket they bought.

People who'd seen the news show had called the box office directly. And somebody's dad, who owned a computer company in Cambridge, wanted to reserve a block of seats together. Although it was open seating, Katani and Mr. Taylor decided to make an exception when the company bought twenty-five tickets.

Ethel had started a trend. Party Favors, home of the best cupcakes in Brookline, put several fliers in their windows and made vanilla and chocolate cupcakes with *Save the Movie House* written on top. Everyone who bought a ticket there got a free cupcake. Montoya's supplied free hot chocolate to anyone who made a donation or bought a ticket. The whole community was psyched. And Yuri, who said, "Americans are so generous," gave free apples to everyone who bought a ticket. Mr. Taylor was completely emotional about all the support. He just couldn't believe how much the people of Brookline wanted to save the old theater.

The dress rehearsal was supposed to begin promptly at three o'clock, with the Hip-Hop Honeys. At three fifteen, the "Hop-pettes," which was how the backup dancers had begun referring to themselves, were still waiting for Kiki, star of stage and screen.

Ms. Ciara was growing impatient. "Where is Kiki?" she asked, looking at her watch.

"She's waiting outside for her father," Anna said.

Suddenly, the doors to the auditorium burst open, and Kiki swished in and breezed down the aisle in a seriously bright, seriously tight red sequined dress.

"Sorry," she said in a tone of voice that really meant "NOT!"

Isabel looked at the color of Kiki's dress and groaned inwardly. We are definitely going to look like a Christmas tree special, she thought.

Anna, who had been tapping her feet with annoyance, asked Kiki what took her so long. Kiki completely ignored Anna, as if she didn't even exist. Anna put her hands on her hips and stamped her foot in disbelief.

The Hoppettes had hoped to preview the video before the rehearsal, but there wasn't any time. Instead, Kiki popped it into the machine and gave Dillon some brief instructions. The boy who was supposed to be in charge of the sound system had walked off the set after their last rehearsal because Kiki yelled at him, so now Dillon had to handle both lighting and sound, which was a lot for one person. Kiki kept promising to get someone else to help out, but word of Kiki's temper had spread, and no one had volunteered for the job.

Dillon was really uncomfortable, too. Kiki kept staring at him all the time. He hated that. And she was doing everything she could to come between him and Maeve. Not that there was anything to come between, really. The guys kidded him a lot about Maeve. "One date with you and she doesn't want to date ever again," his friends said. "Way to go, Dillon."

It was clear to Dillon that Kiki was just playing some kind of a weird game. She paid little attention to him at all unless Maeve was around. Then she hung on him like she owned him. He couldn't wait until this talent show was over, so he could go play basketball.

When the music started, the Hoppettes fell into position behind Kiki, who went on stage first, followed by Isabel, and then, finally, by Anna and Joline.

Anna was right, Isabel thought. While Kiki looked good in her red dress, they looked like Christmas trees. All they needed was a few ornaments hanging off their dresses and the audience would start singing Christmas carols. Katani said it didn't matter, though, because parents really just wanted to see their kids perform.

The music started out slowly, with Kiki singing the melody and Isabel harmonizing. It sounded okay, but Maeve had been right when she suggested that it would have been better if the parts had been reversed.

They sang the first verse of the song softly, and then Anna and Joline came on the stage. When they got to the chorus, Kiki turned to Dillon and yelled, "Hit it!"

Dillon cranked the music and slipped the tape into the video machine for the next cue.

A hip-hop beat took over and the girls started their dance routine. After another chorus, Dillon started the videotape per Kiki's instructions. The projection screen at the back of Isabel's set lit up with hundreds of dancing Kikis all edited together as if they were a chorus line ... zillions of Kikis dancing across the entire stage.

Kiki had gotten just what she'd wanted. Every time the Hoppettes crossed the stage, they were first blinded by the light from the projector, then covered with projected Kikis: Kiki in close-up, Kiki doing a high kick, Kiki dancing her heart out. There were Kikis everywhere.

Everyone in the audience was trying not to laugh.

"I'd think this was very funny if that weren't Isabel up there," Avery said.

"They should change it to a comedy show. They'd probably win first prize," Charlotte said.

Maeve didn't say a word.

They watched in horror as the Hoppettes, blinded by the light, ran smack into each other and collapsed in a heap.

"That's it," Anna jumped up.

Dillon flipped off the tape and turned off the music.

"This wasn't supposed to be The Kiki Show," Anna said. "This was supposed to be the Hip-Hop Honeys!"

Anna stood face-to-face with Kiki. "What is this video, anyway? I thought your father was this famous video maker."

"You know he is!" Kiki said.

"Well this looks like someone's father making home movies," Anna yelled.

"I edited it down," Kiki said. "To just the essentials."

"You mean, all about Kiki the Wonderful, Kiki the Amazing, Kiki the Fabulous ..."

"Enough, girls!" Ms. Ciara stood up. "Do you need help solving this dispute?"

"*We* were supposed to be in the video," Anna said, turning back to Kiki. "Where are we?"

"What are you worried about? You're in there. Each of you still has your own close-up. It's just more toward the end of the number than the beginning," Kiki explained.

"Prove it," Anna said.

Ms. Ciara spoke up. "The real issue here is safety. I think the light from the projector is blinding the Hoppettes. And I'm sure your intention was to project the video onto the screen and not the dancers."

There was some laughter from the audience. Kiki shot everyone a look, but her cheeks flushed. Maybe things were getting just a little out of hand. *But, wait a minute. Look at all the work I've put in,* thought an annoyed Kiki.

"My dancers aren't supposed to be in *front* of the projection screen, they're supposed to be over there!" Kiki said pointing to a small space at the very back of stage left.

"No we're not!" Anna was appalled.

"I did the choreography," Kiki said. "I think I should know where the dancers are supposed to be."

"We won't be anywhere if we walk out," Anna said.

"All right, let's take it down a notch," Ms. Ciara said. "Everyone take a deep breath … Kiki, as choreographer, and just so there won't be any further confusion, why don't you show us where you want the dancers to be."

Kiki walked to the very back of stage left and stood in a tiny space.

"No way." Anna folded her arms across her chest and stood her ground.

"We didn't rehearse it that way," Joline had to admit.

Even Isabel, who was always trying to find a peaceful solution, was amazed. "I think we were dancing more toward the middle of the stage before."

"Well, obviously you're traveling across the stage too much. A lot of amateur dancers make that mistake. That's why you need to start farther back," Kiki said.

Isabel was stunned to silence. Kiki had just changed tactics again.

"As choreographer, I want to make an official change, because some people clearly didn't understand my instructions." Kiki glared at Anna as she spoke. "You all need to dance in that space over there. Do you understand?"

"This is not what we're supposed to be doing," Anna whined to Ms. Ciara. "We've never done it this way before."

"Why don't you all go sit down?" She pointed them toward the audience. "I'll talk to you after rehearsal is over."

Anna and Kiki went to opposite ends of the row. Joline sat in the middle.

Maeve moved over a seat and let Isabel sit with them.

"Do you think you guys are even in the video?" Maeve whispered to Isabel.

"I think we're in it somewhere. Her father shot a lot of footage of us," Isabel said.

"Let's hope so," Maeve said. Much as she enjoyed seeing the mean girls fight, she knew how much Isabel was counting on dancing with the Hoppettes.

"I was wondering," Maeve said to Charlotte, Avery, and Katani when Isabel got up to get a drink of water. "How hard would it be to put a dance routine into the magic act?"

"Do you think they'd let us do it this late?" Charlotte asked.

"Isabel could do a little dance number with Marty," Avery said. The girls groaned. Avery had become obsessed.

"Let's see how it works out," Katani said. "Ms. Ciara is getting annoyed at any new changes."

While the Hoppettes talked to Ms. Ciara, the BSG waited for Isabel at Montoya's.

She looked really tired. There were big black circles under eyes. She looked like she needed a decent night's sleep ... maybe two or three nights' sleep.

"How did everything go?" Katani asked. "Did you get it all worked out?"

"Maybe," Isabel said. "But Anna and Joline are not happy with each other, and Anna really hates Kiki."

"Do you want anything?" Nick came over to the table.

Isabel looked at everyone's hot chocolates. Maeve and Katani were sharing a muffin. Isabel would have really liked something, but she had just stopped by for a minute.

"I can't stay," she said. "We're going to pick up my father at the airport."

Isabel realized she had her fingers crossed. She was so used to something happening at the last minute, she didn't quite believe her good fortune.

"Isabel," Maeve said. "We know you want to dance for your father."

"That's right." Isabel smiled.

"So, we were thinking maybe we should add some kind of dance routine to our act, I mean if Ms. Ciara would let us." Maeve suggested.

Isabel looked at everyone. "You'd do that for me?"

"Sure," Katani said. "That way you wouldn't have to worry about the wicked stepsisters."

"Wicked stepsisters? I don't understand," Isabel said. "What does that make me, Cinderella?"

She realized by the looks on their faces that she was

right. They likened her to Cinderella—how pathetic.

Avery looked embarrassed. She was the one who had thought of the comparison. "Not Cinderella ... Isabella," Avery said, as if disclosing the name she'd chosen would make it all right.

"I didn't know you thought of me as Cinderella," Isabel said.

"We don't," Katani said. "Not anymore. Not since you stood up for yourself and refused to make the costumes."

"I think I should stay where I am," Isabel decided.

"But what about the wicked stepsisters?" Maeve asked.

"They'll be okay," Isabel said.

"They ripped your dress," Maeve reminded her.

"It could have been ripped when I bought it," Isabel said.

The girls exchanged looks. Not one of them believed that Isabel had bought a ripped dress.

"Look, thanks for caring," Isabel said. "But really, I can take care of myself. And the last thing you all need is to add a dance to your act. Ms. Ciara already made you cut one whole trick."

They were about to protest, but Isabel was standing. "I've got to go meet Aunt Lourdes," she said.

"Oh, yeah," said Avery, suddenly remembering to say it. "Tell Elena Maria thanks for moving the brunch to Saturday morning. I'm really glad that I can still come."

"I'll tell her," Isabel said.

She started toward the door. It was an awkward moment.

"Izzi," Charlotte said.

"Yes?" Isabel turned around.

"We can't wait to meet your father."

Isabel beamed. If there was tension remaining, it was erased by the last remark. "I can't wait for him to meet all of you."

Avery and Charlotte left right after Isabel. They had something they had to do. They had decided to chip in and buy a ticket to the talent show for Miss Pierce. But before they dropped it off, they went to the Tower to compose a special note.

Thank you!

Dear Miss Pierce,

Thanks so much for teaching us how to do the Houdini trick! We wouldn't have a magic act if it weren't for you.

We want you to be our guest and witness the trick you helped create, so enclosed is a ticket. The show is at 7 o'clock on Saturday night and it's at the Movie House.

Hope you can come!
Sincerely,

Charlotte Ramsey,

Avery Madden,

and the rest of the
Beacon Street Girls.

"What do you mean, if she is able to come?" Avery asked Charlotte. "You know she doesn't have any other plans."

"I don't want to act as if we know that," Charlotte said, "because it really isn't our business."

"Okay," Avery said and signed the letter next to Charlotte. Then they slid the letter under Miss Pierce's door.

AN IMPORTANT ARRIVAL

Mr. Martinez was booked on the final Detroit/Boston flight of the day. As the ticket counters closed down, Elena Maria, Isabel, and Aunt Lourdes waited together. The last of the people piled off the plane, greeting loved ones as they made their way through the gate and toward the baggage claim area.

It seemed that everyone had already gotten off the plane. Even the flight attendants were rolling their luggage cases outside and getting into the city cabs that were lined up at the curb.

Isabel's heart sank.

"When did you last talk to him?" Aunt Lourdes asked.

"He e-mailed me this morning," Isabel answered.

"Did you check your messages before we left for the airport?" Elena Maria wanted to know.

"There wasn't any time," Isabel said, feeling stupid that she'd dragged them all the way down here when there was probably a message waiting for them at home.

"I can't believe he didn't come," Isabel said. She was fighting tears.

"Come on," Aunt Lourdes said as she watched them closing down the gates for the night, "let's go home."

Aunt Lourdes put an arm around Isabel's shoulder.

But Isabel turned back. "Wait," she said. As they turned to

go, Isabel had spotted something out of the corner of her eye.

Aunt Lourdes turned to look. "It looks like a tree," she said, but the girls were already rushing toward their father, who was struggling to carry the largest papier-mâché tree she'd ever seen. The tree was easily twice as big as he was, and though it was light, it was incredibly awkward.

"He brought my tree!" Isabel laughed. "He knew I missed it, and he brought it as carry-on luggage!"

Aunt Lourdes knew better than to question how Mr. Martinez was able to make that happen. When you were given such a gift, you took it. No questions asked.

They were talking so much that the cabbie had to ask for the address three times.

They drove through the tunnel and up into the lights of downtown Boston. The cabbie took the scenic route down Storrow Drive and along the Charles River.

"What a beautiful city," Mr. Martinez said to his girls.

"It really is, Dad." Isabel sighed. Then she hugged him again and laid her head on his shoulder. She was so happy that he had come, and knowing that he was there, she knew that she didn't want him to leave … ever.

Isabel was hoping more than anything that her father would fall in love with Boston. She knew it was impractical with the family accounting business in Michigan, but she wanted him there just that badly. It was her secret wish.

Her mother was in bed when they got home. The new medication made her a little sleepy, and it was after 11 o'clock. They had told her they were going to see a movie, and she had been way too tired to go with them.

Aunt Lourdes peeked in. Isabel's mom was sitting up in bed reading. When she saw her husband standing behind her sister and daughters, her smile was worth all their efforts.

CHAPTER
23

Musical Brunch

When Elena Maria had heard about Avery's game being postponed until Sunday, she'd had no problem moving the brunch to Saturday. "This party is so all the Beacon Street Girls and their families can meet Dad. We can do it for Saturday."

Isabel and her aunt had decorated Aunt Lourdes's apartment like the Mercado in Mexico City. But it was far more fanciful that any real market. There were colorful lanterns, piñatas, and lights everywhere. The papier-mâché tree that Mr. Martinez had carried all the way from Troy, Michigan, stood in the center of the room. Isabel had fastened bright papier-mâché parrots and tiny white lights to its branches, parrots that her grandparents had given her father when he was a boy.

Mrs. Martinez hugged both her girls and said they had given her the best present she had ever had in her life. And she shook her head in wonderment at how they had kept the secret of their father coming to Boston from her. When both parents saw the party and decorations, they were so overcome that they just kept shaking their heads.

"Girls, I think maybe we should just open this restaurant for you now," Mr. Martinez said.

And when the BSG and their parents exclaimed over the decorations, the Martinez family beamed with pride. Avery's mom, who had traveled to Mexico with Avery's dad once, remembered the marketplace and was particularly delighted.

Elena Maria served Mexican coffee and hot chocolate first. The hot chocolate was a bit different than the kind they loved at Montoya's, with cinnamon and a hint of some other spice none of the girls could name.

"I've forgotten what it is," Isabel said when Katani asked her what the spice was. "I know it's some kind of chili."

Katani must have looked surprised because Isabel went on to say, "Just a trace though, my father swears that Elena Maria simply waves the chili over the glass and doesn't put it in at all."

Just then, Isabel's mother and father came into the room holding hands.

Maeve thought they were the handsomest couple she had ever seen—just like Antonio Banderas and Catherine Zeta-Jones in *Zorro*. Both of Maeve's parents agreed with her when she told them that. It was so good to see them agree on something, anything, that it didn't matter to Maeve what happened next. The rest of the day could be horrible, the show could bomb, but she would be happy because today she'd had this one moment with her parents. A little seed of hope began to grow in Maeve's heart.

Isabel introduced her parents to each person.

"Ms. Kaplan, Mr. Taylor, I'd like you to meet my parents."

They all shook hands in a super friendly way, the way grown-ups always do.

"Very nice to meet you," Mr. Martinez said to Mr. Taylor and Ms. Kaplan. "You are the couple who run the theater."

"Mr. Taylor runs the Movie House," Ms. Kaplan said. It seemed awkward to Maeve to hear her mother refer to her dad so formally. But no one else seemed to notice.

"I've heard wonderful things about your theater," Mr. Martinez said.

"Speaking of which," Katani said, overhearing, "I have a very important announcement to make." Katani's confidence had soared since she started assisting Ms. Ciara. Secretly, Maeve thought she was getting a little too confident. Like now, right in the middle of the party, she could just interrupt everyone like she was the one in charge. On the other hand, Maeve also had to admit that Katani had done a really good job getting kids to put posters around town.

Avery started to clink her glass until her mother shot her a look.

Katani cleared her throat.

"As of ten o'clock this morning, the tickets to tonight's seventh-grade talent show were officially sold out."

Avery led everyone in a loud, "Woo-hoo!"

"So we saved the theater? We did it?" Avery asked, unable to quite believe it.

"Barring any unforeseen circumstances," Mrs. Fields said. She turned to Mr. Taylor. "I know that this is just the beginning," Mrs. Fields said, "But it's a heck of a start."

"I want you all to know that I have also completed the papers for the Movie House to become a nonprofit," Mr. Taylor added. "We can take grants and run all kinds of exciting new programs. It might take a while though. You know government regulations." The adults laughed when he said, "Remember *Mr. Smith Goes to Washington*." Maeve had to explain to everyone later that this was an old Jimmy Stewart movie where Jimmy takes on the Congress of the United States.

"I've worked with a lot of nonprofit organizations at my law firm," Katani's mother said. "I think maybe I can help you fast-track this."

Maeve's mother grabbed her hand and gave it an excited squeeze. Maeve squeezed back and put her arm around Sam's shoulder. Wow, Maeve thought, I even like Sam today.

"My mom and dad have been involved with nonprofits too," Isabel said.

"Not in Massachusetts," Mr. Martinez said. "But I've worked with several in the Detroit area."

"It might be worth looking into," Mrs. Summers said. "Especially since the kids are proving the educational value of the Movie House. And the community is certainly showing a lot of support."

Elena Maria rang a bell to summon them to their tables. The first seats were assigned. But after each course they would switch to a new group of people. That way, Elena reasoned, everyone would have a chance to get to know each other. Everyone oohed and aahed over the way Isabel had set the table to look just like an outdoor café in Mexico City.

Suddenly, there was a big crack and all the lights went out.

Kelley shouted, "Ha!"

For a second, no one else said anything ... assuming that the lights would come back on. No such luck.

Elena Maria started to panic. "My empanadas, they will be ruined."

Isabel rolled her eyes. Her sister was beginning to sound like some diva TV chef.

"Llewelyn, can you help?" Katani's mother asked her

husband, seeing how distressed Elena Maria and Isabel were looking. Then she turned to the group. "My husband's an electrician," she explained.

Llewelyn Summers, a big bear of a man with a can-do attitude, was happy to check things out. He followed Aunt Lourdes and all the girls plus Sam into the kitchen, where he immediately recognized the problem.

Elena Maria had things plugged in everywhere ... coffee pots, electric fry pans, electric mixers.

"These old apartment houses aren't always up to code with electrical plans. The circuits are probably overloaded. Unplug everything. I'll head into the basement and see what's up," he said.

"Will it take long?" a worried Lourdes asked. "This has never happened before."

"If it's a circuit breaker, it won't be a problem. If it's a wiring issue ... that's something else. Now," he said with a big smile, "show me to my kingdom." When Lourdes looked at him quizzically, with an even bigger grin, he said, "The basement! Katani, why don't you and your friends come down with me ... and we'll have a lesson about circuit breakers." He winked at Katani and she smiled knowingly.

Katani knew what the wink was about. Her father was determined that all his daughters would learn about electricity and plumbing and even a little bit about mechanics. And he never missed an opportunity to teach his girls how things worked.

The vision of a basement with dusty cobwebs and leaky ooze dripping down on her freshly washed hair did not play well with Maeve. She had on her favorite pink top and black pants, and she was about to say, "Pass."

But, as if sensing her discomfort, Isabel's aunt said to

them all, "Don't worry girls, this basement is quite clean. The landlord keeps a washer and dryer down there for everyone. Let's go."

All the girls and Sam, who to Maeve's consternation, kept mimicking a spider crawling along her arm, followed Lourdes and Mr. Summers out the door and down along the side of the building. The adults stayed upstairs enjoying coffee and juice and getting to know one another. Mr. Ramsey and Mrs. Madden were deep in conversation about Africa. She had never been and desperately wanted to go on safari there—a dream of hers since she was a little girl.

In the cellar, Mr. Summers showed the girls where the circuit panel was and pointed out all the switches, which each powered a certain part of the apartment. He showed the girls how all the switches were going in one direction except for three.

"Girls, we are in luck. This is a simple matter of pushing this switch back to go in the same direction as the others and I think our problem is solved." He pointed to Isabel and said, "Why don't you do the honors."

Isabel reached up and pressed each switch back. They could hear clapping upstairs.

"Thanks, Dad," said Katani.

Her dad smiled and said, "I'm hungry—let's go eat empanadas."

Suddenly, everyone heard a squeak.

"Omigosh," grimaced Isabel. "I think it's a mouse."

Squeak ... Squeak ...

There was a rush for the door. Not even Mr. Summers, who was over six feet two, wanted to meet a mouse. There was something about rodents that made even grown men squeamish. Mr. Summers was no exception.

Upstairs, Elena Maria, with her father's help, had laid out the first course of empanadas. They were a Martinez family favorite, small pastries with chicken or beef as filling. Elena Maria served them with a cilantro salsa she had made.

Avery and her mother found themselves seated at the same table with Charlotte and her dad.

"This is quite a special event," Mrs. Madden said, looking around. "I understand that Isabel did all the decorating and that Elena Maria is doing the catering."

Avery thought her mother sounded strange, as if this were some fund-raising event she was attending, and not simply a brunch for some friends.

Mr. Ramsey bit into his empanada. "These are fantastic. You all have to take a bite.

"Charlotte told me that Elena Maria and Isabel dream of opening a restaurant someday," Mr. Ramsey added. "Judging from this feast, I'm sure it would be a success." Everyone chatted for awhile about their favorite foods. Mr. Ramsey made them laugh when he told them about his visit to a rain forest, where he ate something that he thought was fish, but later turned out to be some kind of rodent.

"Have you ever *been* to the Rainforest Café?" Mrs. Madden asked, "Out at the Burlington Mall? It's got a rain forest theme—I quite enjoy it."

Mr. Ramsey had to admit he never had been there.

Avery was surprised to think of her mother going to a mall at all, much less outside of Boston. Avery's mother was strictly Newbury Street, with the occasional side trip to Fifth Avenue in Manhattan.

"What?" Avery's mother said when she noticed the look her daughter was giving her.

"I just didn't know you had ever been to the Burlington Mall," Avery said.

"I have a whole life you know nothing about." The words were formal, but her voice was playful.

Mr. Ramsey laughed.

Avery looked at Charlotte.

"In which rain forest was it that you ate the rodent?" Mrs. Madden asked. There had been a lull in the conversation so the rest of the room heard the question.

"You ate a rodent!" Sam said with enthusiasm. "That's so awesome." Everyone cracked up.

"Charlotte and her father have been to a real rain forest," Avery said. "When they lived in Australia."

"I wasn't aware that there were rain forests in Australia," Mr. Taylor said.

"Oh yes," Mr. Ramsey said, and he was off. He loved talking about travel. Every once in a while, someone would comment on how interesting it all was. Charlotte was getting nervous that her dad was acting like a teacher and everyone would get bored. But, just as she was going to nudge him under the table, Elena Maria said it was time to change tables.

It was like a big game of musical chairs. In fact, that's exactly what it was. The guests milled around, weaving in and out of tables while Elena Maria played music. When the music stopped, everyone sat at the table closest to them.

The second course Elena Maria served was huevos rancheros.

This time, Charlotte found herself at a table with Mr. Taylor and Mr. and Mrs. Martinez and Isabel. The adults hit it off immediately. Mr. Martinez was a bit of a movie buff; he had taken a film course while in college at Michigan. They talked about Cocteau's *Beauty and the Beast*, which Charlotte had seen when she was living in Paris. Everyone at the table thought it was brilliant, even Charlotte.

"Not that there's anything wrong with the Disney version," Mr. Martinez said. "It's terrific, actually. And you know that I am, of course, a big fan of animation." Isabel loved daily cartoons, and she often entertained her family and friends with her own cartooning skills.

"You could show some of the old cartoons in the Movie House," Mr. Martinez suggested to Mr. Taylor. "As a nonprofit, that would be a logical way to go. There are good film schools in Boston, you might be able to come to some kind of arrangement to show those movies to their students."

"Boy, that's an interesting idea," Mr. Taylor remarked.

All of a sudden, Sam started coughing violently and had to drink a glass of water. Elena had mistakenly given Sam her father's rancheros, which were heavily spiced. He spewed his eggs and salsa half way across the table at Maeve, who stood up and yelled, "Gross." Her mother gave her a look and told her to go to the kitchen and wipe her top off with a wet paper towel and club soda. Katani said she would help her. That was all Avery, Isabel, and Charlotte needed to hear. They leapt out of their seats and started to rush after their friends.

"Isabel, bring Sam some ice cream. Ice cream is the best way to cool off from too spicy a dinner. People think they should drink water, but they should really drink milk products," said Mrs. Martinez.

Ms. Kaplan pounded her son on the back and helped him drink a cool glass of milk. In a few minutes he was perfectly fine. So fine that he jumped up and waved his fists in the air. Kelley, who had been sitting at the same table, jumped up as well, and yelled "Yay!" Sam went to high five her and she reached over and hugged him. Sam had such a look of surprise that all the adults started to giggle.

Kelley let go of Sam, put her hands on her hips, and said to the group, "You are not being very polite."

Mrs. Fields, who had been sitting next to Kelley, nodded toward Katani's mother and then stood up.

"Kelley," she asked in a very quiet voice. "How would you and Sam like to join me in the TV room? I have *Shrek*. We could eat our breakfast in there and watch *Shrek*. What do you think of that?"

Kelley looked very serious for a moment before she answered, "Is that polite?"

The adults bit their lips to keep from laughing. In her own way, Kelley had impeccable comic timing.

Mrs. Summers smiled at her daughter from across the room. "Darling, it's very polite because you asked so nicely."

Katani breathed a huge sigh of relief as she watched from the kitchen. Her family knew that once Kelley got wound up, it was difficult to get her to settle down. Her grandmother had averted a potentially embarrassing scene. Katani knew these were all her friends and no one would care, but still, sometimes she just wanted everything to go smoothly.

Sam, who was relieved to be released, looked over at Maeve, who could see him from the kitchen. She just rolled her eyes.

She whispered to Katani, "I think there really ought to be a law that you don't take little brothers out in public until they are at least fourteen."

The music started up again. It was time for the third course. They all stood up.

"I'd like to talk to you more about your theater plans. I

might have some ideas that can help you," Mr. Martinez said to Mr. Taylor.

"That would be super," Mr. Taylor replied. It was amazing, when he thought about it, to see how many people were reaching out to help him. Even Maeve's mother was doing her best to come up with ideas to keep the Movie House afloat. It was touching. She suggested that they have a Valentine's weekend special and show the most romantic movies ever made. Everyone tossed out their favorite choice. Maeve's mother announced that her favorite was a sweet, funny little English movie called *Enchanted April*. Maeve's father was the only other person who had seen it. He nodded ever so slightly in his wife's direction as she spoke.

Katani soaked a towel in club soda and gave it to Maeve, who dabbed at the salsa stain.

"It looks okay, Maeve. Let's go. I don't want to miss that dessert," Katani said, pointing to the tray of little custard bowls on the counter.

The last course Elena Maria served was dessert. There was fine Mexican coffee, and more chocolate for the girls. And she served a coconut flan that melted in your mouth.

Elena Maria had stopped the music at just the right time so that all five BSG sat together for the final course.

"This is cool!" Charlotte said.

"It was so nice of Elena Maria to do this," Avery said.

"And your parents are really nice," Katani added.

"Your whole family is wonderful," Maeve said.

Isabel looked around. Sitting here with her family and her new friends, Isabel was happier than she ever remembered being.

If it had taken getting on stage with the Queens of Mean to bring her father here, then that was just the price she had to pay.

CHAPTER

24

Showtime

It was ten minutes to curtain time. Charlotte looked out at the faces of the audience. The place was packed. Katani had been right. Maeve declared it officially SRO, which in theater speak meant *standing room only*. There were actually several people standing toward the back of the room. Isabel and Avery stood behind the curtain with Charlotte.

"Look at how cute your parents are," Maeve said to Isabel.

It must have been the fourth time Maeve had said that to her today. Isabel smiled. Sitting there in the third row, they *were* cute; holding hands and chatting with each other. Somehow, it made Isabel feel happy and secure.

"Omigosh," whispered Maeve frantically. "Is that her? Is that Razzberry Pink? The front row on the left ... look!" Katani, Isabel, and Avery struggled to see. Charlotte looked over Maeve's head.

"That's her. Isn't she ... amazing? And she's really, really nice, too," Charlotte added.

"That's more pink than I ever wanna see in my life," retorted Avery. Pink was definitely not her color.

Sit back, and enjoy the show!

A NIGHT WITH THE STARS!
ABIGAIL ADAMS SEVENTH-GRADE TALENT SHOW

☆ **Remembering Vaudeville**
Abigail Adams faculty

Mustard Monkey ☆
Riley Lee, Josh Trentini, Torin Chang, Sammy Andropovitch

☆ **Abigail Adams Cheerleaders**
*Henry Yurt, Nick Montoya, Patrick Hawk, Pete Wexler,
Billy Trentini, Felipe Garcia*

The Magic of Harry Houdini ☆
*Charlotte Ramsey, Avery Madden, Maeve Kaplan-Taylor,
Katani Summers, Isabel Martinez & Marty the dog*

☆ **Revival March/John Philip Sousa**
Betsy Fitzgerald, Kelsey Marsh, Amber Bedel, Lucy Kim

For Good from the Broadway Hit *Wicked* ☆
Maeve Kaplan-Taylor

❂ ❂ ❂ ❂ ❂ ❂ ❂ ❂ INTERMISSION ❂ ❂ ❂ ❂ ❂ ❂ ❂ ❂

☆ **Funny Boy**
Shawn Carter

Funny Girl ☆
Elissa Babcock

☆ **Fire Baton**
Keisha Vasser

Cabbage Patch Ventriloquist ☆
Chelsea Briggs

☆ **The Hip-Hop Honeys**
*Kiki Underwood, Anna McMasters, Joline Kaminsky,
Isabel Martinez*

The Road Not Taken/Robert Frost ☆
Michael Deer

☆ **Gymnastics Floor Exercise**
Samantha Simmons

Thank you for your help in saving the Movie House!

"I think she looks awesome," said Katani.

Ms. Pink was wearing pink jeans, pink cowboy boots, and a pink tweed jacket with a pink boa around her neck, and of all things, she was engaged in a very animated conversation with Mrs. Fields.

They were talking away like they were old friends.

Funny, thought Katani. She'd never seen her grandmother with anyone like Razzberry before.

Katani could see Kelley in the front row. Kelley gave the girls a thumbs-up. Katani returned the gesture and walked with her clipboard back to the dressing room to tell the cast that the show was about to start.

"Five minutes!" Katani announced as she read the list of acts in order of appearance. Just this morning, Katani and Ms. Ciara had made some last-minute changes to the list, and Katani wanted to run through them, just to be sure everyone knew.

Katani had enlisted her father to help backstage in case any electrical problems came up. He'd already helped Dillon with some last-minute modifications for the Hip-Hop Honeys' number.

Avery and Charlotte were surveying the audience, trying to see if Miss Pierce had shown up.

"I don't see her anywhere," said Charlotte, sounding disappointed.

"I don't think she came," Avery said, shaking her head.

"Places, everyone," Katani said.

At exactly seven p.m., the curtain opened and Mrs. Fields, who had left her seat, stepped onto the stage.

"Good evening everyone, and welcome to the Twenty-Third Annual Seventh-Grade Talent Show," Mrs. Fields said. "As you know, this year's class has mounted the show despite some major setbacks, including a problem with the school auditorium. For a while, it looked as if there would be no seventh-grade talent show this year. But some very resourceful students persuaded us that the show must go on. And so, here we are."

The audience applauded.

"As you are well aware, this is a charitable event. And, unlike in other years where audiences had little opportunity to see the effects of their donations, this year, you can see those effects right in your own community. Look around at this historic old theater. I'm proud to announce that your presence tonight will solve a short-term crisis that the theater is facing. With your ongoing support and the help and determination of young people like these, I have no doubt that we will be seeing movies here for a long time to come, and who knows, maybe even more events like this one.

"What you're about to see tonight hearkens back to the days when the Movie House was a legitimate theater. A magical transformation has taken place here. Tonight's show will start out with the teachers making terrific fools of themselves in an effort to break the ice—another school tradition. Later, you'll see a cheerleading squad made up of some very unusual characters. There's a rock band, hip-hop dancers, a ventriloquist, magic, and music, music, music. So relax, let the lights come down and enjoy the show."

ʘʀ

As announced, the teachers went first. This year, the theme was vaudeville, complete with bad jokes, pratfalls, and a soft-shoe number performed by several of the homeroom teachers. After each segment, Ms. Ciara would bounce across the stage carrying a sign that said LAUGH,

APPLAUD, or BOO. By the end of the number, the audience was laughing and booing at everything. The icebreaker worked.

Riley's band went on next. They played rock, traditional stuff, and they played well. By the end of their number, the audience was clapping to the downbeat or at least tapping their feet. Maeve looked at Riley with admiration. He was a very good performer. Maybe even good enough to be a rock star someday, a dream he confessed to her once in the library when they had been working on a history assignment together.

The curtain closed and the rock group broke down their set and packed up their equipment. While the magic show was setting up, the cheerleaders went on in front of the closed curtain. Henry Yurt was out in front leading the cheers, and the rest of the cheerleaders tumbled onto the stage and performed the strangest acrobatic act anyone had ever witnessed, complete with wigs, pompoms, and the megaphone from the prop room. Legs and arms flew everywhere as the boys gave their best imitation of a girls' cheerleading squad. Red-wigged Henry cheered in the loudest girl's voice he could muster, and, though the others tried to follow his lead, their voices kept cracking, and it was all they could do to keep from busting out laughing.

They finished the ragtag act with a pyramid. Henry got a running start and overshot the pyramid completely, his red wig flying off his head and into the lap of a dignified older woman who was sitting next to Avery's mother. To her credit, the woman didn't scream, but held the hairpiece at arms length and wiggled it so that Henry would reach it. He did, and thanked her politely; he even bowed. Then he stuck the wig back on his head, although it was kind of twisted around, with the pouffy sides in front and the bangs over one ear. When he had it securely back in place, Henry ran across the front row and up the stage-left stairs to try the pyramid again. This time he nailed the landing. The pyramid was complete. Then, on Henry's cue, they collapsed onto the stage and got up to take their bows. The audience was laughing and clapping enthusiastically at Henry's antics.

"What is going on out there?" Avery asked Maeve.

"Two words," Maeve said. "Henry Yurt."

They all laughed.

Maeve poked her head through the curtain to get a better look. "I see your mother, Avery," Maeve said. "She's sitting with Charlotte's dad."

"Is Miss Pierce here?" Charlotte asked.

"I don't know. I don't see her, but it's really dark," Maeve said.

"Kelley is giving the cheerleaders a standing ovation."

"They're going to be a tough act to follow," Maeve said.

"Don't worry about it," Charlotte said. "Your solo is going to be faaaabulous." Maeve chuckled, because as good a writer as Charlotte was, her talent didn't transfer into acting. Maeve crossed her fingers. After the last fiasco with Dillon and not telling anyone where she was, she really wanted to make everyone proud tonight.

Marty barked.

"Shh," they all said, turning to him.

He looked so cute. Katani had made him the most adorable little suit. He wouldn't tolerate the pants, and had long ago shredded them, but he wore the jacket, which matched Avery's. They looked like a matched set.

As promised, the girls had tied Marty up, something he didn't seem to understand at all. The applause was getting to him. Every time he heard it, he wanted to run down into the audience and collect some treats. So it was probably a good thing he was tied up. But the real reason they had to keep him tied, of course, was Kiki and her allergies. That was the agreement they had made with Ms. Ciara.

"Our little Marty is about to become a star," Charlotte said and kissed the top of Marty's head. He gave her a sad look and glanced at his leash. "Sorry little guy," Charlotte said. "That's the price of stardom."

Maeve helped Charlotte drag the Houdini Box over the trapdoor, which was at the back of the stage. The show had been using the rear curtain as a backdrop, partly because it was old and velvet, and partly to hide the movie screen. The trapdoor was so far to the rear of the stage that it was almost off stage all together, which was the general idea, since this was originally a way to access the orchestra pit during the vaudeville years. But with the rear curtain partially opened, the trapdoor stood center stage, just where they wanted it for the Houdini trick. When Avery emerged from the tunnel, she would come out behind the closed portion of the rear curtain far over at stage left where the lighting and sound systems were set up. It was the perfect trick. And they couldn't have done it anywhere but here.

"Everybody ready?" Katani asked when she heard the applause dying down.

"Yessireee," Avery said.

"You bet!" Maeve said.

"Let's go!" Charlotte said.

Avery strapped the new set of rabbit ears onto Marty. This time she'd gotten him used to the headgear, and Marty seemed much more comfortable in them.

"Down," Avery said and he popped back down and disappeared inside the huge hat.

Isabel stood off to one side watching with Katani.

"Your set looks beautiful," Katani said.

"Thanks." Even Isabel thought it looked pretty good: stars, constellations, the Milky Way, all sparking in the full spectrum of stage lights. It was a magical set for a magical show.

"Actually, your sets are amazing. Did you ever think of going into set design, like for Broadway shows?" Katani asked.

Isabel nodded. She *had* thought of it. Her art teacher told her there were many ways to be an artist: artistic director of a theater company, animator, set designer. It all sounded so cool. And he said it was much easier to make a living doing that than just painting. But Isabel couldn't decide. Since she was only in seventh grade, she wasn't going to worry about careers just yet. She would just keep painting and see where she ended up. It would be more fun that way.

"Ladies and Gentlemen," Charlotte's voice boomed. "I would like to welcome you to the world of magic, where everything you see is an illusion, and nothing is ever as it seems."

Both Charlotte and Avery were wearing tuxedos. Even Marty (though still inside the magic hat) was dressed formally. The only one wearing an actual dress was Maeve, and it was a beauty, all gold and silver and midnight black, with sequins in the pattern of lightning bolts. Her mom had found it at a secondhand store, and she'd had it tailored for Maeve. With her red hair and stage presence, Maeve almost seemed magical herself.

The whole picture was so charming that people started to clap the minute the curtain opened. From where Isabel stood, she could see her parents' faces. They immediately recognized her work. She could tell they were proud.

As Charlotte began to wave her magic wand, flowers

materialized out of thin air. As she gestured to each constellation, it became illuminated. Charlotte pulled the endless scarf Katani had made out of one of her sleeves and handed it to Maeve, who kept pulling and pulling until the scarf wrapped around every object on the stage at least once. Then, Charlotte tapped her magic wand again, and the scarf disappeared completely.

Charlotte introduced Avery, who had been standing off to the sidelines. "Meet Avery Madden, escape artist, magician, and animal trainer extraordinaire!"

For the first trick, Avery hypnotized Marty. The trick was an immediate hit, with Marty going stiff and playing dead.

"For my next trick, I'm going to pull a rabbit out of a hat!" Avery announced.

"Oh boy, a rabbit." Kelley clapped her hands together, having seen the trick before and knowing full well that the so-called *rabbit* was Marty.

There were some giggles from the audience.

"That's right, Kelley." Avery couldn't help breaking character just a little. "A rabbit." Kelley laughed with delight at the inside joke.

Music played. It was the kind of flute music they play in old cartoons when they're taming a cobra. Avery waved the magic wand three times as planned. "Abracadabra," she said, and tapped the hat. Very slowly, the tiny ears began to emerge. Marty, the consummate showman, played it to the hilt. He raised the ears so slowly it was almost as if he were playing a cobra instead of a rabbit. Finally, when both ears were above the rim of the hat, Marty popped his little head out and grinned at the audience. Then he hopped out of the hat and jumped up on the stool, standing on his back feet and hanging both paws in the air, looking just the way a real bunny rabbit might look.

"I didn't know he was going to do that!" Charlotte whispered to Avery. "That is so cute!"

"I taught him last night."

Teaching Marty tricks at the last minute was always iffy, but this one had paid off.

"That's not a rabbit, that's Marty," Kelley said, clapping her hands together. "Yay, Marty!" Kelley started another standing ovation, and, once again, the audience joined her.

They all saw it coming. The applause was just too much for Marty. And hearing his name called like that sent him over the edge. Before any of the Beacon Street Girls could grab him, Marty made a mad dash for the audience, going from person to person, looking for treats.

Katani ran after him, handing out treats to a surprised group, who gave them to Marty as he moved down the line. He was about to start on the second row when Isabel grabbed him.

"Oh no, you don't, little guy," she said.

Marty harrumphed.

Usually they tied Marty backstage out of the way. But this time Katani opted to hold him instead. Marty wasn't happy about being constrained, not at all.

"Watch Avery," Katani said to Marty. "She's about to do her Houdini trick."

Marty sighed and harrumphed again. But when the lights went down, he settled in to watch Avery as Houdini.

Charlotte introduced the next trick. She gave some background history on Harry Houdini, the escape artist. Then she told the audience that it was rumored that Avery Madden was a long-lost relative of Harry Houdini. And now, to demonstrate, Avery was going to do one of the escapes that Houdini had made famous.

Avery was nervous. It surprised her. Her hands were clammy when Charlotte secured the scarves around them. They had practiced so the scarves looked like they were tied tight, but the type of material allowed her to untie them really easily. Avery had wanted to use chains like the real Houdini, but Ms. Ciara and Avery's mom said "No way!"

Avery's feet were sweating, which was difficult, since once she was inside the box, she had to open up the trapdoor with her toes. Plus, it was stifling in the box. They hadn't used all the lights at rehearsal, or else Avery hadn't noticed how hot it could get under them. Already, she could feel her stage makeup starting to run. Whose idea was that, anyway? she wondered. Avery hated the idea of wearing makeup at all, much less this heavy pancake stuff. It was making her itch.

Charlotte pushed Avery down inside the box and closed the cover.

"Now, in a feat too daring to imagine, Avery will escape from the scarves and the box before the music finishes. There is only enough air in the box to last until the end of this song. Let's hope she can do it. Good luck, Avery!"

"Good luck, Avery!" Kelley yelled.

Once the music started, Avery had only twenty seconds to open the latch and jump down through the trapdoor to the mattress below. If she didn't do it exactly right, Charlotte would open the box and find Avery still inside, hunched into a ball of sweat, makeup running down her face. And though Charlotte had been exaggerating about the lack of oxygen, it was still very hot in the box. Avery had to do it right.

The music started and Charlotte's voice faded into the background. The only sound Avery could hear was her own breathing.

Avery escaped the scarves easily. The fact that she was sweating probably helped with that part. Avery stretched down, feeling for the latch. She found it, started to turn it and slipped. She tumbled inside the box. She could feel the box move, and she could hear stray laughter from some of the audience in the front row who had obviously seen it too.

"You okay in there?" Charlotte's whispered.

There were only about five seconds left. Avery reached for the latch again. She was sideways in the box, and she couldn't tell which way was up. Avery reached for the latch again, but this time she found the side panel.

"Five seconds. Four. Three." Charlotte was counting down. Time was rapidly running out. What if Avery couldn't get out? Charlotte was really nervous. Maeve could have show business, she thought.

Avery twisted herself in the box, reached a fourth time and *finally* engaged the latch. Giving it all the strength she could muster, she freed the lock. As the final bars of the song played, Avery slipped into the darkness below, just as Charlotte opened the box.

Charlotte looked down at Avery through the hole.

"The box is empty!" Charlotte said, surprised, reaching inside. With one hand, Charlotte held up the empty scarves and, while the audience clapped, she reached into the box with the other hand and relocked the floor latch. Maeve pulled the magic box off the floor, while Charlotte casually put her foot down over the latch. Maeve and Charlotte held the box up to the audience to show that it was really empty and that Avery had indeed escaped.

The audience applauded wildly. They were still applauding as Avery made her way through the blackness of the tunnel and up the other side to the back of the stage. As planned, the stage light was on, and she found her way easily.

Avery broke through the curtain and took her bow. It was the perfect ending to an almost perfect act. Avery walked over and grabbed Marty, Charlotte, and Maeve, and they all took their bows together, with Avery keeping a tight grip on Marty so he wouldn't break free and make another run for the audience and the possibility of more treats!

When they broke down the set, they tied Marty backstage. Then they sat down next to him and watched the rest of Act One.

The show was already a success. Betsy's Sousa band number went next, and it was so lively that everyone in the audience clapped along. The march music kept the energy up and was the perfect lead-in to Maeve's ballad, which Katani had scheduled for the end of Act One.

When Katani had heard Maeve sing "For Good" from the Broadway show *Wicked* in rehearsal, she knew that it was going to be a showstopper and just the thing to end Act One.

Katani nodded to Maeve to get ready, and gave a sign to Billy Trentini to open the curtains. When the curtains opened, the stage was dark. The only light was a spotlight that shone down on Maeve. Dressed entirely in black, her red hair full and shiny, Maeve looked like a cabaret singer. The audience seemed to sense that they were in for something special and grew still.

Maeve dedicated the song to her friends, the Beacon Street Girls, to her mom and dad … and Sam.

Dillon stood offstage, just watching the number. There was something magical about Maeve, her red hair, her great smile, that made him so happy. When she finished, there wasn't a dry eye in the place. She had nailed her song. Maeve beamed as the audience clapped and whistled.

"She's quite a professional," Isabel's father said to Mr. Taylor.

"She will be, someday," Maeve's mother said. Her parents exchanged a look of tenderness and pride that Maeve could see all the way from the stage.

When she came off stage, she almost ran headfirst into Dillon. He caught her by the shoulders. "Ooo!" Maeve said. "Dillon."

"You were great, really great," he said as he looked at her shyly. Maeve felt equally shy as she said a quick thanks. They sort of stood there for awhile, staring at the ground, as other kids walked by them. Finally, Dillon mumbled something about really liking her dress and then he said he had to go, and rushed off. His face was all flushed. Maeve took a deep breath. She knew Dillon still liked her, and she liked him. But what should come next? She wasn't sure. But she couldn't think about that now. She was too psyched about her performance to think of anything else.

CHAPTER
25

The Queens of Mean

While Dillon was busy watching Maeve's act, Anna had stolen Kiki's videotape out of the machine.

"What are you doing?" Joline asked when Anna presented it to her.

"I'm going to watch it," Anna announced. "I don't believe we're even in it."

"Kiki said we were," Joline said.

"Well I'm going to make sure before I go out there as one of her backup dancers, I can tell you that much," Anna said.

"How are you going to make sure?" Joline didn't understand.

"I'm going to watch it, that's how!" Anna said.

"Where? There's no place to watch it around here."

"I've got that all figured out," Anna said. "Follow me."

The back door up to Maeve's apartment was open. There was a little TV in the kitchen and it had a videotape player, which Anna had seen the day she and Kiki went upstairs to find Isabel.

"But what if someone catches us?" Joline hesitated. She was scared. Wasn't it illegal to be in somebody's house if they didn't know you were there? But Anna forged ahead, and Joline did what she always did ... follow Anna.

"No one's going to come up here now, not with their 'precious' Maeve out on stage."

It wasn't if they were strangers breaking into someone's house, Joline thought. They were there before and the Taylors knew them. It wasn't so bad, she reasoned. And she also had to admit that she was curious to see the tape. Lately, she was feeling taken advantage of by Kiki too.

Anna and Joline stood in the darkness watching the tape. Anna fast-forwarded through hundreds of Kiki frames.

Kiki hadn't lied, not exactly. The backup dancers were there, all right, but only at the very end of the number. And they weren't dancing. They were standing awkwardly, watching Kiki dance.

"Do you believe me now?" Anna asked Joline.

"Why did she cut us out?" Joline was really mad.

"Because she is really selfish," Anna said. "She didn't want us looking better than her."

"Then why did she need backup dancers to begin with?" Joline didn't understand.

Anna said, "Because *Ms. Cool* wants all the attention."

Anna had succeeded in getting Joline just as angry as she was, maybe even more angry because Joline felt betrayed. During the last few weeks, Joline had started to think of Kiki as her new BFF. But that was never true. For whatever reason, Kiki had just been using her all along.

Anna pulled another tape out of her backpack.

"What's that?" Joline wanted to know.

"It's a surprise," Anna said.

"What are you going to do?" asked Joline nervously.

"Are you in or not?" Anna challenged Joline.

"I'm in," Joline said. She wasn't sure this was a good idea, but Anna had never been wrong before. Besides, Kiki *so* had it coming. How dare she keep Anna and her out of the video!

They snuck quietly back down the stairs.

While Dillon was with Maeve, Anna slipped the second tape into the machine. Then she and Anna stood on the sidelines and clapped for Maeve, just as if nothing had happened.

CHAPTER

26

The Hip-Hop Honeys

So should we just walk out or what?" Joline whispered to
Anna as they broke for intermission.

"No way," Anna said. "She'll know we did
something."

"What about Isabel?" Joline asked.

"What about her?" Anna said.

"Aren't we going to tell her we're walking out?" Joline
wanted to know.

"Hey, Isabel wants to dance for her father. Without us
there, he might actually be able to see her."

"You're bad," Joline said, but there was admiration in
her voice.

Anna and Joline got to the dressing room just as Isabel
was doing up her dress. She stood in front of the mirror,
looking at her dress. "I don't know," she said to both of
them. "I still think we've got the Christmas thing going."

"It looks great on you," Anna said with a sickly sweet
smile.

It was the first time Anna hadn't complained about the

dresses. It was also the first time Isabel could remember that Anna had spoken a kind word to her. That in itself should have made her suspicious. But she was too nervous thinking about her parents in the audience to give Anna's change in attitude a second thought.

After intermission, Katani had two stand-up comedians in the lineup. Then there was the girl who twirled the fire baton.

Katani had counted on the momentum of the first act to carry these entries, but as the first comedian performed badly, the audience, especially the kids, was starting to get restless. Katani began to panic. What should I do now? she wondered. She looked around for Ms. Ciara. She was on the other side of the stage. Then she saw her father watching the comedian. He was shaking his head in amusement at how awful he was. Katani really panicked now. Her father laughed at every bad comedian there was. Things must be really bad. Katani beckoned to him to come over.

"What's up, honey?" he asked her.

"Dad, I'm scared. This act is not going well. The audience might get up and leave. I don't know what to do," she stammered.

Seeing how nervous she was, Mr. Summers put his arm around his daughter.

"Honey, do what the quarterback does when he's in trouble."

"Dad," Katani whined. "I don't play football."

"Katani, when the game is going poorly—change the play."

Katani looked at him with confusion in her eyes, and then suddenly the light bulb went on.

She motioned for Keisha the baton twirler to come over.

"Keisha, how good are you at this baton twirling?"

Keisha looked at Katani strangely. Nobody in school knew Keisha very well, including Katani. She hardly talked, and she wasn't able to rehearse for the talent show because the Movie House only had an insurance policy for one night. Keisha could twirl her fire baton for the night of the show … that's it. Keisha's mother brought in a tape of her daughter with her baton club to show Ms. Ciara. Nobody else had seen her twirl.

When Keisha didn't answer her, Katani said, "Keisha, this is no time to be shy. You see that audience out there? We need fantastic right now! Can you do it or not?"

Keisha put her chin up and said, "Watch me!"

Keisha stood behind the curtain. Just before the music started, Keisha's mother rushed on to the stage and lit the ends of the baton. When the curtains flew open, the Trentini boys went crazy. They marched up and down the side of the stage, raising their fists, going, "Awesome!"

And Keisha, the shy girl, was exactly that … totally awesome. She twirled her brains out, and when the flaming baton went up in the air the audience held its collective breath. NO problem. Keisha caught the baton, twirled, and bowed to the audience for her finale.

When she walked off the stage, Keisha was an Abigail Adams celebrity, and the show was back on track. Thank goodness!

Next, Katani put the ventriloquist, who was using an old Cabbage Patch Kid as her dummy, on stage. The material was funny, but the girl had laryngitis and couldn't project her voice, so Katani closed the curtain and had her stand in front of the curtain, so at least the first ten rows could hear her. This setup also allowed the Hip-Hop Honeys to get ready behind the curtain.

Charlotte and Avery wanted to watch Isabel dance from the audience. They left Marty snoring next to Katani and tied to a post. Maeve was still backstage, and so was Katani.

There were no seats in the front, so the girls walked to the back of the theater and stood with the other SROs. There was one empty seat.

"Do you think it belongs to someone?" Charlotte said, motioning Avery to it.

It was off by itself, half obstructed by a pole.

"Not anymore," Avery said. She could see someone heading toward the door. "Sit," she said to Charlotte.

Because the seat was off by itself, Avery was able to balance on the chair arm. They couldn't wait to see Isabel's number.

The curtain opened to reveal Isabel's set. The audience clapped just for that. Isabel hadn't had time to do what she wanted, so she took her teacher's suggestion of splashing huge splotches of colors on big canvas frames. On top of it, her art teacher had helped Isabel paint words big enough for the audience to read. Words like, "Oh, yeah," "Just do it," "Hippity hip-hop," "Kitty cat rock," and "Purr." Isabel also added Anna, Joline, and Kiki's names on there with a cartoon of each girl's face. It was really cute.

Joline looked over to Anna, who refused to look back. Joline wished she was anywhere but waiting to see what was on that videotape.

Kiki entered stage, followed by Isabel.

Charmed by the girls' bright smiles, the audience applauded warmly.

Backstage, the applause had awakened Marty. He opened one eye, then both. He looked around for his Beacon Street Girls, but they weren't there. Katani was on the other side of the stage, holding her clipboard, and Maeve was helping Dillon run the lights.

The music started as a ballad, with Kiki singing melody and Isabel the harmony. It started slowly, when suddenly, Kiki turned around and yelled "Hit it!" Dillon turned on the tape, the cue for Anna and Joline to enter, but they were nowhere to be found. Kiki and Isabel started their hip-hop dance as planned.

But something was terribly wrong.

Instead of being awestruck, the audience was giggling. Then laughing. Then wildly applauding.

Kiki turned slightly to see what everybody was looking at. The twirling, dancing Kikis had been replaced by *Fantasia's* dancing hippos!

"It's the hippo hip-hop!" someone yelled from the audience.

Certain that it was planned, the audience applauded again.

If Kiki was fuming, Marty was delighted. The combination of laughter and applause was just too much for him. As far as Marty was concerned, any applause was for him. Show business was in his blood. He just had to get to the audience to get his treats.

Marty pulled on his leash as hard as he could. It might have been his superdoggie strength, more likely it was because he was tied loosely, because after a few seconds, Marty broke free and ran across the stage, dragging his leash behind him. He took a flying leap and jumped into the audience as if it were a giant mosh pit. He landed on the lap of the elderly lady in the first row. Of course, the audience howled. Marty was part of the act, they thought. With the same aplomb she had shown when Henry's wig had fallen in her lap, the lady held Marty and gave him a few tastes of her popcorn.

Kiki was livid. "Pull that tape out of there, you idiot!" she yelled at Dillon, who reached down to get it. But he wasn't fast enough for Kiki, who had broken character and was marching across the stage, her face as red as the dress she was wearing.

Kiki was so angry that when she saw Anna smirking at her she ran offstage toward her. She was about to grab her when Ms. Ciara caught her arm.

"No you don't, young lady."

Actually, it was too quiet. At first, the audience had thought this was all part of the act, but with the extended silence, they didn't know what to make of it.

And poor Isabel stood frozen in place. She couldn't move. It was her worst nightmare. She looked out at her parents, her eyes screaming, "Help me."

"Sing," Maeve whispered loudly to Isabel.

But nothing happened. Isabel couldn't move.

"Do something," Katani said to Maeve.

Maeve looked around and spotted Riley's acoustic guitar. She took it and headed on stage.

Maeve handed Isabel the guitar. Then she started to sing "De Colores," a Spanish song she had practiced with Isabel one day. Only this time Maeve was singing the harmony.

Harmony without melody was a strange sound. If you didn't know what Maeve was doing, which the audience obviously did not, she might seem like a bad singer. Having heard her previous number, this change totally confused the audience.

Isabel had no choice. She had to join in. If Maeve wasn't afraid to make a fool of herself, then Isabel couldn't be either. Isabel played a few chords on the guitar. Then slowly, softly, she started to sing.

Together, their voices were a perfect blend.

The audience went silent and listened to every word. "De Colores" was unfamiliar to the audience, which made it all the more unique. Luckily, the words were in English, or Maeve would have been in deep trouble.

This time Kelley didn't have to start the standing ovation. The whole audience was on its feet before the song was even finished. And Isabel's father was clapping harder than anyone.

CHAPTER
27

Out of Bounds

Sunday was sunny and bright, the perfect day for the final game of the girls' soccer championship.

Everyone was there to watch the Twisters and the Tornadoes.

It was a perfect day to celebrate. Despite the Kiki/Queens of Mean fiasco, the talent show had been a huge success. The sold-out performance paid for itself and alleviated some of the tax burden on the theater.

Kiki's father approached Maeve and her parents to suggest that Maeve record a few songs at his studio. He thought she had *potential*. But Maeve's parents said she was way too young. She was disappointed, but didn't make too big a deal of it because in her heart, Maeve kind of knew her parents were right. She wasn't ready for the big time ... just yet.

The Beacon Street Girls sat together watching Avery ref the last big match between the Twisters and the Tornadoes. Maeve's dad was sitting with Mr. Martinez. They were deep in conversation. Mr. Martinez had so many wonderful ideas for Mr. Taylor on how to convert the Movie House to a viable nonprofit, and Mr. Taylor asked him to be his accountant. Taking on the Movie House as a client meant that Mr. Martinez would have to come east more often, which made the entire Martinez family happy.

Who knows, Isabel thought. If things went well, maybe her dad would open a branch office here. Or relocate altogether … it could happen.

Everyone was doing their part to help the Movie House. Already Avery's mother had been talking about doing another fund-raiser for them. Fund-raisers were her thing. And the Movie House would be more fun than most of the charitable causes Mrs. Madden took up.

There were two minutes to go in the game. The Tornadoes were ahead. Megan's mom was yelling from the stands. She was so loud that all of the other parents were turning around to look at her. None of the parents could seem to believe she was acting that way again. The girls just looked at each other. Katani mouthed "out of bounds."

"It's only a game, for goodness sake," Mrs. Martinez said loudly, but the comment was lost on Megan's mother, who was yelling so hard she couldn't hear it.

It was getting tough to take. The opposing team was floundering, which was just the way Megan's mom wanted things. But Megan wasn't doing any better. What had started as the best game Megan had ever played was descending into chaos and missed shots.

Everybody in the stands knew there was only one person to blame.

"Out of bounds!" Megan's mother yelled. It was her favorite call.

Katani turned to Charlotte and Isabel, "I told you so."

"I guess some people never learn," Isabel shrugged.

Suddenly, unable to stand it another minute, Avery blew her whistle.

The game stopped. Everyone looked around, trying to figure out the call. There was no such thing as *out of bounds*, which is what Megan's mom kept yelling. But they all watched in amazement as Avery stood there staring up into the bleachers. She didn't speak or move. She just kept looking directly at Megan's mom.

Everyone held their breath to see what Megan's mother was going to do. Marty stood at attention, ready to leap in and protect Avery at a moment's notice.

Megan's mother stood up and stared back at Avery.

Katani counted, "Ten, nine, eight, seven, six, five, four ..."

Megan's mother sat down.

Avery blew her whistle.

The Twisters won the game in double overtime. And with the help of her teammates, Megan was able to score the winning goal of the season.

As they walked off the field, Mr. Taylor approached Avery and Charlotte. "I forgot to give you this," he said, handing them an old leather-bound book. "The cleaning people found it this morning in the lobby. I saw your names in it, and figured, in all the excitement, you must have forgotten where you left it."

Charlotte recognized the Houdini book immediately. "She came!" Charlotte said to Avery, who still didn't quite understand what was going on.

Charlotte flipped open the front cover and discovered the book plate. *This book belongs to: Charlotte Ramsey and Avery Madden.* Below the book plate was a simple inscription: *Thank you for a magical evening.*

"Miss Pierce," Avery said, finally getting it.

"I can't believe she came," Charlotte said.

At least for that one magical evening, Miss Pierce must have decided that it was okay for her to be out of bounds.

Avery and Charlotte were hurrying to catch up with the rest of the Beacon Street Girls and tell them all what had happened when, out of the corner of her eye, Charlotte saw something ... could it be? It was.

Suddenly, Avery, Charlotte, and Marty were off and running ... chasing a vision in pink.

Epilogue

Because of her performance, Keisha, the baton twirler, made a lot of new friends, most of them boys who were totally in awe of her baton fire power. Billy Trentini in particular thought Keisha was a great athlete and couldn't stop talking about her. "Did you see that baton go flaming in the air? It totally rocks," he kept saying ... over and over. Keisha was beginning to get a little annoyed.

Anna and Joline were assigned twenty-five hours of community service, which included helping Mr. Taylor clean up after Saturday matinees and reading to elderly people at a retirement home around the corner from the theater. Mrs. Fields made them write an apology to everyone who was in the talent show. The parents and teachers were really upset about their bad behavior, but most of the seventh grade at Abigail Adams just shrugged it off. After all, it was the Anna and Joline show. No surprises there.

Mrs. Fields made Kiki go help out in the kindergarten after-school program for a week. She hoped Kiki would learn how to be patient and to share.

Henry Yurt and the other cheerleaders were asked to perform at the high school cheerleaders' annual fall banquet. They received a standing ovation.

Isabel was asked to help design sets for the eighth-grade play. She said okay, as long as she had help painting.

Kiki's father asked if he could use Marty for a TV commercial. Avery thought that would be just "too cool."

CR

To be continued ...

Out of Bounds

BOOK EXTRAS

- Book Club Buzz
- Charlotte's Word Nerd Dictionary
- Trivialicious Trivia

Book Club Buzz

5 QUESTIONS FOR YOU AND YOUR FRIENDS TO CHAT ABOUT

1. Which characters in *Out of Bounds* go way out of bounds with their behavior?

2. Do you think Avery did a good job of dealing with Megan's mom? What would you have done if you were Avery?

3. How do all of the different talents of the BSG come alive during the talent show?

4. Why are the Beacon Street Girls so worried when Isabel starts working with the Empress and Queens of Mean?

5. What makes dancing in the talent show so special for Isabel?

Charlotte Ramsey

Charlotte's Word Nerd Dictionary

BSG Words

Cutified: (p. 4) adjective—*completely cute; dressed for cuteness; as cute as can be.*

Charmball: (p. 4) noun—*someone who makes other people happy ... or not!*

Snurp: (p. 9) noun—*a combination of a snort and a burp.*

Other Cool Words

Panache: (p. 5) (pa-NASH) noun—*having lots of style and flair.*

Sleight of hand: (p. 6) (SLITE-of-hand) noun—*magic tricks that require you to move your hands fast enough to trick the eye.*

Trompe l'oeil: (p. 17) (TRUMP-LOY) noun—*French, a kind of painting that means "trick of the eye." The subject looks very real.*

Ineptitude: (p. 39) (in-EP-ti-tood) noun—*inability to perform a task.*

Vaudeville: (p. 45) (VOD-vil) noun—*a form of theater pre World War II that consisted of a series of live entertainment acts.*

Diaphanous: (p. 48) (di-AF-a-nuss) adjective—*almost see-through, filmy.*

Mortgage: (p. 49) (MORE-gaj) noun—*money you borrow from a bank when you want to buy a house.*

Triptych: (p. 66) (TRIP-tik) noun—*three pieces of artwork fitted together.*

Symbiotic: (p. 69) (SIM-by-ah-tik) adjective—*two things that are different that benefit from living or working together.*

Pensive: (p. 103) (PEN-siv) adjective—*dreamy and thoughtful.*

Intermittent: (p. 128) (IN-ter-MIT-tent) adjective—*stopping and starting.*

Entourage: (p. 182) (On-too-raj) noun—*a group of people who help you or entertain you—rock stars usually have entourages.*

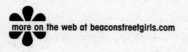
more on the web at beaconstreetgirls.com

freaked out **trivialicious trivia**

1. What is the name of Avery's famous noise?
   A. Burp
   B. Slurp
   C. Yurp
   D. Snurp

2. Whose mom is out of bounds at the Twisters vs. Tornadoes game?
   A. Jen's mom
   B. Megan's mom
   C. Molly's mom
   D. Ashley's mom

3. What song does Henry Yurt sing in Ms. Ciara's music class?
   A. "The Star-Spangled Banner"
   B. "Sweet Home Alabama"
   C. "Happy Birthday"
   D. "Who Let the Dogs Out"

4. What is Kiki's father's job?
   A. Freelance writer
   B. Dentist
   C. Music video producer
   D. Actor

5. Whose name does Katani put on her *Save the Movie House* proposal?
   A. Kelley's
   B. Maeve's
   C. Charlotte's
   D. Isabel's

ANSWERS: 1. D. Snurp **2. B.** Megan's mom **3. C.** "Happy Birthday" **4. C.** Music video producer **5. C.** Charlotte's

more *out of bounds* Trivialicious Trivia at beaconstreetgirls.com

CR

Sneak Preview!
Promises, Promises

Who's running for seventh grade president at
Abigail Adams Junior High? Dillon, of course,
and none other than the Yurtmeister. But some
surprising developments may spell trouble for the
Beacon Street Girls, in #5: *Promises, Promises.*

"Guess what!" Katani and Avery said at the same time.

"Go ahead," Katani said, slumping back in her chair.

"No … you go ahead," Avery said, rolling her eyes.

Katani and Avery looked at each other and motioned for
the other one to go first. Exasperated, they both turned to
face Isabel, Maeve, and Charlotte, and said at the same time,
"I'm running for class president."

They turned to look at each other again.

"What?" Katani asked. "What did you say?"

"I said I'm running for class president!" Avery announced
excitedly. "Coach G put off the fundraiser until spring. So
now I can run. Isn't that great?"

Avery glanced around the table. "Hey," she said. "I
expected whoops and cheers, but all I'm getting are goofy
looks. What's going on?"

Avery turned to Katani, who looked like she had

swallowed a canary. "I thought you said you didn't want to run?" Katani said.

"I NEVER said I DIDN'T want to run. I said I COULDN'T run because I had too much to do. My mom said if I cut one thing that I could run. Now because the fundraiser thing was pushed back … I can run. Isn't that great?"

No one said anything. Isabel appeared confused, Maeve stared at the ceiling, and Charlotte looked nauseous.

"Uhhh … what did YOU say, Katani?" Avery asked.

Katani looked at her shoes.

"What did you say?" Avery asked again.

"I said the same thing you did. I'm running for class president too," Katani said.

"You're running for class president? What's up with that? I didn't know you were even interested, Katani!"

"Well, the more we talked about class president, the more important it seemed. We talked about it at the game yesterday, and Charlotte said she thought it would be a good idea."

Isabel and Maeve looked at Charlotte, who looked like a deer in headlights.

"I thought you decided not to run, Avery … and Katani is a leader … like you," Charlotte finally squeaked out.

No one knew what to say. The Beacon Street Girls' lunch table was an island of quiet in a lunchroom sea of chaos. Isabel looked to Maeve, usually so good at filling in the silence, then at Charlotte, who looked totally miserable.

They all seemed frozen in that awkward moment and then Avery started eating again as if nothing had happened.

"I'll withdraw," Katani said finally, picking at the food in front of her. Her eyes were down, as if she dared not look at anyone else in the group. Isabel thought it was the closest she had ever seen Katani to crying.

How could Avery keep eating at a time like this? wondered Maeve.

Tell your BFFs to meet you on Beacon Street!

Join the Tower Club at **BeaconStreetGirls.com** for Super-cool virtual sleepovers and parties!

Personalize your locker and get $5.00 to spend on Club BSG gifts
with this secret code 🐾

SECRET CODE
ITTS59778

MARTY💲MONEY™
VIRTUAL RESERVE NOTE

CLUB
BSG®

BEACON STREET GIRLS

MARTY💲MONEY is **not** legal tender.
MARTY💲MONEY can only be used on
www.BeaconStreetGirls.com to purchase
virtual gifts online for your Club BSG friends
and **cannot** be used to purchase "real world"
gifts at the BSGshop.

FIVE MARTY DOLLARS

BEACONSTREETGIRLS.COM

To get your $5 in **MARTY💲MONEY** (one per person) go to **www.BeaconStreetGirls.com/redeem**
and follow the instructions, while supplies last.

Collect all the BSG books today!

#9 Fashion Frenzy □   **READ IT!**
Katani and Maeve head to New York City to experience a teen fashion show. They learn the hard way that fashion is all about self-expression and being true to one's self.

#10 Just Kidding □   **READ IT!**
Spirit Week at Abigail Adams Junior High should mean fun and excitement. But when mean emails circulate about Isabel and Kevin Connors, Spirit Week takes a turn for the worse.

#11 Ghost Town □   **READ IT!**
The BSG are off to a real Montana dude ranch for a fun-filled week of skiing, snowboarding, cowboys, and celebrity twins ... plus a ghost town full of secrets.

#12 Time's Up □   **READ IT!**
Katani knows she can win the business contest. But with school and friends and family taking up all her time, has she gotten in over her head?

Also . . . Our Special Adventure Series:

Charlotte in Paris □   **READ IT!**
Something mysterious happens when Charlotte returns to Paris to search for her long lost cat and to visit her best Parisian friend, Sophie.

Maeve on the Red Carpet □   **READ IT!**
Film camp at Maeve's own Movie House is oh-so-fabulous. But is Maeve's new friend, Madeline Von Krupcake the star of the Maddiecake commercials, really as sweet as the cakes she sells?

Freestyle with Avery □   **READ IT!**
Avery Madden can't wait to go to Telluride, Colorado to visit her dad! But there's one surprise that Avery's definitely not expecting.

Katani's Jamaican Holiday □   **READ IT!**
Katani's first Caribbean vacation is more mystery and adventure than lazy beach days, with a mysterious old lady, a lost heirloom necklace, and a competitive businessman scheming to take over the family banana bread bakery.

FREE Club for you and your BFFs on BeaconStreetGirls.com!

If you loved this book, you'll love hanging out with the **Beacon Street Girls** (BSG)! **Join the BSG** (and their dog Marty) for virtual sleepovers, fashion tips, celeb interviews, games and more!

And with **Marty's secret code** (below), start getting **totally free** stuff right away!

To get **$5** in **MARTY $ MONEY** (one per person) go to **www.BeaconStreetGirls.com/redeem** and follow the instructions, while supplies last.